The Wizard King

Miranda Mayer
www.mirandamayer.com

Content Editing:
Two Girls Friday
www.twogirlsfriday.com

Cover Art by:
Mt. Hood Creations
www.mthoodcreations.com

Photography:
Julie Savage Lee Photography
www.julieverdini.com

Models:
Robyn Wodiuk
Breck Warren

Stylist:
Morgan Shanafelt
morganshanafelt.carbonmade.com

Costumes:
Lady's Costume
Mt. Hood Creations
Gentleman's Costume
Morgan Shanafelt

Photo Shoot Location:
Timberline Lodge, Government Camp, Oregon
www.timberlinelodge.com

Thank you to all for being part of this project.
Miranda Mayer

The Wizard King

A fantasy by

Miranda Mayer

FOX DEN
PUBLISHING
Oregon

Miranda Mayer

The Wizard King

Copyright © 2014 by Miranda Mayer

Fox Den Publishing may be ordered through booksellers or by contacting

Fox Den Publishing
PO Box 39
Brightwood, OR 97011

Fox Den Publishing rev. date 12/31/2013

Dedications

To my precious little boy. Your existence has given my
life so much greater meaning, and every day spent
watching you grow is a gift I will ever be grateful for.

To the cover and content crew; I could not have this
wonderful, professional product without your
excellent efforts. Thank you!

As always, to my husband. You, like our beautiful
child, are everything. You are my family and my life.

Miranda Mayer

Table of Contents:

Miranda Mayer

1. First Impressions

Arnsword bumbled around the corner of the archive shelf, leaving the area of Anatomy and Medicine, and nearly tripped over Ynith where she sat cross-legged amid several stacks of books in the next section of shelves. It was late morning, and it was rare for anyone to be in the archive besides those that staffed it. Both Ynith and Arnsword were surprised to see the other there.

The first thing that struck Ynith about Arnsword was that he was a clumsy exercise in slants and corners. He was too narrow and lean, his shoulders sharp, his lines harsh, his clothes hanging and draping heavily from his edges. His severe face was long, his cheeks drawn, emerald-green eyes large with heavy lids. He stood with a posture that bespoke an aloof boredom; his pelvis hitched out to his side, his shoulders slanted, and his long, bony back hunched and indifferent. His hair was cut short, and it was unkempt, sticking straight up in places at all angles, his sideburns long and in disarray.

He glanced down at her, appearing unmoved while he circumvented her on his gangly legs, settling into an area of shelving containing several hundred books on Rhoic Dynasty period history. He glanced at her again, and then again, choosing a book from the shelf which he opened, leafing through the pages in silence. He tried to seem interested in his book and oblivious of Ynith whereas she merely studied this awkward stick-figure for a brief moment and then turned her attention back to the towers of books around her. She pulled a few more off the shelf in front of her and sorted them onto her stacks.

"What in the name of Furos are you doing besides making a mess of these books?" The words emanated from the rickety figure in the most condescending tone; his stiff upper lip and haughty gaze rankling Ynith at once. He was seemingly interested after all. She looked up at him, puzzled by his puzzlement. His long, black broadfall breeches were baggy on his thin legs, and looked like folded paper at the knees. The fashion was to have close-fitting leggings; she couldn't imagine he could pull that off at all with his bony legs. He wore a black waistcoat, a white shirt with a rumpled collar and the high-collared black robe of a final-year sagging from his shoulders and flopping about his arms. The fabric was pleated liberally and surprisingly elegantly off of the short yoke on his back, the full, swaying hem hovering at his ankles. The deep gold piping at the seam of the yoke and down the front panels was indication of his year. The bright pop of white on his knuckles and neck made even small movements noticeable and distracting to Ynith, who was trying to concentrate on her task. It didn't help that he was quite fidgety and awkward.

"I'm re-sorting them. This section is in particular disarray, the Docent asked if I could fix it and order other sections," she retorted, perhaps a bit too defensively. "I'm nearly finished with these last two shelves, I'll be moving on to the magics and out of the way momentarily." The young man arched his brow dubiously and snorted, turning his attention back to his shelf for a while. He couldn't help himself, however, and his face invariably pivoted back towards the delicate creature hunched cross-legged on the floor in a nest of literary towers. Her red-piped, black robes rumpled around her, signifying to him that she was but a year behind him. She wore the standard black linen jumper gown that young ladies were required to wear beneath her robes, with the plain white button-front chemisette with simple sleeves that drooped over her delicate knuckles. The bony character was most apt to gaze at her at any given opportunity, and seemed intent on pestering her as much as possible.

"How are you choosing to sort them? I hope you're thinking it through properly," he added. She frowned and looked up, her pretty brow furrowing in annoyance.

"I am sorting them mostly as they were sorted before they were jumbled up, perhaps with a few improvements," Ynith grumbled defensively. She picked up a rather worn and crumpled sheet of coarse wood-pulp paper and proffered it to him. Written in a messy hand was an outline of the subject matter contained on that shelf and a structure of how to organize the texts. There were a few newly inked words that had been recently added to the pages in a careful, quite artful hand along with a few scratches and arrows.

His eyes quickly scanned the page, and at length he nodded in concession, but still offered a dubious frown as he feigned interest in a tome about the Frain Dynasty. He pulled it off the shelf and flipped it open to a random page, pretending to skim the dense text, but she could feel his gaze on her soon after that. Ynith rolled her eyes and went back to work. She was determined not to allow this strange character to ruffle her feathers.

There was a brief, pleasant moment of silence that was disturbed only by the hollow sound of Ynith's fingers thrumming one of the books as she figured out which tower it should be set on. She nearly forgot he was there. Then he cleared his throat, revealing he had stealthed his way right up behind her and was presently reading the titles of the books on the top of each pile.

"Don't you think the book on the Alrian Isles ought to go on top of this pile?" His long, skeletal finger pointed to a squat tower of varied historical atlases.

"It's not an *atlas*. It's a historical text," she muttered in annoyance, glancing irritably up at him. Gazing up at him from that angle made him look even taller and skinnier and more austere. He did not believe her, and stooped, grasping the book and opening it up to verify this claim. Having proven Ynith correct, he quietly slid the book back onto its stack. Ynith glowered, and straightened her back, jutting out her chin defiantly. With a barely controlled voice she said:

"The *Docent* trusts that I am capable of doing this task correctly. If you believe that I cannot be trusted to do the job, feel free to speak to the Docent. In the meantime, I'd like to finish this. My legs have fallen asleep sitting here and I have pins and needles," she snapped. Arnsword withdrew his hand as if she'd burnt it with her words and stepped back.

"Ap... Apologies," he muttered, almost in a bewildered manner, surprised by the irritation in her tone, and apparently quite unsure how to respond to it. He sidled away, and vanished into the stacks. When he was well out of sight, Ynith huffed out in exasperation and got to her feet, managing to do so without upsetting her circle of book towers. After verifying he was no longer there, she lifted her hems up to the shabby green ribbons holding her stockings up at her knees, and gingerly stepped out of the circle. She then minced around on her prickly feet until the stinging started to abate. She ambled up and down the narrow aisle between the two bookcases. When she walked briskly down the aisle to the end and turned around once more, she saw the unmistakable silhouette of the scarecrow standing in the light of the high-set arched window. He was at present bending down and reaching for one of her stacks.

"Please!" she shouted angrily, "can you not leave it alone?" He straightened himself momentarily and squinted down the aisle at her.

"I've decided that I want one of the books in your pile here," he replied, pointing one of his osteal fingers to the books. He bent down again, and Ynith hurried towards him. He pulled a book right from the middle of the tallest stack, upsetting it. In doing so, the falling books avalanched into the other towers, setting off a chain reaction that could not be stopped. Before she got to him, her neat stacks were reduced to a shuffle. If anyone had done it intentionally they couldn't have done a better job than he. Only one short stack had survived the devastation. When he looked up, Ynith's face was beet red and her small hands were gripped into angry fists against her thighs. She gritted her teeth at him, and a tear rolled down her cheek. *"GO AWAY!"* The words burst from her mouth with great force and ire, her normal poised and controlled voice was raw and imbued with fury. His green eyes locked on her face for an uncomfortable moment, and they were filled with utter confusion.

"S..sorry," he stammered. With a strange attempt at a conciliatory smile, he hugged the book he'd taken to his chest, hesitated twice as if wanting to say something, but gave up and scurried off into the stacks. A loud, frustrated, anguished scream rose up from the stacks with a resounding clarity as soon as he'd gone. Ynith then flopped down obstinately onto the ground and started brusquely gathering up the books, her eyes burning with frustrated, salty tears.

She was angry at herself for being so upset over the books. It was her assigned task and she was being a big baby, but she was tired from a night of little sleep to begin with, and she also felt she had so much to prove to the Docent, and here a simple task would now take her twice as long to complete; *what will he think of me?* Ynith was very upset, and gave in to her tears, hiccupping through them as she tried to make order of the chaos scattered around her.

She sorted and sniffled, occasionally pausing to wipe her tears with the edge of her long cuff. She also had several more bookcases to do apart from this one. Only a few moments later, she was interrupted again:

"What in the name of Elgos was that, young Ynith? Are you unwell?" Ynith turned her red and brimming eyes up to see the Docent himself, whose eyes were wide with concern as he wrung his hands.

He was a sweet, quiet sort of fellow; aged somewhere in his mid-sixties perhaps, his hair more white than grey, his body permanently hunched from years of sitting over a book. Rumour had it that he had once been one of the more powerful wizards of his time, but chose to set aside his conjurings for a less demanding occupation. She couldn't imagine this old bear being capable of destructive powers. He squinted at her with his clear blue eyes and pushed his little pince-nez spectacles up onto the upper bridge of his nose. He was in his robes as always. His were less elaborate than the Professors' robes, and were worn and threadbare. The entire faculty wore cassock-like garments; his were shapeless, older of fashion and shabby in places.

"I apologize for my outburst, Docent," she said, her voice shaking. The Docent studied her flustered expression and glassy eyes, and a sympathetic smile spread across his lined face.

"Do you need a rest dear girl? You've been at it all morning, I confess I forgot you were out here. Poor little thing. How awful of me to forget about you. Your shout did quite startle me out of some very deep contemplation, which I probably needed."

"I would not decline a little break, sir. But it wasn't the work that caused the outburst. I am not trying to make excuses for this mess, but the whole thing was caused by a rather rude and thoughtless archive visitor. I had all these books organized, and now they're all a mess again," she sighed shakily, her voice still wavering from the edge of tears.

"Visitor? There's only been me and the Everath, the hapless fellow. Has *he* been a nuisance to you?" She paused and looked at the old man with an expression of incredulity. She tried to speak a couple of times but couldn't form a word. She then blurted:

"The Everath? The Everath was here? Are you sure there was no one else?" she repeated, her face twisted in bafflement. The old man sighed,

"Yes, he is the only one this morning that has come through the doors, I was sitting right there," he nodded gravely. Then his expression lightened and he waved his hand dismissively. "He is not exactly what one imagines a prince to be, eh?" he chuckled. She shook her head in stunned agreement, her mouth agape. Then a look of pure horror washed over her pretty features.

"I just screamed at the prince?" her face turned waxen and the tears began to fill the brim of her lids again. Her fingers hovered just over her lower lip and they trembled slightly. She knew that the Everath attended the academy, but had no idea who he was. The girls were mostly segregated from the young men.

"Oh, don't worry about that. He is an impolite and admonishing character by nature. Trust me, I know him better than most. And because he isn't overtly going about saying: 'hey ho, I'm the Everath,' it's only to be expected that people won't know they're addressing a royal when they shout at him—which I suspect is something that happens a good deal more than one expects. You are not the first, and he isn't the resentful type. I honestly think he *wants* people to be frank with him—but most of the time they are not, and are too busy cowering in deference at him. He's a tolerable sort of chap deep down, in spite of that condescending veneer. I've known him many years. Don't fret little Ynith. Come, stand up." He reached out and took her hands, pulling her to her feet. "Leave the books as they are; nobody will notice anyway since hardly anyone comes into the archives this time of day. Let's go and have a cup of tea and sit down by the hearth in my office. It's my tea-time anyhow. You deserve a nice break for all your work today. You can take this up later." He took her hand and looped it around his arm, pressing her hand there so he could pat it kindly as he walked. Ynith strode alongside the old man, her robes fluttering around her legs.

They wended their way through the labyrinthine shelves of the archive, moving with a comfortable silence towards the private offices that the Docent occupied. She'd never been inside them. He released her arm to open the door, and then ushered her into the warm, cozy space. She moved into the office area, and looked about. Three heavily upholstered, spongy chairs hunched like old, sagging boulders by a fire which burned low; the embers dancing beautifully on the sooty coals. "Sit, girl, sit," he gestured towards a chair. She complied, surprised by how low she sank down into the squashy upholstery. She scooted to the edge in order to appear more composed, her eyes taking in the rich colours of the rug that covered the whole floor, with its ruddy-coloured fringe that edged the room. He had a few crammed bookshelves against the wall as well, and his desk was a clutter of papers, books, dirty tea cups and what appeared to be a stuffed bird, although most of its feathers had come off.

The Docent disappeared through an archway, and returned carrying a bundle of firewood and a heavy black kettle. He knelt in front of the hearth and jabbed some frayed pieces of kindling into the orange embers. This welcome new fuel made the embers pop into life as flames, and when the kindling was snapping along, he put the larger pieces atop them.

He hung the kettle over the flames, and then shuffled back to fetch more things. Ynith scanned the faded tapestries insulating the stone walls, which depicted scenes of the desert countries. One showed the execution of the legendary ogrein Othrick, his twisted body under the feet of the great knight Alnord, the disembodied head being held aloft by the knight's mail gauntlet. She smiled to herself, as she studied the woven features of the Knight, recalling that he was a Shalmeen; which meant he was one of her ancestors.

Her eyes then took in the grayish garlands of cobwebs occupying the upper walls, draping with some eerie grace over a collection of figures and items lined up along the top of the book cases—some so caked in dust, they were unrecognizable. The Docent brought clean cups, and a little tray table upon which he set a nice pile of small cakes.

He steeped the tea and poured it from a finely-made formal serving kettle that hung from a tall, gracefully turned matching silver plated floor-base. She took the cup and sat as politely as she knew how on the edge of the precipitous chair, feeling awkward doing so in the clumsy, coarse robes and the rough linen gown she had to wear when in school.

Ynith was one of the only girls allowed out of the ladies' wing to work in the administrative areas. There were only thirty one girls total in the school of over five hundred students. The girls ranged in age from six to twenty, although the elder girls outnumbered the young ones significantly.

The boys were allowed free rein everywhere except the girl's wing, which was a part of the oldest building of the academy complex, annexed entirely for their use. It included the dormitory, the refectory, a small library, a large common room that was comfortably appointed, and a decent sized room for projects and work. They also had their own small well-maintained courtyard to enjoy the outdoors in privacy from the boys.

Most of the young men used of their free rein to invent ways to spy on the girls. They were constantly getting in trouble for scheming their way into forbidden areas to catch glimpses of the young ladies in their isolated part of the school. They hoped to catch a glimpse of an ankle perhaps, or to see one of the ladies wearing her hair down. There were some prospects about the academy that allowed them to look into the girls' dorm windows and they never seemed to run out of ingenious new ideas on how to get to them. It was a constant and unending thing to hear of some boy or another being caught and reprimanded for trying to sneak a peek into the ladies' domain. This was something many of the girls found most amusing.

Girls came and went from the Darvath; some took their studies seriously, and some left to be married. Ynith had come there as quite a young child. She had nobody to go home to; nobody who didn't have questionable motives about her to begin with. The Darvath was not only her school, it was her home and it had been for many years.

"You're a timid little thing normally, Ynith, I'm a bit astonished at your temper today." The Docent was gazing at her as she looked about his office, his eyes filled with humour and kindness.

"It was unbecoming and childish, I know," she said ashamedly. The Docent sat down with his cup of tea and bit into a cake, chewing thoughtfully. He then shook his head;

"I don't know about it being unbecoming or such, but it still surprises me. Your temperament and steadiness is what earned you the privilege of assisting me here in the archive. Please don't think your outburst today has had any influence on my opinion of you, it hasn't. We all have our limits—and Arnsword knows very well how to push someone's limits. Still, I heard that scream, but I still can't imagine all that noise coming out of such a little creature," he chortled delightedly. She smirked and then snorted with laughter.

"I let him bother me too much, perhaps. A prince indeed." They laughed together. She gazed at him, her eyes twinkling with humour. She liked the Docent very much; he was so kind. It was her third day with him, and she had the whole year to look forward to working with him—possibly more, depending on the way things turned out. Her eyes quickly wandered around his office, which was in such disorder. She resolved to help him manage it, and to attack the dust on the top of the shelves at first chance.

"I don't have much experience working with young ladies like yourself—you are the first I've had assigned here, but I dare say you have been a great delight to me these few days. More competent than most of the layabouts I've been assigned from the boys' wing; and patient, and efficient. AND..." he stressed, raising the hand holding half of a little cake, "I can sit down and have a nice tea with you and you are not bored or embarrassed by it as the young men would be. We should make this a daily routine, don't you think? Tea before nuncheon, at the tenth-hour I think, and maybe something light at threeish? What think you?" She nodded with a smile.

"Good. I like company with my tea; especially with young ladies that flatter an old man with a smile. Here, have a cake, my dear," he lifted up the plate and let her pick one. She nibbled on it delicately and sipped her tea, her cheeks flushed and heart warmed by his words. It was the first time in a decade she'd felt that comfortable with one of the school's faculty. The professors were kind to her; they always were, but not familiar like this; not comforting and humourous. She glanced at him as he ate another cake with great relish, pouring some more tea. She wondered in passing why he'd never become a professor, and remained a Docent. The rumours of his legacy in magic were numerous and flattering, in spite of the sometimes less-than favorable view of magic-bearers.

The old man seemed content to chat about little things and keep the conversation light and pleasant. She polished off her last cake, drank three cups of tea, and then declared it was time to go back to work. The old man shook his head, "you should perhaps join your lady friends at your wing for nuncheon."

"I'm full of cakes. We chose to take such a late tea, I am not hungry, not to mention that I'm almost finished with the histories.

I'd like to work my way through magic to the biographies today and get them all done. I'm looking forward to the transcribing, and want to get to it quickly."

He smiled at that, and stood as she did. "I'm looking forward to showing you the ropes on transcribing texts. I have seen your artwork, and you have a lovely hand; you will write some beautiful books." Ynith blushed and smiled. She wanted a hasty escape because the three cups of tea were catching up to her, and she needed to make a brief detour to the wash chamber before going back to the stacks.

"Thank you, Docent." She curtsied politely and made her way to the door.

"Very well. Do you need help sorting the mess the Everath made?" he called, taking a step towards her. She lifted her hand and waved dismissively.

"No, it wasn't that horrid, I overreacted." He smiled and sent her back into the stacks. She ran off to the wash chamber, and then eventually made her way through the shelves with renewed energy, and a glow in her soul from the special attentions of this fatherly figure. She turned into the row she'd left and stopped short.

Her pile of books was gone. On the floor where the pile had been was the outline page she'd left behind. The books were filed tidily back onto the shelves, ordered as she had them based on the outline. She knelt and picked up the outline, much mystified. On the very bottom of the page, underneath the outline, a line of nine new words had been scrawled in careful, beautiful script. "I am very sorry that I made you cry."

Miranda Mayer

2. Better Acquainted

Ynith woke up several days later with a smile. It was the week's end, and she had been invited, along with another student, to accompany the Docent to a social visit away from the school for the day and evening. This was a heady privilege and an unexpected surprise. The Docent asked her only the day before and was not very detailed in what the activities would be or their ultimate destination, but she did not care, she was excited to get out of Darvath, for she rarely ever did. She was even more delighted with the opportunity to shuck her heavy school robes and to feel like a girl again.

Ynith shared a room with a large gawky girl by the name of Treen. She was not a pretty creature by any means, with a long, hawkish nose, and long teeth that made her look horse-like. Her eyes drooped like that of a hound, and she had mousy, thin hair. She always wore it in the tightest of buns that pulled the corners of her eyes into a squint, and she had little to no grace at all. She was however, gifted by the gods when it came to academics. Her inability to maintain any meaningful social interaction was a great obstacle for her, but when it came to learning, she was brilliant;

and it was very likely she'd end up becoming a docent and then ultimately a professor someday.

Treen was overtly jealous of Ynith's special appointment to the archive. She believed she deserved the honour more than Ynith. Ynith could not really disagree based on academics; Ynith's studies were excellent, but Treen's were outstanding. However, it was understood that Ynith's manners and sweet nature had earned her the position as much as her level of learning. The administrators knew that Ynith would get along with the Docent who was notoriously difficult with most students. Treen would drive an affable but impatient old man to distraction with her overzealous efforts. Ynith, after these few days wondered at that now.

The Docent seemed more than affable, he was doting. She saw no impatience or intolerance in him at all. Everyone spoke of his having a short temper and she had been the only one to display that character flaw so far. He was mostly a happy fellow when she was about; he hummed tunes, and scripted alongside her, chatting about banalities and fussing over tea, which he seemed to cherish the most. He discovered Ynith had a particular blend of tea she enjoyed called Summer Pudding, which was a mix of black tea and some fragrant berries, and that she had a taste for some walnut biscuits his sister sent him every week, and he made great effort to insure she had what pleased her most when she was working in the archive with him.

Ynith's appreciation and politeness was most gratifying for the old man, who saw very little of either in the students he'd been saddled with before her. She could not know that it was her very nature that made him happy. He was growing to adore the girl very quickly, and it was becoming most important to the Docent that he think of her wellbeing beyond the archive, as most of the faculty had hoped he would in pressing him to accept her assignment to him. So he decided to include her in his weekly visits to his sister's home. He had not been collected enough to tell her this, he only told her to dress prettily for a day abroad, for he would be taking her someplace nice to enjoy the day. Ynith did not press him for more information; she merely smiled and nodded, imagining an afternoon outside Darvath and the company of at least one person she knew she enjoyed very much. That was all she needed to know.

Treen was particularly standoffish that morning because Ynith was going on an outing with the Docent. She ignored her all through breakfast at the refectory and now sat at her desk sulking, pretending to write something, although her quill hardly scratched at all. Ynith was positioned at the single vanity the girls shared. Ynith made use of it for the most part. Treen occasionally poked her face in front of the hammered silver mirror to adjust the position of her hair bun. Ynith was fashioning two little twisted buns behind each ear, and arranging curls of her lovely silken black hair around her face and her coif.

"I find it quite peculiar that you should be going on an outing alone with an old man," Treen mumbled acidly. She sat at her desk on one of the two wingback chairs, writing something as she spoke. Treen's leg shook underneath the table, a silent communication of her irritation. Treen was the only girl she knew that still wore the drab black jumper-gown and sleeved chemisette at endweek. Everyone else shucked the robes and uniform and put on whatever loveliness they could wear just so they could feel civilized and ladylike for the three days of rest. Not Treen. She did not wear her robes, but the black gown was invariably wrapped around her slight form, her ink-stained cuffs hanging limply from under her hand.

"It isn't peculiar at all. He takes students with him often on his outings. The only peculiarity is that I'm a girl, and since I'm the first from our wing to be assigned to him, it's bound to seem different," Ynith replied with a deliberate airiness. "It's nothing out of the ordinary, really. Besides, there is another student to accompany us; one of his prior assistants." She stood and looked at her underpinnings in the mirror, tucking the shoulder of her shift under the stays and turning to look at the line on her back. Satisfied, she reached for her strapped petticoat, tugging it over her head. She shifted it to encircle the high waist before fastening it just underneath her bust, adjusting the straps on her shoulders to sit on her other underpinnings.

"Should I wear a chemisette or a fichu? I don't want to be *too* warm…"

"I couldn't care less what you wear; do I look like someone who cares a jot about being fashionable?" Treen snarled. Ynith's shoulders sagged a bit and she sighed.

"I'm sorry, Treen. I certainly didn't mean to irritate you," she moved to her small armoire and opened it. Inside were four identical robes for school, six neatly pressed black linen gowns (two were in the laundering basket), a small row of the heavy white cotton sleeved chemisettes that went with the gowns hanging from pegs on the door, and standing out from the uniformity on one side of the armoire, three thin, wispy little muslin gowns. One was pristine white, one was forget-me-not blue and one was an elegant silver-grey and partially embroidered with an intricate pattern down the front and along the hem. She wasn't quite finished with the project.

She picked the white gown, and took it off the hook, laying it out delicately on the bed. She took a wispy triangle of fabric from a small drawer and drew it over her neck and shoulders, pinning the ends to the front of her stays. With a final adjustment to her underpinnings, she loosed the stomacher of the gown and stepped into the gauzy material. She pulled the back on like a jacket and buttoned it closed under her breasts. She then tightened the ties around the high waistline, and tied a bow, tucking the ends underneath the bib which she then lifted up and closed the buttons on. With a tug here and a tuck there, she looked at herself again. With a bit of doubt, she sighed, wondering if she looked too plain to be out and about. This dress was the nicest one she had—at least until she finished the grey one.

Ynith was beautiful. Nineteen, sheltered and modest of nature, Ynith had no idea how stunning she was. She was a petite thing, with light-grey eyes and fair, soft skin. Her face was sweetness embodied; her eyes wide and curious, full of kindness and temperance, her full lips smiling, her cheeks flush with life and beauty. In her white gown, she was elegant and charming.

She put on a simple straw bonnet adorned with sky-blue ribbons and a flouncy white feather, and tied the ribbons under her chin. She picked up her only shawl and most treasured possession; a wide and long skein of the finest goatswool fabric, intricately woven into a beautiful pattern in burgundies, royal blues and a rainbow of jewel tones. She wrapped it around her shoulders and turned to Treen, whose leg still shook frenetically underneath the desk. She markedly avoided eye-contact, and continued writing. The small clock on the bookshelf struck the ninth hour, and was immediately followed by the sound of the clock tower as it began its cranking and whirring across the court from their window. It tolled as well. The bell was loud but they were accustomed to it. Ynith gave one last glance into the mirror, and waited for the tolling to finish before looking at Treen.

"I'm off then. The coach will be here any moment. I hope you have a good day, Treen," Ynith muttered. She slipped out of the room. She heard Treen snort defiantly as she closed the door. With a sigh, she moved with purpose down the narrow hallway of the dormitories, passing the open-doored apartments of many other girls who hung about in various states of leisure, some of whom smiled warmly at Ynith as she walked by in her finest clothes, envious of her escape.

In her deep red slippers with the matching silk ribbon ties around her slight white-stockinged ankles, she padded down the steps into the garden common, which she crossed like a pale blossom passing through a garden of roses. After a quick scurry through the main hall, she exited the ladies' wing and crossed through the vaulted halls that connected to the main building. A few of the male students roaming about in plainclothes glanced at her as she flitted through, a few making appreciative noises. She ignored them and headed to the main doorway, heaving the great portal open successfully before any of the boys could make it to assist her. She tugged it closed, and turned just in time to see one of the school's older coaches pulled by a heavy team come 'round the bend on the white drive of crushed oyster shells.

In the window was the smiling face of the Docent, who admired her prettiness with an adoring grin. He opened the door for her, and handed her in. She smiled shyly at him and sat down next to the second student; a young man by the name of Hestin who she knew of but had never met until today. He was an upperclassman and was only a few weeks shy of being set free from the Darvath Academy. He was a stoic, handsome fellow, who made no effort in hiding his appraisal of the newest passenger. The coachman made a little clicking noise and the coach began to travel forward, pulled by two cinnamon coloured light-draughts.

"Ynith, I don't believe you've been introduced to your predecessor," the Docent declared. "This is Hestin, and Hestin, this extraordinarily lovely creature is your successor, Ynith, and she's doing a bang up job at it too. Infinitely more meticulous and competent at her work, by far."

"Well, if I had been young and pretty and a girl would my competence have been improved?" Hestin retorted with a chuckle.

"I would hope there is much more of value to what I offer than my youth or supposed loveliness, especially to you and the archive, Docent," Ynith replied. The Docent smiled and nodded.

"Ynith, you are a skilled organizer and showing to be a tremendous artist and scribe. You are also a delight, and it's not just your pretty face that makes you so—though I will not lie and say that it does not make having you as my assistant all the pleasanter; the gentle company is infinitely more desirable. AND," he added with a grin, "she takes tea with me every day."

"Well *that* alone is a critical qualifier, taking tea is one of our Docent's most treasured rituals," Hestin informed Ynith as if this were a great secret, whispering loudly. "I am very pleased our Docent found someone who shares an appreciation for the finer things. I see now where the extra competence points for Miss Ynith have come from. I can rest now that I know I was not *completely* inept. I just didn't care to take *tea*." He offered her a humourous smile, which she returned shyly. "I confess, however, Miss Ynith, that this is the first time I think anyone has ever seen the Docent gush so liberally about anyone before, so you must be *quite* remarkable." Ynith blushed and looked away.

"We've only worked together less than two weeks, give it time," she whispered uncomfortably. Hestin shook his head and grinned. The Docent reached across to pat her hand as if to assure her there would be no time where his good opinion of her would ever change.

They rocked as the carriage trundled onto the main road from the pristine shell-roads of the academy campus. The roughness of the ride increased by tenfold immediately, and Ynith's bonnet feather waved about like a banner as they swung along with the body of the coach.

"Hestin, Ynith has reordered a number of the research sections using your outlines, but I dare say, she has taken your guides and interpreted them beautifully. She has an intuitive sense for organizing books. And she has taken to organizing my offices as well. She got up to the top shelves yesterday, and washed everything down. It's starting to look too clean in there for the likes of me."

"Thank you Docent," Ynith's cheeks turned red. All this interest was nearly too difficult to bear. She turned her attention to the window, watching with a child-like excitement as the landscape opened up to reveal the rolling hills of Evronell. She was ashamed by how little she actually saw of the world outside of the Darvath, and in spite of her being a bit cowed and intimidated by being outside of her comfort zone, she could not hide her excitement for doing something out of the ordinary. She often lamented her sheltered life when the other girls came and went on family visits and sometimes on voyages to exotic places with their family and friends for weeks at a time. She never had that opportunity. She remained at the Darvath. For the better part of her life, her entire domain consisted of the girls' wing at the academy and very little more. She watched avidly as the hills slipped by, at the pop of gold of a newly thatched cottage roof, or a field dotted with sheep that looked like little ivory puffs of wool, tottering about on four spindly legs. She lost herself for a moment, forgetting there was a conversation still active inside the coach.

"Well, I cannot say I ever aspired to be the best organizer of books. But it was a pleasant an occupation as any could be at the academy, and I do admit that I will miss the musty old books when I'm gone from here," Hestin's voice startled her attention back into the coach.

"Our Hestin is to inherit a grant. After he leaves here; he will be a true gentleman," the Docent informed her proudly.

"I intend to pursue my studies beyond the academy, as my father did."

"Your father's patronage of the intellectual arts has advanced much knowledge in the sciences; that they have. He would be proud to see you continue your family's support of the pursuit of information," the Docent beamed. Hestin nodded gravely.

"I am sure. What of you Ynith? What shall you do when you are finished with the Academy?" Ynith flushed and lowered her face, her fingers wringing around her shawl. She didn't have a place to go—and there were few occupations available for anyone of the fairer sex. She was here by the patronage of distant relatives who knew not what to do with a rich orphan. She cleared her throat and looked outside uncomfortably.

"I am not certain yet. I have until next year to decide," she muttered in a faint voice. The Docent sensed her unease and changed the subject, bringing up instead her run-in with the Prince. Hestin's laugh was open and hearty, and he chortled a great deal when the Docent described her frustrated scream.

"Eh haha hahah, you shouted at the Everath! That is brilliant!" Hestin laughed, slapping his knee delightedly.

"I did not know," she pleaded, which only made Hestin laugh harder, "and I didn't shout *at* him per say, but *because* of him." Ynith's smile was subdued, her laughter stiff and uncomfortable. She had not told of the gesture of apology, and how thoughtful the stork was. She hadn't seen him since to thank him and offer her apologies for her inexcusable outburst.

"No one can deny that the young man is a bit of a buffoon…"

"Hestin!" the Docent admonished.

"He is only a bit awkward." Ynith mumbled in Arnsword's defense, feeling guilty for speaking of him where he could not defend himself.

"Oh no, you will see, buffoon" Hestin chuckled. The Docent showed a subtle reaction to Hestin's words, as if he'd been disrespected by them. But he remained quiet and sat back a bit. Ynith thought Hestin was being disrespectful as well. Hestin was oblivious to the subtle change of humour in the coach. He crossed his leg and gazed out the window with his eyes still smiling at the humour of the tale. In spite of Hestin's belittling attitude towards the prince, Ynith could not deny that he did cut a handsome figure in his wheaten breeches, top boots and elegant pine-green frock coat over a goldenrod and ivory striped waistcoat. He had his face meticulously shaven and groomed save for a pair of handsome sideburns, and his expression of humour had melted away the initial stoicism he bore when she first climbed into the coach. His bicorn sat beside him on the bench, its white feathers dancing with the movement of the coach.

The weather was very warm, and it was decided to lower the top of the coach so they could ride in fresh air. The atmosphere within was getting close and uncomfortable.

"If we are to be jostled about like molded jellies, then we should at least have the comfort of a breeze and the benefit of a view!" the Docent declared. So the livery stopped, and they sat patiently while the footman wrestled with the rickety top, trying to fold the stiffened leather and spindly wooden frame down and secure it so they could continue on.

Their comfort was instantly improved by the open top. Ynith was so happy to see all around her, and to look at the landscape she so rarely saw. Soon enough they were on their way again, the fresh breeze blowing the single feather on her bonnet to and fro— the view made her nearly forget the jostling altogether. She was feeling increasingly excited about this day. She did not let Hestin's nature dampen her spirit; she was looking forward to whatever the Docent had in mind. As if he'd read her thoughts, the older gentleman turned to her and smiled openly.

"So, my dear, are you not even slightly curious about our destination today?"

"Of course I am, Docent, however I would not presume to ask. I am so thrilled simply to be invited. I get out of the Academy so little. Even if we did nothing but ride about in circles, it would be a great occasion for me. And I like surprises," she added with no shortage of delight.

"Do you not go home for visitations?" Hestin asked. The Docent did not allow for a possible reply, knowing she did not have one. The Docent had tried very subtly to hint at Hestin to cease the questions of a personal nature, but the young man again seemed oblivious to subtlety. Even Ynith was able to see the old man's effort to catch the young man's eye and to relay the message with a very slight shake of the head or furrow of his shaggy silver brow.

"Well, my dear, we are visiting my sister, the Lady Farnham. She is a wealthy widow who lives on a fine estate a few miles from here. Her home is unfortunately located for society. She has only a very small village and only two sizable houses to pay her visit within reasonable distance. She is sorely lacking in society and discourse, and begs me to visit and to bring her fresh new faces as frequently as possible. I visit here often at endweek, and most of the time we spend the three days in the most dull and stick-in-the-muddish way possible; at least from the perspective of the young and the lively. But we do take company on occasion when we are there. Sometimes we have other family present, but they too prefer a more peaceful time than I imagine you or Hestin would prefer. She has promised good, lively company today for your first visit, Miss Ynith. So there should be many diversions. She is already doubly delighted that you are coming, for she longs for a young lady to talk to. Do you sing, Ynith?"

"I have been taught music and singing," she replied, shifting uncomfortably, her voice immediately tentative. The idea of singing in front of a group of people seemed quite daunting.

"Be prepared, for my sister's piano has been neglected for too many years, and she will surely ask you to sing." Ynith blanched and shrank back against the seat of the coach.

"Oh dear, am I frightening you? Oh, my dear Ynith do not be frightened. Please, be at ease. This is my family, and my family will delight in you no matter what you do. Whatever the rest of the company thinks should be meaningless to you, they are of no consequence." He reached out and patted her hand. She smiled wanly and remained largely silent the rest of the way.

The Docent was attentive to her feelings, and kept the conversation light. It was the first time in his entire career he'd been presented with a creature like Ynith. She was a thing to dote upon, and someone who gave him pleasure to see and speak with, and she was very good at her job on top of that. She was the young person whose manners and humility and modesty made the young men who he'd come to know seem like boors.

He knew of her situation, her deceased parents, and the fortune behind her. He knew of those who sought to remove it from her when she was very young, and the fight undertaken by a distant but caring uncle, who found a way to protect her and her fortune—which was to remove her from the society of her relatives at once. She arrived at the academy at five years old, a timid, frightened mouse. The faculty members that knew her loved her. They had petitioned the Docent heavily to have him accept her as his assistant, despite his policy against having any young women working in the archive, but they knew of his sister and they knew it would be of advantage to a girl with no true advantages. For, in spite of the fortune that ostensibly awaited her, she had no home to return to, no family that awaited her, no circle of friends or patrons to welcome her. Even with Shalmeen blood, she had very little to look forward to when the time came for her to leave the Darvath. Ynith had changed Docent Oreth's entire perception in her short time with him, and he vowed to do what he could to help her find some balance in her life, and to forge a future beyond the academy.

The Docent Oreth's sister was perhaps the best wager for that—she was extremely well-connected and unlike her brother, she actively partook in her advantageous society whenever she could. The siblings were related to the throne; Lady Farnham and the Docent were brother and sister to the Queen Consort. However Lady Farnham was the one that kept that connection alive, unlike her brother who did not care and preferred his books.

The Everath was the Docent's nephew, and this is why he had taken quiet offense to Hestin's ridicule. He knew people talked about Arnsword in a less than stellar light, but he did not like to hear it first-hand. But very few people knew of the connection and were free to assume they were safe to gossip maliciously.

The Docent set aside his annoyance, and thought ahead to their arrival. He knew his sister was simply dying for something to do and someone to focus on. When he told her of the appointment of this young lady to his archive, she was immediately interested in meeting her, and when the Docent had shared Ynith's unfortunate story, Lady Farnham was doubly determined to take the girl under her wing. She had been all a-titter all week, sending notes to be assured he hadn't forgotten to invite Ynith, and more notes to insure that Ynith had accepted, and more letters to ask what he knew of her preferred foods and tea, and was in raptures when he told her Ynith liked the walnut biscuits Lady Farnham's pastry chef sent to Darvath each week.

Oreth knew his sister would be good for Ynith and Ynith would be invaluable for his sister, whose own children and grandchildren were spoiled and inattentive to her. She spent most of her time alone in her great house, or surrounded by the vapid attentions of the scarce, low society that attended her. Ynith would receive her attentions with gratitude and kindness, and return his sister's thoughtfulness with the friendship and companionship she desired. It was a perfect arrangement as far as the Docent was concerned. And it also meant he would be able to spend as much time with the delightful girl as possible.

For Oreth, Ynith represented an unusual and unique enchantment. She was gentle, sweet, cultured, and polite; she also had incredible talent, was well-spoken, educated and interesting to speak to. He relished these qualities the moment he discovered them. She was so quiet on the most part; very few people knew this of the girl, so he felt most privileged to be one of the only people who knew the depth of this young woman. He also appreciated how pleasant her company could be for a lonely old man. He knew his sister would also appreciate that there was much more to Ynith than her peaceful, timid demeanor. He knew there was fire underneath and Ressa would love that about her.

The faculty members that had sought out Oreth's help for Ynith as a whole agreed this was the best choice for the sweet-tempered, pretty girl, and they supported her appointment to the Docent's archive. Even more so, they desired the opportunity to find a place in society so when she graduated, she would belong somewhere. In spite of her title and her money, Ynith was quite the little foundling, and the faculty of the Darvath felt especially responsible for her. Oreth, once he became familiar with Ynith, was most delighted to be the provider of this opportunity for the young woman, and looked forward to seeing her blossom under the devoted care of his excellent sister and to possibly even become a fixture in her household, and in part, his.

Ynith's eyes, the moment she entered the large, opulent parlour locked with horror on the unmistakable shape of the Everath. She could scarce believe it. He was here! His shape was cast against an etched window—he was apparently stalking about a beautiful conservatory through a set of paned-glass doors, and it was no doubt that same scarecrow frame she remembered from the library, more defined now for the lack of the school robes.

She did not actually see the Lady until she was upon her, arms open, her hands clamping over-affectionately on Ynith's face. "Oh my goodness Oreth, what have you brought me here? She is so beautiful! Where did you find this elegant little creature?" She dropped her hands and took Ynith's. It was only then she allowed her eyes to stray from the gangly silhouette in the window to the gloriously warm face of the remarkably elegant Lady Farnham.

"She is a student, my dear. My new assistant would you believe it?" He feigned along with his ebullient sister that he had not already shared all this information already.

"*No!*" she exclaimed. "No, no, no, this little creature is too delicate to be sitting about darkened halls and roaming amid hundreds of dusty and cobwebby books. She should be in a place such as this," the Lady exclaimed. "Come, sit with me. Take off that bonnet my dear, and come sit."

Ynith's eyes kept moving back towards the shape of the Everath, who seemed to be enraptured by something growing out of a planter. She was mortified. She did not resist the gentle guidance from the lady, and she followed, resigning herself to the abject humiliation to be expected once the Everath decided to make an appearance. He seemed to be deliberately avoiding the brouhaha that their arrival caused.

Little did Ynith know that the time leading up to their arrival was thick with anticipation as the Lady impatiently waited for the sound of their coach approaching the house. Their arrival set her into raptures, and her company also felt it necessary to echo her delight and repeat her exclamations as well. It was a loud and chaotic welcome for someone who was not accustomed to such noise. Ynith would have liked to avoid the brouhaha too, and quietly envied the Everath for his freedom to escape it.

She quickly tried to take in the company surrounding her. She spotted an older gentleman with a strange, ferrety looking wife, and Hestin immediately fell into an animated chat with the man— they were apparently familiar. They moved away together towards the windows to get away from the Lady's shrill excitement. A younger, very plain woman sat in a chair looking quite sallow and uninterested, and an older woman sat beside her peering impassively upon Ynith as she was guided towards them. Both women were stiff and distant at first glance. As soon as the Lady came within range of them, they made reedy exclamations of welcome that rang quite insincere. They both seemed almost overtly displeased by the noise and fuss, except when the Lady's eyes crossed over them; then they both smiled listlessly and nodded in agreement with whatever exclamation the lady made.

"What is your name my dear?" the ferrety woman asked. Ynith answered confusedly while being gently shoved onto a long settee, and had a cup of tea forced into her hand no sooner did her posterior fall upon the soft jacquard upholstery. Her bonnet, which had been in her hands, disappeared. She kept a tight hold of her shawl, however, when hands reached for it. Only seconds later, a plate full of very rich treats was proffered to her, and all the while, everyone chitty chatted and clucked. Skirts rustled in front of her, and she caught glimpses of the faces of the ladies between them.

She remained rigid and befuddled while the Lady and the ferrety woman, in addition to two servants bustled about her. The

Docent had settled in across from her, and immediately began actively chatting with the other lady and her daughter, whose blank faces melted into affability immediately upon his warm attentions. The ferrety wife of the unknown gentleman was laughing at something, and the servants still hovered in front of Ynith. The other gentlemen chortled loudly in their corner, and Hestin lit a pipe. Finally, the servants vanished, the Lady and the ferret woman had somehow found time to sit down, and everyone in the immediate vicinity turned to Ynith in unison expecting an answer to a question she had not heard. Ynith's face grew pale and stricken and the Lady took instant sympathy upon her.

"Oh, the poor child, look at her, like a muskrat in the light of a trapper's lantern. Our fuss has discomfited you, hasn't it, Ynith? I'm quite certain you must be very unused to all this noise and commotion."

"I was just about to mention that," the Docent muttered.

"Oh, Ynith forgive me. Forgive us!" Lady Farnham exclaimed. "We have all been so verbose and involved that we have scarcely allowed you to get a word in edgewise. How very inconsiderate of us!" Lady Farnham continued.

"Inconsiderate, indeed," Mrs. Ferret parroted, and then the word was echoed twice more out of the mother and daughter's mouths.

"Ahhh. Your Highness," the Lady stood as Arnsword entered the room from the conservatory, and everyone followed suit. Bows and curtsies, low and respectful followed. Ynith felt clumsy as she curtsied, watching him with her face lowered and eyes rolled up. He looked less awkward this day. His society clothing was far better-fitting than his school togs, his hair combed, his sideburns trimmed. He nodded quietly and mumbled something and everyone sank back down into their seats. The three visiting women had fallen distinctly silent and withdrawn when the looming character appeared, as if trying to disappear in his presence. It was then he noticed and recognized Ynith with what was most evident surprise, and she saw a distinct flush on his face for it. She matched it with an embarrassed, wan smile and a drop of the eyes.

The prince could not help but take her in in this altered state. Her raven hair, and large stormy grey eyes ringed with strikingly dark lashes, framed by her delicate brow had been most appealing the first time he set eyes upon her. Now, in this setting, it was almost impossible to tear his gaze away from her. Her mouth was a rose pink, full and delicate. The white gown made her features appear almost magnified. He was floored by the sight of her. He'd already noted her prettiness even when she was garbed in the plain school robes in the gloom of the library, but this was a marked and most noticeable improvement.

"Your Highness, you know everyone but the young Miss Ynith," the Lady said. He smiled at her and she blushed, nodding faintly.

"We have met once, at school. But we were never formally acquainted. I am Arnsword," he offered his hand and she stood and took it, curtsying deeply as he greeted her. She wasn't sure of what proper protocol was when shaking a prince's hand, but she avoided eye-contact while he lifted her fingers to his forehead. When he released her hand, she curtsied again. He indicated that she sit, and she did, squirming a bit in discomfort.

"Your Highness, Geros here wants to shake up a game of Pirate's Dice, care to join us?" Hestin called across the room most boldly, rudely interrupting. The prince glanced back at the young man briefly and barely bothered to hide a sneer.

"I would kindly refuse, if I may. I am not in a gaming mood."

"Docent?" Hestin asked.

"I too am not game for gaming," he chuckled at his own cleverness. Hestin shrugged and they both moved to a small round table where one of them produced a handful of six-sided dice and began to rattle them on the table while talking loudly and sipping tall fluted glasses of dark ale delivered by a waify footman. The Everath moved with little grace into the circle of seats, and settled in beside Ynith. She retreated a little further into herself, both sorry and humiliated by her behavior and embarrassed by the prince's bold gaze.

The Lady leaned towards her brother when Oreth gestured to her, and they joined together with the ferret lady, the other two ladies and partook in a private conversation. Ynith suspected she had been given introductions during their chaotic settling-in period, and she had missed them all through the madness. She still had no idea who the women were.

With the surreptitious glances in Ynith's direction, she suspected the Docent was filling them all in on what he knew of her. She was left entirely to the attentions of the Everath, who leaned back into the corner of the settee, and turned to face her a bit, crossing one long, thin leg over the other. He wore a blue velvet frock-coat with a black collar and cuffs and gold buttons with a gold waistcoat, blue breeches and the whitest stockings she'd ever seen. His eyes looked animated and his expression less disengaged today.

"Did you receive my note?" he abruptly asked in a very low voice. Ynith nodded shyly and then turned to look at him. Her gaze was tentative but she respected him enough to look directly at him when he spoke to her. He seemed surprised by this, perhaps unaccustomed to being looked at so openly when spoken to.

"It was very kind of you to finish the work, but it was not necessary, and I must also apologize for my inexcusable outbur..." she began to whisper. He shook his head and interrupted.

"No apologies, please. I was insufferable and made you angry. It was rude to question everything and then undermine your efforts as I had," he assured her. He shifted slightly so he faced her a bit more, and leaned forward with an expression of confidence in her. "I am not a kind person most of the time and I don't usually care much, honestly. However I confess your tears had a particular impact on me." Ynith was astonished by the honesty that flowed from his mouth. They leaned away from one another for a moment, as if each needed a second to process the other's words, and then the Everath asked in a murmur; "would you like to see the conservatory? I don't like to whisper in company."

"I would," Ynith replied quietly. He stood and offered her his hand. She took it and stood in turn, taking a moment to adjust the drape of her shawl and fixing it on her arms before walking beside him, small next to his towering, lean frame. They passed through the doorway which he closed behind them. He sighed out loud the moment the latch clicked, and smiled stiffly at Ynith.

"Gods, this is less confining isn't it? What a relief." She nodded in agreement. He looked around the huge space appreciatively. "I like hothouses." Just as he said this, a little Jewel hummingbird with a sapphire coloured hood and ruby belly darted near his shoulder, hovered and then buzzed away. Ynith giggled, and the Everath looked squarely at her with bemused eyes. He studied her quietly, an odd smile on his face.

"I knew you attended the academy, Your Highness," Ynith blurted, a bit uncomfortable from his quiet scrutiny, "but I did not know who you were."

"Call me Arnsword. Please. You treated me like an ordinary person before; I wish you would continue." She nodded, and added:

"But only in private company. I don't want to be informal in front of them." he agreed with a terse smile and looked about. The huge conservatory was a great oval shape before them, packed tightly with exotic plants, flowers and full-sized trees. Hummingbirds darted through the leafy canopy, feeding from the array of beautiful blossoms. There were chairs and furniture scattered through the many stone paved garden rooms, and they chose to sit near the door so they could be seen from the other room. The prince was convinced that if they could see them, they would be less likely to come to disturb them.

"I had no idea *you'd* be here today," he declared, sinking down into one of the fine chairs. Far off, on the other end of the glass-covered garden, a groundsman was watering and tending to some plants. It gave them both something to look at besides each other. "I understood someone rather special was to join us for the day, from the Lady's frequent chattering, but I wasn't really paying her much heed, in truth," he said with frankness. "It was a pleasant surprise to see it was you. It is an opportunity for me to apologize in person." He tried to be casual but could only come off a bit forced and clumsy.

"Thank you. And likewise. I was only told of this outing last evening. I had no idea who else would come or where I was going. You seem familiar with the Lady and the Docent, do you know them well?"

"I do, but I confess I have a much closer relationship with the Lady. She is my aunt, the Docent my uncle. The Docent has always been sequestered in his own world at the Darvath. Even as I have attended it, I have spent little time with him. My aunt is most strongly connected to my household, and spends time with my family during the year. She has been a fixture throughout my life. As my aunt is a frequent guest at the royal houses, I can be easy and familiar with her. She leaves me alone to do as I please, and doesn't fuss too much when I'm here. She also seems to understand me best out of all of my family. I have great respect for Aunt Ressa.

"I come here quite often when away from school; it's closer than my own home, and considerably less irritating. That is, when it's not full of half-wits like the Tayeens and imbeciles like that Hestin fellow. The Misses Aldrins are neither here nor there, like mice, you only realize they've come and gone by the crumbs they leave behind." Ynith kept her mouth shut, and let him go on. She felt a tug of a grin on her lips and did not want to succumb to laughter at the expense of others, but his words were rather amusing if not slightly cruel. Still, she found it funny that he would feel so comfortable with her as to speak so freely of his opinion.

"The Tayeens are considered the highest echelon of society around here under the Lady; they are not even titled. They are rich—and purchased an estate from the throne; they come from Arath where he earned a fortune in shipping. She is vapid and ridiculous and has a quick and sharp tongue. Watch her," he warned. "Did Hestin pester you much? I'd watch him too, he's a notorious swine with ladies, and has smirched the virtue of several unfortunate girls over the years. They were bustled away from the school in quiet, never to be heard from again; probably mired in some back-country convent raising a child they never wanted. I was most dismayed to see him here today. The gall of that arse to speak to me as if I were one of his insignificant compatriots from the Darvath," he snarled.

"You are very frank, Your H… Arnsword. I'm not sure how to react to it." Ynith muttered suddenly. He looked at her wide eyes and flushed ears and laughed a strange and haunting laugh, nodding in agreement. He then changed the subject.

"You were working in the archive. I didn't know young ladies worked the archive."

"They didn't until me. We aren't permitted to roam as you young men are. We are permitted in the classrooms and the dormitories only."

"Hm. You seem sharp enough, I suppose—to earn a greater roaming area. I paid attention to your stacks, you know, before I knocked them over (which was not deliberate, I must reiterate). I did my best to follow what order you had them written in. You did a lovely job; you improved upon the provided guideline in my opinion."

"Thank you, again."

"No, no, no. Please. It was no favour." He paused. "I am frank. I suppose it's a side effect of being raised a royal, you grow very free with your words when people always acquiesce to you no matter how awful you are. You didn't. It was refreshing."

"I didn't know you were the Everath. I thought you were just some annoying…"

"It doesn't matter. It takes courage for any lady to stand up for herself these days. I like the school for that. It creates very opinionated and knowledgeable and hence infinitely more interesting creatures than the ridiculous ladies that populate the parlours of so many homes. It's too bad so few ladies are sent there; my sister could use a few years in that place, as well as a few of my cousins."

"We aren't exactly welcomed back into society afterwards, are we?"

"Unfortunately, no. But there are some places where someone like you could find your niche. What course of study do you follow?"

"I have chosen a broad course, most subject matter, no specific arts. You?"

"I have chosen to study the arts of magic. I hope to be a master at it."

"I never heard of a mage-prince," she giggled, letting go of her reserve. She was, however intrigued. She had always loved the subject, but had never been able to excel at it. Instead, in her free time, she studied magical theory whenever she could. Because she could not practice magic, she was inclined to search mostly for whatever reading materials she could find on the forbidden, dark magics, which always fascinated her. It was her small, guilty pleasure. And she enjoyed the challenge of it, because texts on those subjects were very scarce and hard to find. Her lively gaze seemed to please him. He shrugged with a strange smile.

"Eh, why not? I showed some moderate talent at it when I was young. I figured why not? What else am I going to study? Law? Medicine? I'm a prince. I won't be a judge or a doctor."

"I enjoy history, arts and literature," Ynith declared, an easiness coming about her as she spoke. He was quite drawn in by her familiarity and her warmth towards him. From what he had observed of her so far, she offered no such thing to anyone else. He knew that in time, Ressa would make her feel comfortable, as she was able to do with Arnsword. For Arnsword, somehow, her outburst and her anger before had revealed to him alone a facet of her being that she could no longer conceal, and so she simply gave into it. That outburst in the archive had earned him a glimpse into who this young woman really was beneath her quiet reserve. It earned him a special, privileged confidence.

So few people were able to comport themselves with any true sincerity in the presence of the Everath, especially the scores of young women paraded through his life. He cut an intimidating figure, and was not handsome by any conventional standards. He knew most of the young women who met him were frightened by his cold eyes and found him unattractive, but they also understood the advantage of his acquaintance, and were all most willing to tolerate his attentions for the possibility of a match with the future king. Arnsword found it all insultingly obvious and it disgusted him. Most people disgusted him.

The attention he largely received from women and girls was one of downcast eyes and uncomfortable, halted, acquiescing conversation with no substance or depth. There was an undercurrent of terrified coolness in every conversation he shared with other females. They all agreed to everything he said, and laughed forcedly at any attempt he made to fulfill his family's expectations and to be humourous or affable towards these courtiers; both expressions of which were difficult things for this cool, hardened fellow to grasp. The ones that forced themselves to show attraction especially revolted him, and he could not help but curl his lip at their forwardness and flirtations, the calculated glimpses and flicks of the fan, the postures that presented their figures and assets to their best advantage. It was all quite predictable and distasteful to him. In the end, he saw them as little more than hollow and meaningless figures that may as well be made of porcelain.

He truly held most people in great disdain and respected very few of his acquaintance. Ynith had somehow bypassed all of his immediate prejudices against humanity almost the second he set eyes upon her. He could not stop looking at her then, and he could not now. She was special. She had some unidentifiable quality, aside from her remarkable beauty that somehow cut through his hardened heart and pierced directly into his nearly empty soul. He knew the first thing he admired about her was the earnest truth in her eyes. She looked at him presently, her expression warm and comfortable as she talked about her preferred subjects. He found that her affection for history, art and literature did not surprise him now that he knew her a bit better. He would only expect it of someone as delicately complex as she.

"I *knew* you would like those things. I see it in your nature already, hidden wit and profundity—unobserved and unappreciated by most, I'll wager. Because you do not offer yourself up freely to others as most women do. You have no such vulgar habits. I recognize that in you just by knowing you these short moments," he declared. Ynith cleared her throat and shook her head, unable to reply to this determination. He gazed at her with his cold, green eyes.

"What of the magics, Miss Ynith. Have you no interest in those? Have you done no conjuring of magic at all? It is the most popular subject matter."

"For those with a talent for it. We are not all born with such abilities."

"You have none at all?" he asked, surprised. He imagined someone like Ynith would have at least some skill for the craft. She seemed to exude some acumen for it; he could sense it emanating from her flawless skin, even if she could not. He saw her shift about for a second or two, and then she replied almost reluctantly.

"I'm not *completely* bereft of the skills, but I am not... keen enough to control them. I failed at all attempts in my primary years, and I did try the novice class in my eighth year but did so poorly. The professor shouted at me so often I decided to stick to subjects that I was more comfortable with; subjects I was more likely to excel at," she sighed. "I was told my lack of control represented a danger to myself and others," she laughed softly when she said it. There was a lilt of regret in her voice. Arnsword again, was surprised. He loved only one thing in his life and that was magiccraft. He was in harmony with it more than most, and he had a sense for it. He knew Ynith was more capable than she imagined or revealed. This intrigued him even more.

"You didn't challenge yourself, Miss Ynith, shame on you." She frowned and then laughed through her nose, shaking her head sadly. It saddened her that she could not tell him that she challenged herself all the time when it came to this subject. Not in practice, that was too dangerous, but at least in gaining as much knowledge she could. But what would he think about her forbidden obsession with archaic, now-prohibited arts? She quietly mused. Her response was the one she had made countless times to herself and others:

"To what end? All my studies are for no purpose in truth. They are but a means to keep me occupied and located, I suppose, when I have no other place. Pursuing magics serves me even less."

He scrutinized her again, his hard eyes softening. "Had I 'challenged myself' as you call it, and learned to master the magics, if I *had* shown acumen for the craft, I would be ridiculed for it. No woman has become a wizard, they are called witches and they are mocked, and they do little more than parlour tricks and fooling people into thinking they're speaking to their deceased relatives." Arnsword let a pause stretch in their conversation while he pondered this. He then said:

"There *are* magics that no one would dare to mock," he suggested, "magics beyond ridicule."

"Pardon?" The hairs on the back of her neck bristled.

"Magics that tap into greater powers."

"You mean the *ancient* magics, the forbidden powers used in the Age of Rains?" Ynith asked, her brows arching in shock. She flushed, immediately overcome with both a sense of guilt and a desire to hear more. She felt as if she'd just been found out. But the Prince merely smiled coolly.

"Nobody would call anyone wielding those magics a parlor wizard, would they?"

"Or a witch?" she added with a laugh, a bit relieved he was keeping the discussion of it mostly as jest. Part of her hoped he had been serious, but then she felt ashamed for thinking so. He smiled stiffly and nodded.

"No. One would be much-respected bearing those kinds of powers." he said as warmly as he could muster.

"Less respected and more feared, I'm sure," she retorted. "I'd rather *not* be a source of terror. I'd rather be a humble little nobody, thank you very much," she concluded. It was interesting that he mentioned the dark magics. It made Arnsword more intriguing to her.

"A nobody? Truly you jest. I think you are exceptional, and every word that comes out of your mouth seems to make you more so," he told her with a strange look on his face. It was like he was attempting a certain expression for the first time and falling just shy of achieving it.

"You are too complimentary; it's making me uncomfortable," Ynith said, her cheeks burning red and a timid smile on her lips. She squirmed a little bit.

"How can I help it? I am quite taken," he said, his face splitting into a fearsome grimace. She shook her head and blushed, laughing effortlessly—appreciating his pains to converse with warmth, yet unable to provide any rational response besides laughing at his boldness.

"Stop, please Your Highness…"

"I cannot control my esteem; it's like an illness." He was being sincere, but didn't know how to make it obvious that he was. She thought him to be jesting or perhaps to be flattering her for some other purpose, but she humoured him, and found his efforts strange and thoughtful. She also appreciated his attentiveness. They were chuckling together when the doors burst open behind them and the Lady came bustling up to them with a happy expression on her lovely face.

"There you are. The two of you were very stealthy in your escape from our mindless chatter. The Docent says you sing lovely Ynith, oh do please come and sing us a song, it's been so long since this house has heard music!"

As Ynith had been prepared for this, she did not quail. She did not think that it would be seemly to make a fuss and protest, and she did not want to call further attention to herself. She settled in and let her fingers slide onto the keys of the ancient instrument. They were narrower than she was used to, but the ivory was worn smooth and shining. She tried not to focus on the truth that the room had eight other people in it all waiting for her to perform. The idea made her nervous. Instead, she concentrated on the unusual instrument at which she sat; it was antiquated and almost garish, inlaid in gold and ebony shaped into frilly leaves growing from twisting vines.

She tested a few notes with her slender fingers, clearing her throat subtly behind the sound of the music. The tones rang out with a strange hollowness; she was used to a tighter string, a cleaner note; but it had a lovely archaic feel to it. She ran the scales from end to end to limber up and then straightened herself again, giving everyone a demure glance before positioning her hands on the keys.

She chose an old song to match the instrument, and began to play the notes, her hands tickling out a melodic introduction, filling the large parlour with sound. The chatting of the visitors ceased immediately and faces turned to look at her. She opened her lips and sang out her first note in a clear, straight, angelic tone, offering only light vibrato, and no unnecessary inflections to taint its purity. Her words were clear and plaintive, her voice strong and filled with the love she felt for the song she chose to sing.

Unfurl the leaves of spring,
And bring the soothing rains,
The wing-ed bards shall sing,
Of their winters long away.

Feathers ride the summer skies
And the sun does kiss the trees
Dragonflies rise as you wander by
And the wind plays with the reeds.

A languid dance,
A quadrille never ending.
Meeting and parting,
Casting and setting,
Turning and changing,
Always to begin again

This song's melody rose and fell like the warble of a bird, and Ynith's high register carried this old refrain and trilled it into the room. Arnsword shifted in his seat and then stood, finding a place to get a better view of the young woman. He frowned to himself, and crossed his arms, leaning against a large column that supported a massive beam above. She was radiant to him; an angel.

The idea that he had made her cry suddenly struck him again with the same sharp agony it had that first day; a feeling utterly unfamiliar to him, it left him so confused. The regret and culpability made his cool heart cringe inside him. How could he have brought this dove sadness? Arnsword knew what he was. He knew he was not like normal people; that he lacked traits that sometimes made him think he wasn't quite human.

He also knew his rank could win him this delicate prize if he wanted her, it would be easy—but that quality that made her special also made him understand that it wasn't a simple matter of possessing what he desired. For once in all of his life, the opinion of this woman mattered. She was so vulnerable and sweet, but there was so much more. He didn't just want her, he wanted her respect and her attentions, her admiration and her warmth, and he wanted her familiarity and her smiling eyes. He had never wanted anything more in his life as he did this young woman. And the idea that it was possible to have all those things, because she was so remarkably different as to see something in him worth heeding was almost unbearable. He'd only known her for a day, but he understood there was something to the irrational attraction to Ynith. It was not to be ignored.

He watched her like a wolf watched a doe, with both fascination and avarice. She played a lifting interlude and then opened her lovely full lips to sing again; her sweet voice set goose bumps onto Arnsword's skin.

We dance to the music
Of dried leaves beneath our feet
The last shreds of summer's warmth
Make the orchard's fruit so sweet.

The mournful cry of the ravens
Are muted by the snow.
A white-furred winter hare
Makes tracks for us to follow.

A languid dance,

A quadrille never ending.
Meeting and parting,
Casting and setting,
Turning and changing,
Always to begin again

Always to begin again.

There was an appreciative applause, and the Lady stood and rushed over to Ynith, helping her up. She had tears in her eyes. "How did you know I loved the Song of Seasons? It was my favourite to sing when I was a girl. It was the song that taught me my scales and how you played, so beautifully! You dear thing, you sang it so magnificently, I was beside myself. You sing like a divine creature. Do come and sit with us."

The Everath was miffed to see Ynith dragged away into the midst of the Lady's small entourage. He didn't want to share her with anyone; he wanted to sit and talk to her some more in the conservatory, to allow her comfort with his company to grow, and to see her laugh and smile at him again. How easy she made him feel, thought he—something akin to normal. He joined the group simply to be near Ynith, and sat quietly by her as they bombarded her with attention. He faded into the background, but his eyes were always on Ynith.

They gathered for midday nuncheon, and Ynith ate in silence while everyone else chatted. She was placed down at the Lady's right, and the prince sat at the opposite end of the table. He took to the garden afterwards to escape the torture of being in her presence but being denied her attentions, and found that the ladies had followed him shortly after. He waited until Mrs. Tayeen pressed to gain the center of her Ladyship's attention as she always did. She monopolized the conversation, and Ynith wandered a bit off the path to take in an unexpected prospect. She was shocked to discover that her Ladyship's estate was set on top of a cliff overlooking the ocean. Their arrival and approach gave them no hint that they were so close to the sea.

Her gasp was heard by the looming scarecrow, and he seemed to materialize beside her. "What is it?" he asked. She glanced at him. Just contact with her eyes stirred his heart.

"The ocean," she pointed. The garden space they'd exited opened up into a wider swath of manicured grass framed by some old beeches and a heavy aged conifer. Beyond, the blue plane of the ocean met the sky with a thin white line. She moved forward over the grass with a look of awe that made Arnsword want to kiss her.

She padded in her dainty red slippers towards the edge of the cliff side. There, a stone pilaster fence skirted the irregular shape of the broken land, and four granite benches offered shaded seating for a lovely view. She stopped at the low barrier and put her hands on the long carved-stone railing, looking down at the water-washed rocks. The wind blew against her body, framing it beautifully in her little wispy gown. Her bonnet sat on a chair in the parlour, and her shawl next to it—she was slight looking now, without her accoutrements. Her side-curls tossed in the breeze.

The tide was low, and the water not very foamy—he wished it was high-tide and there were lots of waves so she could feel the vibration of the water meeting the cliffs. He sat here often when he visited, even in dead of winter and watched the sea-birds kite on the rough winds over the water, and found strange comfort in their distant, hollow cries. But the view did not draw him today. He instead took pleasure in looking at her as she gazed out over the ocean. She then turned to him suddenly, smiling, setting his heart apace again. He could see the pure delight and wonder in her eyes, and she offered it only to him. The Everath invited her to sit under one of the beeches with him.

"Ynith, at the risk of being so bold and to make you even more uncomfortable," he began,

"It is an illness, Your Highness. I understand," she laughed easily, her manners open and earnest, her wonder and happiness making her forget herself. He felt empowered by her comfort with him.

"Well, since I have a viable explanation for my inexcusable forwardness, I would ask you, if you would come here again and again—give me something to look forward to at the end of week."

"I could not presume to say yes, Arnsword, for it is not for me to invite myself."

"The Lady adores you, that is evident, and she has wanted a young lady to keep company with for so long. She will surely wish to secure your company in earnest once this end week has passed and you can return without the addition of the other distractions and guests. She will want your good company; company that isn't as meek and retiring as Miss Aldrin. You would be a good thing for her, and I have no doubt you will be asked to come whenever you are free, should the Docent be willing to part with you. I know my aunt very well."

"If that is the case, I would not refuse; not only; and no offence, for your preferences, but also because I would like some change from the walls of the Academy. I think the Lady would become increasingly less overwrought the more frequently I visit, and it can be a pleasant way to spend a few days between classes and archiving." He nodded; the pleasure on his face perhaps not quite as obvious as it would be for anyone else, but Ynith was able to see it. She smiled gently and looked out to sea.

"Wondrous. Another delightful surprise to discover we were by the sea. I paid no attention to the sky for sea birds, or saw any clue in the landscape. I suppose I have no basis of comparison since I've never seen the sea before, I had no idea what to look for."

"It is rather abrupt, but it was meant to be. The prospect is artfully hidden by the design of the park, and only the back of the great house gives view of the ocean," he explained. You can go an entire day without knowing the water is just within reach. One must know the paths to find the prospects inside the park itself. It is a private setting, lots of trees, right up to the cliffside," he said. Ynith sighed happily. But her uninhibited moment of contentment was yanked away from her with a single, innocent question.

"Do you not leave the Darvath, Miss Ynith?" he asked. Instantly, her unfettered easiness dissipated, and Ynith's entire demeanor stiffened. She shook her head, her lips pursing with regret, her eyes darkening a bit. He furrowed his brow, asking why without uttering a word. She did not respond, but he was certain she understood his silent query. He studied her now pained face for a moment, speculating answers for himself and then asked in the most frank manner:

"Do you not have a family, Miss Ynith?" She paused and leaned back a bit, and then looked away, glancing at him quickly and then away again. Her ease and warmth of moments before had shifted into discomfort, and she twisted her hands together into a tight clutch. Her words came out clipped and matter of fact.

"I do. I have an expansive, rather influential family. I was born to the house of Shalmeen," she started. Arnsword knew of this house. It included a Duchy and several Baronies. He knew that the Duke and Duchess of Shalmeen were killed—he wasn't sure of the details. Immediately, selfish thoughts consumed him. This was a good sign; there could be no objection to her from his family. She was a duchess, they could have no problem with that. And, she was a duchess from a well-respected house no less. His family had some history with the Shalmeen that he knew of, but it was eons ago, and surely irrelevant now. The chain of realizations was halted when more words came forth from her alluring lips. He focused immediately on her, confused and intrigued by her quick change of bearing.

"I was very young when my mother and father were killed. I don't have any memory of them. I had only a title and fortune that my extended family vied for. My uncle chose to send me away for my protection, and the protection of my birthright. He believes I would be in imminent danger against some of the less tactful of my family members. I've no idea what exactly has come of my childhood home, or anything of my past. If you know our history, there has been some underhanded ways of trading up the titles and fortunes among certain branches of our House. So here I am," her voice broke and faltered. She cleared her throat, and said in a weaker tone, trying to inject some humour unsuccessfully:

"I am nobody, nowhere, until when I do not know. What happens when I must leave is still a mystery to me," she said through a forced smile. "I have nowhere to go and have had nowhere to go since I was a little girl. The Darvath has been my home, the faculty my family I suppose," Ynith said pointedly.

She shifted a bit, her back straight. "That is why I do not get out much, why I have never seen the sea, and why I find such extraordinary pleasure in the events today, for this has never happened for me. I've never spent a day like today before." She realized she sounded like she was wallowing in self-pity and she reined herself in, biting back the rush of emotion telling him all this created. He did not back down however.

"Never? You've never sat in someone's parlour, played cards or sang songs? Traveled abroad?"

"No," she said, but lifting her voice a bit, she continued: "but I do take some brief excursions to the village in Evronell." She tried to imbue this with as much zeal as she could only to fall short miserably while sounding wretched instead.

"There is very little to see at the village proper," Arnsword muttered unthinkingly. This caused her to feel the burn of embarrassment. The village visits were important to her, paltry and meaningless as they were for everyone else. She hated for him to see how awfully small her expectations were. She was embarrassed by it. She wished she hadn't even started talking about it at all.

"For me that is sufficient," she said, cringing at the sound of shame she could not keep from her voice. "One does not miss what one does not have," she laughed sardonically and then shook her head, trying to shake away how pathetic she felt. She never spoke of this to anyone before. She never allowed herself to feel self-pity for how sheltered her life was. Not until Arnsword asked her. And then she felt unworthy all of a sudden; dim-witted and petty to be so upset over a stupid conversation. She unexpectedly felt the keen and unmistakable, familiar feeling of being utterly alone. She felt the cumulative resentment of putting on this façade of forced cheerfulness time and time again when she watched her classmates come and go, live their lives, share stories of their travels and their families, of their romantic interests, and hearing them talk about the marriages they hoped to enter when leaving the Darvath. She hated hearing about their futures and their prospects, their fulfilling time away from the limited world she was forced to call her own. Her throat tightened, and for the first time under his scrutiny, she was filled with humiliation and an overwhelming sadness.

Arnsword stared frankly at her, his eyes unrelenting, the weight of his gaze almost palpable.

"Miss Ynith, dearest Ynith, you are forced to content yourself with so very little," he mumbled, his voice, although cold on the surface, heard by anyone else would have sounded almost mocking, but she heard in it what was meant to be heard. It revealed a touch of empathy, and that little shred of concern was enough for Ynith's throat to constrict and for her emotions to rush forward in a way she'd never felt before. She wished him away, so he could not see her losing control of her poise. She wished him away so he could not witness how very much she lamented her solitude.

Arnsword may not have been a master of emotion for himself, but he was most astute and observant of the creatures he mostly abhorred. He could not help but see that speaking of this upset her much more than she let on, and that she was barely succeeding in controlling the emotion this discussion had caused. His concern was too much for her to bear. She was unaccustomed to it. Her face had gone pale and her voice sounded weak. An alarming sensation cut through the stork-like man, the same one he felt that first day when he'd caused her such distress. He'd done it again! He should have let it alone the moment he saw her darken. He boldly reached out and took her hand.

"Miss Ynith, I am sorry, I believe I might have made you cry again." She turned her large, unassuming eyes upon him and graced him with a weak smile, shaking her head, tendrils of her hair brushing her face in the wind. More sympathy, more concern, it was only making it harder to keep hold of it all. Her eyes were glossing over, and she became wan.

"No, you haven't, I promise. It is simply that sometimes, it is difficult to think about the unknowns and how few choices I've been allowed to make for myself. I usually throw myself into the day-to-day and try to forget about everything before me and everything that waits," her voice wavered, and he squeezed her hand. He had never once in all his life adored anything more than he did this strange, tiny, beautiful lady. He didn't even know he was capable of adoring or coveting anything at all until he met her. He could see her resolve losing ground and he wanted to stop it before she lost control. He knew she would be embarrassed by her own feelings.

He stood, reaching to take her hands and help her up. He thought perhaps she required a soft chair and a cup of tea to brace her failing spirits. Something to keep her from falling into the well of despair his probing and questioning had opened. He felt utterly responsible for Ynith's sadness. She had scarce gotten to her feet when the welcome distraction of the Lady and her entourage arrived.

"There you are! Your Highness, forgive me but you simply *must* stop stealing our Ynith; she is only here for the day, and I must be watchful of my time with her, for she will be gone for a whole eight days again! My dear brother is a fortunate man to have you Ynith. Come inside now. We are going to start a game of Velspa. You must learn to pla…" The Lady Farnham stopped short when she finally noticed how pale and distant the young lady looked.

"Miss Ynith should go indoors. I believe she feels a bit faint," the Prince fibbed on her behalf. He took her arm and led her around the bench, and escorted her to the private family parlour where the Lady insisted she lie down on a long reclining chair. She sat on the edge of it, and offered Ynith some tea, shooing everyone out.

"So much excitement for a little bird that has been for so long in a cage," she whispered.

"I'm not feeling ill nor am I fragile, I'm just…" she hesitated.

"Sad," the Lady finished. Ynith nodded, and her chin trembled. Arnsword was no longer present, and the lady's sympathetic gaze was enough for Ynith to give in. She felt no shame, for the Lady had no true understanding of what the source of her sadness and embarrassment was, so she no longer risked being humiliated by it. She began to weep. The Lady scooted up a bit, and pulled a kerchief from her sleeve, handing it to Ynith. She did not ask any questions, she did not press; she merely caressed Ynith's cheek when she took the kerchief and used it to dry her cheeks and eyes.

"You poor thing. I can only imagine. He doesn't understand; he can't. He has been free to do whatever he pleases most of his life," Ressa told Ynith. How she knew this was the thing that prompted it all, Ynith did not know, but she knew that she was wrong. Arnsword did understand. She had him all wrong. "But we shall change all that for you. First thing is to make sure you know you have a place here with me whenever you are free from your studies. I've told Oreth this, and he is to relinquish you if he cannot leave, and my coach will be there to collect you the evening of every Eighthday. Understood?" Ynith smiled weakly and nodded. She waited until Ynith was able to wrest her tears under control again, and she took her hand and gripped it tightly.

"And I may presume too much by speaking of this now, but I feel it necessary to caution you. The Everath is most attentive to you."

"He has become my friend after a silly misunderstanding," Ynith explained.

"Good. I am glad. But do be cautious of him," she paused, as if trying to find the words. "He is a strange creature, and he has a past of questionable actions. He can be cruel sometimes, even though in essentials, I truly believe my nephew is a decent enough soul. But Ynith, I... I question his capacity for truly caring about someone. He is hard and sometimes thoughtless and lacking of empathy."

"He is much concerned about my wellbeing, my Lady. You saw his concern, he lacks no empathy; he just expresses it differently," Ynith said her voice cracking.

"I did. It is the first time I've ever seen him give anyone any seemingly genuine concern, but I immediately feel myself questioning his motives and sincerity simply based on his past. You could be the thing to change him, of that I can believe, but again, I am merely cautioning you... you are a sharp girl behind those watchful, innocent looking eyes, I am not blind, I know what I see," she snorted and they both shared a laugh. Ynith had been given little chance to truly see the woman that was Lady Ressa of Farnham during this chaotic day, but she was immediately given a great deal of information in that one moment. She was a great deal more than the overwrought, fussy creature that she'd given herself to be most of the day. She was watchful and wise like her brother. Ynith immediately knew she would love this woman through and through. "Please promise me you will take care. I think you know what I mean."

"I will."

"Now, sit back and rest. You are here through dinner, and everyone wants something to do. If you do not wish to play a game, then I suggest perhaps you find a nice book to read and sit in this plush little chair while we do. I have ordered that you are brought calming teas. You do not think you are ready to emerge from here now?"

"Not yet. There is much activity… noise, and my head aches."

"Understood. I'll look in on you soon. Make yourself at home my dear." The Lady rose and studied the girl one more time while Ynith finally took her in in earnest. The Lady had once been a great beauty. She was fine in feature, tall and willowy. Her once golden hair was now silver, and her face had a network of pleasantly arranged lines that revealed a lifetime of smiles and laughter. She wore a gown of a fine slate-coloured silk with brass-coloured trim that was sewn to the edges of her neckline, waist, sleeves and hem. The front of her bodice was ornamented with similar trim arranged in an artful scroll. Her neck was appointed with a massive sapphire pennant hanging from a simple chain, and two earrings to match hovered below her ears, hanging from delicate filaments of white gold. She had glassy blue eyes exactly like her brother's that looked upon Ynith with a kindness she rarely saw. She smiled at the girl for a second before bustling away in a flare of her train.

3. The Trials

Ynith rested her head down on her pillow and sighed. Treen was in a deep sleep. Her usual quiet snores were a familiar comfort to her. She stared at the divided rectangles of moonlight that were cast on the ceiling from their two large windows, and let the tears slide down the side of her face in silence. She was embarrassed, and confused. Her strange status as someone of consequence and yet nobody had been a source of much consternation through her life. She'd only been permitted to speak of who she was to certain members of the faculty, and she was used to keeping to herself. All of a sudden there were people who mattered and they knew who she was. Everyone wanted to discuss a sensitive subject with her, and she wanted only to run away.

She'd remained sequestered in the private parlour at Gallevin House the rest of the evening while the Lady entertained her guests. Arnsword wanted very much to pay her further attentions but had been prevented in doing so by the Lady, who insisted she should be left in peace for a while. The Lady made her promise she'd return the next endweek, and stay the whole three-day period of rest. She said it would just be she and the Lady on the most part, with the possible company of Arnsword, who when in residence, ordinarily spent most of the time out or reading in the library. She declared that Oreth could not *always* be counted on to be present either, but it was a strong possibility.

She thought about Arnsword, and what she felt about his strange advances. Part of her was frightened of him. He had a coldness to his demeanor in general. A sort of intolerance of people; it changed when he was addressing her; but it was nonetheless there. He unsettled her sometimes, but a small part of her welcomed his attentions. She wasn't sure why. Perhaps it was flattering to her to be attended to by a Prince. Perhaps it was her vanity; having attention paid to her when she was so often ignored. She was not sure why, but she decided in the end to make nothing of it. It was their first and only true meeting, and he was probably simply amusing himself. It seemed impossible for someone to be so enamoured so quickly.

She turned over and faced the wall, thinking about his interest in the magics and how strange it seemed to her that a Prince would choose such a pursuit. It was a less-than-popular choice as a profession. Perhaps it was the most intriguing and most often sought-after subject by students, but to prepare for a future of magic using was never lucrative nor was it something anyone of high blood would pursue. In general; Wizards were regarded as second-class citizens, and given little recognition for their occupation; in fact, it was a social detriment in many of the higher circles. It held as little prestige as being a lawyer. She found it puzzling.

His mention of the dark magics was something that clung to her mind. She wondered if his interest was in historical wizardry and how much he'd dabbled with it. Her own interest in it was acute, and she desired to speak to him further about it, but feared his reaction. Was his intention in bringing the subject up done merely in jest, she wondered? Or did he have an interest like hers? She knew it was forbidden to use the ancient crafts. Even the study of it was frowned upon, and finding any reading material on the matter was extremely difficult. Ynith prided herself in having found as much as she had at the Darvath as it was. She doubted Arnsword would have been as relentless in his search as she had been. Surely he brought it up just to shock her.

His pursuit of conventional magic still puzzled her. She decided it was simply a matter of rebellion against his family; doing something useless to annoy them. She imagined he brought it all up to impress or shock her. He couldn't possibly know her furtive interest in it. Could he? She closed her eyes and tried to sleep. In spite of being made completely exhausted by the events of the day, sleep did not come easy.

The following morning at breakfast, Treen and other ladies in her dorm were full of questions. Many girls already knew who was there and how long she'd stayed—she imagined that Hestin must have been sharing information about the excursion and the rumours had spread quickly. Ynith rarely did anything that would qualify as a viable source of gossip, so there appeared to be even greater motivation for everyone to speak of her. Talk of Arnsword was not complimentary, and some girls giggled that Ynith had received special attentions from him. Although one of the eldest girls, Auria, felt it necessary to point out that it was a great compliment to receive attentions from a Prince, and that any one of those girls would be dishonest if they said they wouldn't welcome it for themselves. Arnsword's reputation was one of a rude and awkward thing, and it seemed everyone tended to forget he was next in line to the throne.

"He does nothing the way it should be done. He has no friends or party that follows him about, he goes wherever he pleases, alone, and he attends none of the society events any prince or princess ought to attend," one girl rattled.

Ynith was sitting in a chair that had been left purposefully open for her so she could sit in the middle of the long dining table. She was also surreptitiously guided to table in the middle of the three, so she could face the inquisition and everyone could hear her answers. The other two tables were largely silent as they listened to the conversation around Ynith. As the servants brought platters, the ladies sat politely with their hands in their laps, all faces pointing towards Ynith, who described briefly the Lady Farnham's beautiful home, the cliff-side and the conservatory.

"Did you see the upper floors? I heard she has a great ballroom in one wing."

"Oh, Ynith, if you are to become her ward, you should persuade her to arrange a ball for us to attend!" Voices around the spacious refectory agreed in a cacophony of exclamations with the idea of a ball.

"I will try, but I make no guarantees, it is not my home after all," Ynith retorted, and there were little squeals of delight in spite of her warnings against hoping too much. The final plate was served and the little bell was rung, and Ynith reached for some bread and ladled some thick, velvety beef stew into her shallow bowl. She picked up her spoon and ate; the sound of silverware on china rung pleasantly about the smallish lady's dining room.

"What's he really like? I've only ever seen him walk by the classroom," Linea asked, delicately serving herself a deviled egg from the elaborate silver platter and then gracelessly gobbling it in a single bite. She was among the newer girls, although she'd arrived at a later age than most. Rumour was that she was sent to Darvath out of punishment for attempting elopement with an unworthy young man. None of these tales had been substantiated by Linea, and although she did seem quite content without this supposed lover, Ynith thought perhaps there was some truth to what she heard, and some exaggeration. Linea was markedly keen on avoiding any discussion that would require her to speak of her past at all. She remained happily in the present, eating deviled eggs and living to hear the sordid tales of others.

Ynith shrugged, and smiled softly. "He's kind to me."

"He never smiles," one elder girl observed at the other table.

"Maybe you'll be able to meet the infamous Adra. She's a viper, from what I hear. You ought to stay away from her," Mina declared. She was an enormous gossip, and knew everything about everyone. It was she who began talking of Linea's indiscretions the moment she arrived. She said she had heard of Linea's scandalous actions from correspondence with friends outside the school.

Mina was referring to the Princess Adra, Arnsword's sister, whose frequent harsh behavior was often described in the gossip periodicals; mostly in articles about courtiers and other people who the Princess publicly spurned and mistreated. Ynith merely pressed her lips together and shrugged before sipping some more stew from her bowl. She had no desire to answer any more questions. Frustrated, but silenced by Ynith's reticence, the girls set to eating their meals and whispering to one another instead. They knew by her cool reserve that she should be left alone.

Arnsword was spent. He'd been locked for more than sixteen hours in the lower levels of the Academy, in what were called the caverns, taking part in the advanced tests. His cheeks seemed even gaunter, and his eyes were sunken. His mind was in a dark place, and he was wallowing in it, staggering through the throngs of male students who ignored him as they made their way about the campus. The Prince's mind came back to the object that had been occupying it for days; Ynith, and he stopped in his path and wavered there a second. Changing direction, he made his way towards the archive building across the courtyard.

Ynith was sitting quietly at the work desk in the private transcription room, her hand moving carefully over the page, her faultless script trailing out behind her perfectly cut quill as she wrote. It was dead quiet; so quiet, she could hear the sizzle of her candle on the wick, and the nib of her quill scratching loudly on the paper. The fire had burnt so low, it was little more than a pile of coals with orange shapes dancing across them, and the occasional bluish flicker of flame.

The Docent was spending the day in the print press room below the archive, where he employed several students in the task of publishing new works, and copying the common texts for distribution. Ynith enjoyed the process of woodblock printing, but she much preferred being in the transcription room. It was a special honor to be among the few allowed to copy the ancient magical texts and other selected and coveted works, which were required to be copied by hand alone. It was a privilege to do what she was doing. Her artful hand and her eye for detail were integral to carrying the subtleties of the original books into the newly bound copies. It was a laborious process, and each book took a long time to complete. The Docent said that each copy could not be valued. The task was considered so sacred, that the room was designed simply for this one purpose.

This was a spacious room, set up to make the wearisome task of transcribing as comfortable as possible, from the perfectly angled writing table to the softly upholstered stool upon which she sat. Here, the shelves lined almost all four walls, some divided into little cubbies to sort the variety of soft papers and binding supplies. Others were crammed with pre-bound, blank books of a variety of sizes, and some had orderly rows of ink bottles of myriad colours. Some shelves held ink powders, mortars and pestles, rows of canisters of special more modern nibs that still were put rarely to use, various quills sorted from goose to swan based on the size of lettering needed, paint-brushes and more. Ynith had her own crow quill at her station, a shining black, fine tipped quill she used for all of her most delicate line work.

One large, arch-topped door was inset into the center of the shelved short wall to her left which led to the Docent's office suite. No fewer than four resting chairs were arranged in a semi-circle around the fire before her, a long, narrow, central table held scrupulously arranged stacks of books in progress, a neat row of reflecting lamps down its center, and four chairs randomly placed along each side. A binding machine hunkered against another shelf to her right. Three copy desks, one which she presently occupied, sat against the long wall in front of three tall, stone-mullioned windows with window-seats built in.

A new shipment of finely cured leather had been just brought in and hung on a special rack. The pieces of leather were fragrant and glossed in tones of burgundy, navy blue, gold, brown, and black. Above her, three mammoth circular candelabras hung.

They were adorned densely with candles. Only one was burning above her, and daylight poured in from behind her. Outside, three stories below, the courtyard was alive with the movement of young men in fluttering robes who were changing classes, but much to Ynith's pleasure their noise did not reach the scriptorium. She hardly noticed they existed at all. Even the loud clock tower on the older side of the academy complex could be easily forgotten in this pleasantly quiet place.

Ynith used her crow quill with a delicate hand to trace out a spidery shape in a rusty brown ink on the margin, before dropping it back in its slot on her desk. She picked up a small jar of salt and sprinkled it over the fresh ink, waiting for the ink to absorb into it before she swept it carefully with a soft horsehair brush into the little trough on the bottom of her desktop. She then picked up an old, worn quill with a blackened shaft and began writing again in a jet black ink, dipping it afresh for her next line or two.

The entrance of the Everath was a shock to her peace, and her hand jumped and ink spattered across the page. She was the only scripting student assigned to the Docent at this time, and nobody was permitted in the scriptorium except those who worked there. The inconsiderate noise was clue it could not be her superior, so she was immediately infuriated by the interruption. She looked up in anger, but her annoyance melted at the sight of the wasted prince. She dropped her quill on the page and stood, bustling around her desk to catch his arm as he stumbled into the room.

"Everath, what's wrong? Are you ill?" she asked, her eyes brimming with concern. He loved her face, the little patch of concerned wrinkles between her brows; the contrast of her stark, black hair against her soft, pale skin; the thick lashes ringing her beautiful eyes. What he'd ever done to merit the concern of such a flower, he did not know, nor did he wish to question it. He reached out and placed his hand upon her cheek.

"You are *so* beautiful," Ynith blushed, shook his compliment off, and frowned.

"You are not well. Come and sit," she partly dragged him to one of the chairs in front of the dying fire. He fell into it. His eyes were glazed over, and he looked almost drunk. His gaze was unsteady and his limbs were listless and uncoordinated. He seemed... odd—or in his case, odder than usual.

"I think what I feel in here," his hands clamped onto his bony chest, which rose and fell heavily under his robes, "is love."

"Arnsword, really. This is no time for declarations; and far too soon for that one. We've only really had one day together. Have you been out drinking?" Ynith stammered. She touched his forehead, and he leaned into her hand, and then grasped it and kissed the palm. She pulled it away, and glowered at him, "Arnsword, stop." He looked at her with regret and then sighed. "I'm going to send for someone from the infirmary. I don't think you are well at all."

"I am fine, only worn out. They held the advanced trials today," he mumbled. Ynith frowned again and sat in the chair next to him. She then saw the state of the fire and stooped on the ground by the hearth, adding some fresh wood and using the poker to taunt the fire into life again. He watched her.

"I've heard of the trials. I'd forgotten. I thought they were held yesterday afternoon."

"They were. They have concluded."

"You've been at it all night?" she asked, incredulous. He nodded, and she shook her head, taking in his state. "You look really terrible, Your Highness."

"What did I tell you? Arnsword; that is my name to you," he grumbled rather gruffly. She took his irritation in stride and sighed.

"Perhaps you *should* go to the infirmary," Ynith concluded. She began to loosen the drawstrings of her cuff protector which was smeared with ink. This single mitt kept her sleeve from dragging into her work, and staining her clothing. Once a ruddy white, it was now blotted in all manner of inks and paints. She slid it off her right hand and put it on the seat of the chair, trying to make herself moderately presentable. She wore the school's clumsy-sleeved chemisette and black linen sleeveless gown. To Arnsword, it looked odd to see her in this now that he'd seen her in common clothes.

Her school robe was hanging on a peg by the Docent's office door. She moved to fetch it, drawing the sleeves onto her arms. As Ynith returned to help Arnsword up, he refused, waving her off.

"Stop, I don't need the infirmary. I would like you to come to Imsgaard with me. Of course, not *with* me per say, that would be improper, but Lady Farnham goes every year, and she can take you as her ward," Arnsword declared.

Imsgaard; thought Ynith, her mind reeling. *Why is he so strong in his pursuit, so determined?* She wasn't sure what to make of it, *now this.* She would be in a permanent state of humiliation and fear if she did. It was one of the four large estates owned by the royal family. Each summer, they would pack up and take some of their court to Imsgaard for a month or two, to enjoy the pleasures of the season.

"I do not want to be alone there anymore. And your status would not in any way be objectionable to them, so we could be together."

"Arnsword, I don't think…"

"No, you must please consider this, it is torture for me to be there, but I am obligated every time to be present. There is nobody there that I have anything in common with, nobody to speak to, and nobody to make the time there bearable for me. I beg you, please; I will ask Lady Farnham." Ynith sighed and sat down in a rumple of black linen and wool, gazing at him for a moment. He stared at her feet which peered out from beneath her hems. She had on white stockings and black slippers with the single shining band of raven ribbon crossing the arch of her foot, tied with a small bow at the center. He thought that very sweet, all of a sudden.

"I don't know what to do with you, Arnsword."

"How so?"

"I'm not… ready for you. Or anyone. These declarations, they are off-putting and make me feel awkward around you, and I do not wish to feel that way."

"I know. I'm too forward. I push too much. You must understand me to understand why I am so determined. I have never…" he paused, and seemed almost fearful to say what was to come next, but then he looked at her face, then her delicate feet with the spare little soft black shoes and the black ribbon bows sitting on top of the creased stockings, and that little part of him that screamed for her love gripped his mind. "I have never *felt* anything, Ynith." He sighed.

"All my life I've struggled to understand people, and their feelings, to understand compassion, to find the capacity to feel it in my heart; it was as if I didn't have it inside me. At least, until I saw your tears. How painful it was to see your tears and to know I caused them. I've been, *dead;* yes… *dead* until I met you. With everyone else it's still the same; I follow the rules of polite society, and what others call 'common consideration'. I feign it all. Except with you. With you I have a heart. You make me, at least for a brief moment when I am with you, just like everyone else. I can't tell you why, I just know that first moment, when I saw you, I could not bear to walk away from you. And then I made you weep, and I felt more horrible than I have ever felt; it was heavy and horrid and it's a feeling I wish never to repeat.

"Your cry of frustration was like a dagger into my heart. I lingered a while, wondering what I must do, confused by these feelings. At length I went back to atone, but you were gone and I felt doubly horrid.

"Ever since that moment, I've done nothing but long to be near you to feel all these things. Even through my trials, which require much concentration, I could not keep you from my mind. Instead of affecting my trials for the worse, my passion for you fed my power. It took everything out of me, but *you* made me stronger."

Ynith stood and then sat again, trying to find a way to make him cease this narrative. It was causing her significant unease. She felt as though he was putting something very weighty upon her, and she wasn't sure what it was. She did welcome his words in one way but in another, she felt as if she'd been burdened with something she wasn't nearly prepared to carry. It frightened her. She didn't like to be frightened of Arnsword.

"I want to kiss you," he declared. Her stomach clenched and she froze.

"Arnsword, I don't... it's not..." She was utterly unable to formulate words to express her confusion. He on the other hand seemed to come to a resolution, and he gazed at her firmly. He stood with renewed strength and grasped her hands, pulling her to her feet.

"Let me kiss you, Ynith. Please, it will give me strength again."

"I b... beg your pardon?" she stammered. She gazed up at him, eyes wide in both terror and concern, and she watched his dark, oddly empty eyes gaze at her, and as they did, she saw the flicker of something; of that love he declared perhaps, the humanity that made him just a bit less frightening. He slid his hands down her cheeks to cup her face, and he admired her beauty and the perfection he saw there. And then he bent down and laid his lips upon hers.

It was surprisingly tender. It was sweet and loving and lingering. He suspired heavily, and hunched his shoulders over her, almost enfolding her in his rickety being. She trembled as he pulled away, still on her toes, and opened her eyes to see his brimmed with moisture. "My heart hurts," he said in a broken voice. "I cannot be without you now. Please come to Imsgaard." She reached up and touched her lips, dropping her eyes and stepping back.

"If the Lady asks me I will go." She wavered a second and then sank down onto the chair, sitting on its edge, gazing blankly into the fire. Arnsword left without another word.

"Looking forward to Gallevin House pretty girl? I am. Without the Tayeens, the Aldrins and the brouhaha, and Hestin gone to visit his family, it should be a nice restful time. I usually bring lots of books to read, because it can be very quiet. My dearest sister has promised not to drive you batty with requests. She told me she plans to give you the oak room apartments, which are in a nice quiet corner of the south wing, and they overlook the oak grove and the cliff-side." Ynith smiled at the old man, who was sitting at his transcription desk beside her. She was working on the page she had been working on when the Prince interrupted her. She had been obliged to remake it completely.

"I am looking forward to a nice quiet three days, Docent. I appreciate you so for including me in your family so easily," she began. "It's a good idea to leave tonight, so we don't waste any more of our precious free days in travel." She then smiled forcedly and glanced at him a few times before finally asking; "do you know if the Everath will be there again?"

"Oh, it's likely he will," he replied distractedly, but then plopped his hand down. "He rarely misses a chance to escape the school grounds. He is not a pest though, that you can count on. He spends most of his time brooding about the place. He seems quite able to tolerate your company, seeing by our last visit," the Docent muttered.

Ynith merely focused on the little tree she was inking in, her hand following the penciled lines quite carefully. When she finished tracing it out, she salted it, lifted out the catch tray that was brimming in ink-saturated salt, and emptied it into the urn by the door. She then went to fetch some more inks, a few tablets of water colours and two fine-tipped paint brushes.

"Docent," she said over her shoulder as she pulled open the huge drawer filled with neat rows of corked ink jars. She sorted through them, the glass bottles clicking against each other.

"What is it, child?"

"The trials... the magic trials; are they dangerous?" He thrust his great whopping swan quill into its pot and crossed his arms, his brow furrowing as he pondered the question.

"Indeed, they are. For those who are not meant to bear the weight of true magic, it can be fatal. But our Wizardly professors are very good at winnowing out the weaklings and the mere magicians before the trials, preventing all manner of disaster. But nobody, not even the strongest of bearers, leaves the trials without being taxed quite heavily for their efforts."

"What *are* the trials exactly?" she asked. His brow wrinkled a bit further and he shook his head.

"I cannot discuss in detail what goes on in the caverns, my dear. It is something all of us who have shared in it must promise. I can only say what everyone else knows, and that is that the trials are a succession of increasingly difficult challenges that the participants must use magic to overcome. Only a few are able to complete them, and those who do leave this place of learning as true Wizards. Those who don't are welcome to try again only once more, and if they fail the second time, they must resign from all use of true magic. They are welcome to do the silly things that entertain house parties—but they will be punished if they do anything more without having achieved full qualification."

"Punished?" Ynith picked up five little bottles she'd chosen and put them in the little indentations carved just for them on her drafting table, uncorking each one with care, and wiping her hands on her apron. Today she did not wear the school gown. She wore a plain sage coloured linen day-dress that she'd been given by one of the other girls only two nights before. She'd traded her steel-coloured muslin gown for it. She was annoyed by the clumsy sleeves of the heavy chemisette when she painted. She traded her gown because she was tired of embroidering it, and the girl who wanted it was quite happy to finish the work and to keep it for herself in trade for the simpler garment. The Docent had approved her to wear this mid-sleeved, utilitarian gown in the scriptorium. She was permitted time to change when she arrived each day. She quickly sewed up a plain apron that wrapped mostly around her skirts and tied in the back, with a small bib that could be pinned to the front of her bodice. The apron was already peppered with ink smudges in black along the hem where she wiped her fingers and the nib of her quills. "What do you mean, punished?" She placed a bowl of water on the level portion of her drafting table and laid a small plate out next to it containing several small pastilles of colour.

She pulled herself into her chair, and sat forward, picking up a fine-tipped paintbrush. The Docent stood and stretched, and started some water for the tea right over the fire that popped and snapped in the hearth.

"There are wizards that are appointed to be what we call Hunters. There are many, for there is much work for them. Think of them as the constables who work on behalf of the governing body of magic users. As you know, magics were once so destructive, so powerful in the past that some measure of control had to be instituted. When the new governing body of the magic bearers finally wrested some control and put down the rabble, they decided it was time to set some guidelines, and limit practitioners," he explained. "We never could have achieved this level of civilization if we had not taken control of our magic bearers. It would be as it was a thousand years ago during the Age of Rains; savage feudal factions warring with wizards taking the front lines, destroying anything they could find. Not to mention the hordes of other bearing beings like the ogreins and the verenmen who at that time were infinitely strong and destructive."

Ynith dipped her brush in the water, and slathered it over a pastille. She then painted the tree a rich brown, her hand moving instinctively along the lines she'd just drawn. All her focus was on what the Docent was saying. Most of this she already knew; it was common knowledge—but the punishment aspect was new to Ynith. Meanwhile, the Docent was busy portioning out some tea into the porcelain pot decorated with simple vertical blue stripes, which he used when not in his offices. In the past week, the Docent had found a cup and saucer set which he had indicated would be hers only to use. It was delicate china, with tiny flowered vines elegantly decorating the shining surface. He set that up next to his blue striped cup and saucer on the small tea table.

"The use of magic has been limited to those that demonstrate only the best capacity for it. Those who do not may not in any meaningful way practice it. There are ways of knowing. Every Magistrate from the time since magic became governed has ensured that those who crossed the line and practiced arts they have been forbidden to practice are duly punished. Depending on the severity of the infringement, the punishments can range from fines to being jailed in a binding cell, preventing them from ever casting magic again. Sometimes the punishment is worse," he finished. Ynith put her brush down and picked up a quill with a gilded shaft. She dipped it into gold ink and started painting the gold into a rumpled inked ribbon that surrounded a block of text. Her grey, heavy lashed eyes flashed up to the upper portion of her table onto the page of the original book and then back to her work, careful to replicate the lines as best she could. The work was becoming a brighter-colored version of the original. She paused and looked up again.

"What would be worse?" The Docent smiled grimly and shook his head.

"There are some who still wish to control the old magics, to pad their arsenal with the most sacred and dangerous of spells and magical sources. They wish to advance themselves and others using spells that are tremendously destructive and powerful; spells that can ruin lives. These are all forbidden. When the governing began, the first Magistrate, a wise wizard by the name of Wetherly produced a stellar piece of magic; a spell that would spontaneously work whenever anyone dares to cast any of the old spells. It's an unusual manifestation, but when someone uses the old magic, every floor of the magistrate's seat, Wetherly Hall, sprouts a carpet of bluebells. It's the sign they need to dispatch Hunters. Once that's done, the one who has cast forbidden magic is supposed to be found, jailed, bound with restrictive spells, tried and possibly hung. Unfortunately, most of the ones who have committed the crime tend to be the sort that would fight back, and the hunters are forced to try, convict and execute them on the spot," he rambled.

Ynith's mouth went dry and her hand hung frozen over her work. She had no idea of this. Had she summoned up the courage to try the theories she studied so extensively, she could have been punished! Most magic that was used in general she knew to be benign; searching for blood connections, finding lost people, tracing out the path of a soul before its death to determine the cause, repelling night stalking ogrein, casting fire. She knew some magicians could make someone appear to be someone else, and could cast illusions, like the infamous Herral who liked to cast great flying dragons into the sky to thrill and frighten his aristocratic audience. Ruining lives, that she had no idea of; she couldn't begin to imagine. Conventional magic had always been something she knew she could touch but it was something she feared she could not control. She had tried, but her professor had all but shut her down, telling her she was worthless in the craft, for she had no capacity to guide her castings, and she could potentially harm or kill herself and possibly even someone else. She was told to give up. She did so quite willingly; glad to leave this difficult art behind her with a valid excuse never to look at it again. What she could not control frightened her. She had been confident she could have excelled at the ancient methods, by what she read in the texts she could find. It was fortunate she never summoned up the courage to try. Now that she knew of this Wetherly and its hunters. Her stomach was tight and felt icy. She shook it off, and looked up at the Docent.

The kettle began to puff out steam and bubble over, water spewing out of the spout and hissing onto the fire. The noise startled her out of her bemusement. The Docent took a towel and lifted it off the hook, filling the pot.

"Do you want cakes today? I do not have the walnut biscuits, but we will have those at Gallevin soon. I also have some almond biscuits that are most delightful," he offered. She smiled at him, and sat up.

"I might want one of both," she said cheerfully. He delighted in that, and rattled about putting the tea cups on their saucers and moving quickly out of the room to fetch his baked goods. Ynith frowned when he left the room, and put her gold tinted quill down. She stood, cleaned the tip on her apron hem and took off her apron, laying it over her chair. She thoughtfully poured the tea, her brow furrowed.

Had Arnsword passed the trials? He never said. He was so spent, nearly ill from it. She hadn't seen him since that day. She was eager to leave that evening so she could see how he was faring and to know more of what happened when he came to her that day. The Docent and Ynith quietly shared tea, the conversation shifted to other less grim subjects. All Ynith could do was glance relentlessly at the huge clock ticking loudly in the corner and silently will it to move faster.

4. Invitation

Arnsword hadn't yet arrived at Gallevin House when they arrived that evening. It was just dark when the coach lurched to a stop in front of the great house. The Lady's ebullient voice could be heard from inside long before she met them at the foot of the stairs and watched them as they stepped down onto the gravel. The coachman dismounted and waited just long enough for the footmen to take down Ynith's small trunk and the Docent's before he led the horses to the carriage house and stable. The footmen preceded the three up the stairs and vanished inside while the Lady took inventory of Ynith to ensure all was well. The Lady looked most lovely this evening. Her hair was arranged in a large curled coif on top of her head with a single weft of buffed, shining hair curled onto her left shoulder. She wore a chemisette of astonishingly sheer net with a thick ruff around the collar, and false sleeves trimmed with lace. Her gown was dark, silk velvet of the deepest red, embellished very simply with a few pearls on the bodice.

"My dear, do you only have that one gown?" she asked brazenly. Ynith glanced down at her white gown and her shawl, and her face turned a lovely shade of pink that could not be seen in the weak light from the doorway. She was ashamed to tell her that she only had two others in her small trunk.

"Forgive me, my lady. I don't have a great many reasons to have more than what I own. Or I didn't, until recently," she replied. The Lady saw her embarrassment and patted her hand assuringly.

"Now, now child, do not let my curiosity make you so uncomfortable, I was merely wondering, that is all. We can go to Narie tomorrow, and we will appoint you with a few more items of clothing for your visits. You *will* need a decent wardrobe; especially if you are to join me at Imsgaard this year." The unexpected mention of this made her flush even more, but the lady did not see it in the darkness. She took her hand and shooed her brother up the stairs.

"No sense in idling about out here. The mosquitoes are right frightful this year, come inside before we are drained of our blood to end like raisins," she swatted about her with her free hand and then led Ynith to the open doorway, which beaconed with its warm, yellow candlelight. "Get inside. With the clouds of mosquitoes, and possibly an ogrein or two lurking about in the shadows, we could end our lives as hollow husks if we remain too long outdoors," she rattled on.

Ynith lifted up the hem of her gown with one hand and followed. Talk of ogrein always unnerved her. She'd never seen one, but almost all the girls had one story or another of encountering one somewhere and barely escaping with their lives. There was a rumour of there actually being an ogrein on the school faculty, but nobody knew if that was true at all. Few ogrein were known to dwell in the general society without succumbing to their predatory nature. There were some cases of this, but Ynith had yet to see it for herself.

Out here in the isolation of the country, there was no telling if there were predators stalking the good people or not. But the Lady spoke of them so casually, comparing them to mosquitoes. It seemed almost a challenge to any creature that might be stealing about the grounds. Ynith hurried indoors.

"You must have at least one or two traveling gowns, and you have no kid gloves, no furs; this is such a shame. Do you not even have a spencer or redingote? We must remedy this in the next weeks, we must."

"Do stop pestering her, sister," the Docent grumbled. "She's worked extremely hard all week with me in the scriptorium. Between attending class and organizing my office, she is probably very tired," he said, "not to mention quite hungry."

"Yes, yes, we've been holding dinner service for your arrival. Come." She dragged Ynith into the dining room where only then was she released. A young lady relieved Ynith of her shawl and ushered her to sit with the Docent and his sister at the end of the table. They partook in a lovely leek potage, followed by quail and exquisite creamed cauliflower. The sweets were some cakes and a crème in a pastillage box. They retired to the drawing room, where Ynith sipped her very first glass of apple brandy and then assisted the Lady in assembling a puzzle of wooden pieces which were scattered over a round table in the corner between the window and the fireplace. They did this while the Docent dozed off in one of the chairs.

Arnsword arrived not long after they'd finally settled in, and he looked much better than he had the other day. She could scarce look at him without her cheeks and ears burning in memory of his kiss. He seemed completely unaffected, and situated himself wordlessly beside the ladies in the nearest settee, crossed one gangly leg over the other and flipped open a periodical which he didn't take his nose out of until the Lady got tired of doing puzzles.

"Oh, goodness, Your Highness I had no idea you'd arrived. I was so absorbed in this confounded puzzle. Are you any good at puzzles?" He shook his head, folded up the periodical and tossed it aside without ceremony onto a nearby table.

"Miss Ynith, I hope you are well," he greeted Ynith kindly. She smiled gently and nodded.

"Indeed, Your Highness, I am quite well, thank you. And you?"

"I am well enough," he said impatiently. "Perhaps you would care to take a hand in Highwayman with me?" he offered unexpectedly. Ynith nodded shyly and stood.

"You do not mind, Lady Ressa?" she asked. The Lady waved her hand at her dismissively and stood.

"I certainly do not mind at all. I would much rather read a bit before I retire for the evening," she took the periodical he'd tossed aside and sat down near her brother and shook it out in front of her face. Arnsword led Ynith to the card table. He'd picked the game because it required only two players, guaranteeing him Miss Ynith's undivided attentions. He picked up the stack of cards and tamped the edges neat. He then shuffled them, his eyes never once leaving Ynith's face. His gaze was off-putting and intense. Ynith fidgeted, making eye contact only in fleeting glimpses.

"Are you unwell, Miss Ynith? You seem unusually restrained this evening," he observed. She shook her head and sighed, watching his unusually long, bony fingers spider about the cards. He dealt her five and himself five and dropped the deck between them, face-down. She picked her cards up and spread them in her hands, pleased to see he'd dealt her two wives and a swordsman. The other two she would have to cast away, but she had a good start.

"I am not unwell. Perhaps a bit tired. I must also confess I was a bit worried for you. You looked so bent and pained when we last met; it has occupied my mind most unendingly since. And then I engaged the Docent in a discussion about the trials and it made me worry all the more."

"Worry for me?" he asked, genuinely bewildered by her concern. He then shook his head and put a card down with a snap, and sighed: "there's no reason for you to be worried for me. I'm *quite* well." She studied what he'd put down and she pulled out her useless leviathan card, and put it on top of his. He arched a brow and took it, tucking it into his hand.

"Hm," she said observantly. She studied his face for a moment and then pursed her lips. "Pass," she said, and then arched her brow; adding: "speaking of passing; did you pass the trials, if I may be so bold to ask?"

"Of course I did," he grunted. "Although, I must beg you keep this in confidence. I have not told anyone in my family of my *dabblings* in the magics. They would think it most vulgar of me, and I'm not ready to explain myself to them," *snap*, he put another card down. It was a swordsman. Ynith didn't want to appear too eager to steal it up. She let herself ponder it for a good, long moment and then with a sigh of resignation, she took it.

"Mark," he muttered with an amused, almost sinister grimace. She frowned, and relinquished her twin swordsmen, tossing them into a new pile on the other side of the deck; this was the deck that would count against her. He smiled wickedly and dealt her two more cards. He could easily see the irritation in her face. She tamped her cards into a packet and put them face down in front of her, readjusted her chair and then picked them up again, fanning them out in front of her nose. She kept her face as straight as possible and she collected what were now three wives and put them down face up in front of her. He scowled and dealt her three more cards. She now had a completely wild hand with only one high-valued card; but at least she had just gotten some points on him. With a triple nonetheless! She seemed quite pleased with herself for getting him back for his mark. He found that utterly charming and he offered her a strange, stiff smile.

"It is good to see you," he admitted. "I've done nothing but think of you."

"Arnsword," she whispered, snapping a card onto the table, "that is not an appropriate declaration in company," she hissed, her eyes betraying her with a little twinkle. He smirked devilishly in his awkward way and picked up her discarded card. She glanced at him and said:

"Mark!" He shrugged and turned the card, putting it onto the discard stack, and she huffed out in great frustration, sifting through her cards for the highest valued one, the wood-nymph, tossing it with ire on top of her cost-cards. She wanted to ask if he was cheating and if he had a match for that card in his hand, but she knew that was not an honourable way to act.

He dealt her another and then took one for himself from the stack. "I hate this game," she grumbled irritably; he actually chuckled at that. She tamped her cards with conviction and fanned them out again. To her dismay, her new card was another wood-nymph. Oh well, she came out even, she supposed, hoping she could collect another one without him making her cast them like he did her swordsmen. After all, she still had a triple on the table. He had nothing yet. She straightened her shoulders and furrowed her brow with resolve. She waited to see what he would do on her discard, but he took from the deck instead and discarded two low cards into his cost pile, in penalty for not gambling. She picked up his last discard as a bluff and he sighed 'pass' as if she were the most predictable creature in the world. He seemed to derive some joyful delight in prodding her.

The game went on in the same genteel, amused humour with someone who seemed not to have the capacity for it. He indulged Ynith, and let her keep cards when it was most obvious they were destined for a set in her dainty hands. Nobody picked up an ogrein card and expected to hear a 'pass'. It was too high-valued. One could only really collect those through the dealing; instead, he pretended he thought she was taking a high-risk bluff. He could not resist taunting her about it a little however.

"I see you have a penchant for the night-stalker," he said as she daintily slid the ogrein into her hand. She glanced up at him by merely rolling her large eyes up from her bent position.

"Your aunt made me think of them tonight, she spoke of them as we arrived," she replied.

"I see," he said. "They are heavy cards to hold, my dearest Ynith; I would not take one so boldly from a discard."

"I have my reasons," she said. "Perhaps I have a triple now, and you just let me have it." He snorted through his nose, and she furrowed her brow, lifting her face and pressing her cards against her collarbone.

"You'd have played it if it was a double and you know it," he said. She frowned, but still managed to hide a playful smile in it.

"I wonder why they are such high value in the highwayman game?" she mused. "They value the same points as a royal set." Arnsword snapped down his card, which she studied and then dismissed.

"They were once much more than the shadows they are today," Arnsword said, his voice sort of hollow as he said it, as if he were partially distracted talking about them. She arched a brow and pursed her lips charmingly, which brought him back to watching her keenly.

"I've never seen one."

"It's likely you never will. There are a few here and there among the common society, some that are moderately evolved, but they do not like humanity as a habit. They prefer to look at us as food than as equals, save for the odd one or two. They don't actually take from humanity very often."

"Indeed. I don't hear of people dying by ogrein hands at all, yet they have such a dark reputation."

"They do kill, don't be mistaken. They're experts at concealing their crimes, and choosing people that won't be missed. And sometimes, from what I understand, they keep feeders, people who willingly give of their life-force in a position of servitude." Ynith wrinkled her nose and twisted her lip in disgust. Arnsword thought that was adorable as well.

"There aren't any around here, are there? Your aunt mentioning them sort of set my skin crawling this evening."

"Who knows? There are probably many more about than anyone really knows. They are shadows, they hide well. But if they take someone, it won't be from our ranks. They take the people that nobody cares about so nobody will feel compelled to come and hunt them. They are pathetic things, even if they do hunt our kind."

"But were once different?" He nodded.

"Once quite powerful." Ynith's brows arched, and she sighed.

"I wonder what happened?" she asked with a soft voice, "to make them so different." Arnsword seemed to know by the confidence of his gaze, but didn't say anything immediately. He merely watched her large eyes turn to look into his, filled with curiosity and a beautiful guilessness that consumed his heart. He wanted so just to reach across the table to kiss her senseless for being as utterly irresistible and sweet as she was. His absorption in his tiny universe of two people was torn apart by the Lady's sudden exclamation;

"Well, I am cooked; it's time to sleep, what think you brother?" Lady Farnham reached out and smacked her brother's knee quite hard and he jolted out of his quiet nap with a look of utter panic on his brow. The Docent then collected himself and grumbled at his sister, rearranging the banyan he'd put on after dinner. He stood up in his embroidered slippers and stifled a yawn. "The girl and I are going to the village for a spell after breakfast; we'll be back for more games and diversions afterwards, Your Highness. I think the hour is late and I am quite spent," the Lady declared, standing beside her brother. Ynith put her cards down gratefully. She had three sets on the table, Arnsword only had two. She hadn't tallied her cost cards yet, but she imagined it would still be a close game. She pursed her lips at him smugly, and glanced at the dwindling deck.

"We can finish it tomorrow night," he said. She nodded, her eyes twinkling at him, and she followed the Lady upstairs, where she was accompanied by her ladyship's prattle all the way to her room. With a promise of an early rise, she latched the Lady out and went to the bed where her night clothes were neatly laid out on the blankets.

Morning was exactly as promised, a leisurely breakfast that Arnsword only joined when the ladies were finished, and then Ynith was bundled off in the coach to the small seaside village where she was measured and patterns for her future garments were shaped right on her body in old linen by a tiny, fussy little woman by the name of Narie. She was a strange, plain little ginger thing of about thirty years who squinted too much and whose brood of children sounded like two armies clashing in battle above—floors. She seemed not to hear the squeals and thumps, crashes and bangs as she pinned and smoothed fabric over Ynith's shoulder, and snipped with a pair of shining scissors to piece out what she'd drawn on her rough linen used for pattern-making.

Lady Ressa Farnham instructed Narie exactly what Ynith would require, what pieces, what accessories, how many gloves and stockings and mitts; how many new shifts and stays, and of what fabric each one should be composed. She only asked Ynith what colours were her preference, but other than that, Ynith's participation was not required, except to be present for measuring, although Ynith did make a point of asking for simple garments and to stray from the fussier fashions she was seeing in fashion plates of late.

"No ruffles!" she blurted to Narie as the Lady was guiding her out. "And try not to add too much fuss on the fronts of things, or use too many bright colours! Just please choose sensible colours," she called out as the door closed behind her.

They then set off for the great house, where Ynith was immediately swept up for a nice stroll at the rocky shore before nuncheon by her princely suitor. After lunch, they went on a sedate ride together for more air and exercise. He seemed unaware of her embarrassment for not having a proper riding habit, and oblivious to her nervous posture as she first rode this serene, borrowed white and soft grey-dappled mare that belonged to her Ladyship.

She rarely rode at the Darvath. But when she did, she preferred a small horse, almost a pony by the name of Stomps, who was a plain bay with black mane, legs and muzzle, was as slow as molasses in winter, and whose gait was so jarring, even at a walk, only few of the ladies tolerated him. She did not have her own horse liveried at the academy as many of the other girls did. Stomps was her only recourse if she wanted to ride.

He was a scruffy, graceless excuse for horse kind, but for the price of a plump, crunchy carrot, he would exercise patience and tolerance as Ynith fumbled to place her nervous limbs in the horns of an old, mouse-chewed sidesaddle, and kept Stomps at a slow walk while everyone else galloped ahead in search of stone walls to leap over. He was not the sort of horse to feel compelled to join the romp, and was perfectly happy to trudge along and circle patiently around obstacles the other riders sailed over.

The Lady's mare Mistral was more fluid and flexible than what Ynith was accustomed to. She had a lithe elegance to her gait, and although she was sedate, she was neither slow nor sluggish as poor Stomps was. She tossed her head, and lifted her legs with great alacrity, her ears pert and alert, eyes bright and watchful. Ynith took a bit of time to grow accustomed to this lively, yet perfectly ladylike horse, and by the time they had returned, was utterly in love with this little dip-nosed marble-coated mare.

The Lady was coming out to ride her own tall, leggy chestnut hack as they rode to the stable, and saw Ynith threading her fingers lovingly through Mistral's smoky-grey mane while the stable hand removed the tack and Arnsword tended to his own horse. "Did she suit you my dear?" Lady Ressa asked. Ynith nodded with a shy smile.

"She was purchased for my granddaughter who shows no inclination for the saddle, sadly. And considering she hardly ever comes to visit anyway, you may consider her yours whenever you please, my girl. I can't imagine keeping such a sweet creature stalled up or ridden only by hands. She could use a good, regular rider. Narie will set you up properly with riding attire soon enough," she assured her. And with that, her groom threw her into the saddle of her shining horse, and she settled her legs into the horns and her foot into the stirrup so fluidly it was unnoticeable. With a subtle nudge, her graceful horse danced rather than trotted around the building towards the park.

Before dinner, Arnsword trounced her at cards at last, leaving her feeling most put out. She was particularly annoyed to see him play a triple ogrein, which meant he was holding them knowing that when she picked hers up it would be useless. *Sneaky,* she thought.

The three days were spent in the same idle occupations. The Lady was content to sit and listen to Ynith sing, or simply play and practice her scales on the instrument she'd once played when she was Ynith's age. Arnsword doted upon the girl in his own way, and hovered and lingered like a great, bony, rickety carrion-bird. There were no visits, no bothersome conversations, just a strange family-like ambience that Ynith had never had a chance to enjoy until now. She was loth to go back to the academy with the Docent come the last evening, and the Lady was quite reluctant to let the fresh face leave her company, but she took comfort in knowing she'd be back in eight days.

"And then after that endweek and week, my dear, it's to Imsgaard we go. Are you not excited? You'll have Arnsword there to make you feel at home, and his whole family to meet," Lady Farnham declared, hanging in the open coach-door, still holding Ynith's hand. She bent forward, indulging the Lady of her last goodbye until her next visit. Arnsword had grown tired of the Lady's fussing and moaning about the new week beginning, so he had left a bit earlier, taking only a moment before his exit to draw Ynith into the conservatory once more, and leading her behind some rather lush greenery to steal yet another kiss from her and to tell her he would not be here at the next restdays.

"I will be at Toreth for a few days so I won't be here for endweek, I am going to miss some classes as well on the eighthday. I will try to spend time with you during the week in the afternoons, if I can and you are able. But I will be gone for eighthday and the endweek. I will then see you at Imsgaard, Ynith. You must promise me again that you will be there, for I fear by your lack of enthusiasm when the Lady speaks of it, that you do not wish to go."

"I would only go because you wish me there, Arnsword," she whispered. "I do not wish to expose myself to judgment; especially to your family, the idea alone frightens me. I've been hearing some terrible tales about your sister."

"You have nothing to fear. I will be there to keep the hounds at bay, and surely my aunt will keep you tucked safely under her wing as well. I will see you at the academy this coming eightday. I will visit you at your work in the archive, if I may."

"Of course," she uttered. She did not know why she welcomed Arnsword's affections. There were so few redeemable qualities about him. He wasn't attractive in any conventional way, he was tall and lanky and bony and severe. He had no warmth of character with anyone except in tiny shreds in her company. He would not delight in the joys she would, he would not reflect her feelings, because he seemed to lack them himself, but for some reason, Ynith felt drawn to him. It was inexplicable. She was willing to face the infamously cutting and cruel creature that was his sister, whose reputation was well-known and something of great discussion in the girl's dormitory now that Ynith had so much involvement with Arnsword. The girls spoke again and again of Princess Adra, and her exploits of cruelty exacted upon the succession of people that had been presented to the family. It struck Ynith cold just thinking about it.

5. The Calm Before the Tempest

The week to follow was consumed with the things one might consider tedium, but to Ynith were comfort. She had quite enjoyed the sense of normality and belonging she felt at Gallevin with the Lady and the Docent. It had made her feel warm and valued. And that feeling carried on whenever she spent time in the scriptorium or the archive, and so she scheduled her entire week around it, spending every possible daylight moment she could scratching out text in the light of the window, and carefully drawing her delicate crow quill along the penciled lines she'd drawn, her eyes dropping from the master to her copy and back, seemingly in time with the ticking of the clock.

She took comfort in the sound of Oreth moving about the space as he prepared tea, and indulged him with a smile when he presented her with the fresh box of walnut biscuits just arrived from Gallevin with an affectionate note from his sister asking for confirmation that she would be leaving for Gallevin the last evening of the eighthday. She reveled in the fragrant tea, the scent of which she now associated with these two people who had brought her such wonderful inclusion into their lives.

She was happy. Ynith realized this one morning on the sixth day, and she could scarce help but smile to herself. She had just left a boring class, and had the rest of the day to spend here. She pinned on her apron and sighed happily, scooting onto her drafting chair.

Oreth arrived predictably with the kettle filled with water, and he sat down at his table to write while he waited for the water to boil. The fire was lively, the room comfortable, the scent of leathers and inks and wood fire were only improved by the addition of the aromatic summer pudding tea she loved so.

She could do this happily until the day she died, she realized. She then thought about Oreth and his age, and her heart hurt for a moment. But she forgot about that painful thought when he plunked a plate with a cake and a little butter-smothered muffin on it on the level portion of her desk. His eyes were filled with unadulterated affection for Ynith and all she could do was beam her adoration back in the form of a twinkling smile.

By the time the light had turned gold, and the three great chandeliers were lit, her back was a bit sore, she was full of tea and she'd made four complete pages. Oreth vanished as he did most afternoons to attend to the archive and the rush of post-class students. He let her stay in the scriptorium during that time because it was the young male students that were the afternoon visitors. It was then Arnsword took advantage of the time to slip in and spend a few moments with Ynith. He did this almost each afternoon.

He watched her quietly from the fireside as she finished up the last of her work before all of the decent light was gone. "Have you had a meal today, besides tea cakes?" he asked her in a strange cold voice. Ynith knew that was just his way of expressing himself, and that his concern was genuine; at least for her.

"I did slip out for nuncheon and eat with the girls. If I hadn't they'd have come to get me, because they cannot go a day without barraging me with questions about you," Ynith replied, never looking up from her page. She heard him snort, and shift about in his chair.

"You spend far too much time in here; it cannot be healthy, hunched over like that all day, never being out of doors, squinting at text day in and day out."

"I like it in here. It makes me happy to be here," she replied archly. She then looked up, and then stretched backwards, groaning a bit as her tense muscles gave way. There were welcome pops and snaps of bone and sinew from the action. She stood set about corking up all her ink bottles and putting the ones she no longer needed back into their respective drawers, and tidying away anything she would not need the next day to continue her work. She then stripped off her wrist cuff and stained apron, folding them and placing them on the chair.

"To each their own I suppose," the Everath mumbled. He grumbled about her work, but he was still considerate of her wants, which surprised her. She would imagine any man besotted by a woman would do his very best to compete for her attentions at all times, to divert her even from the things she enjoyed. But not Arnsword. He interrupted only to speak of things that might concern him, but he did not demand her attention away from her pursuits, he only conversed with her while she engaged in them. He waited patiently until she was finished tidying up, and then sat with her by the fire for a few moments. He contented himself with her company no matter what she was doing—even if she wasn't spending the time paying attention solely to him. Arnsword was happy to just be with her, and to know she welcomed his company.

"I am hungry now," she confessed. He nodded.

"I will walk you to the ladies' wing so you can eat."

"I have to change into my school gown. Will you wait for me?" He nodded once, and looked at the fire. She slipped into Oreth's anteroom to quickly change her clothes and then remerged carrying her school robe, which she donned as she approached Arnsword. He helped her place the garment on her shoulders, and then offered her what she imagined amounted to a smile, but it was strange and haunting, and with his hand hovering just at the nape of her back, he guided her to the door. She paused, and angled herself to face him a bit before they left the room, and reached out to squeeze his other hand before they slid out of the scripting area and offices and into the archives.

"I am leaving early, tomorrow morning," he confessed to her as they entered the archive. They walked side by side down the labyrinth of aisles. She looked up at him, and nodded.

"I'm terrified about the trip to Imsgaard," she replied. With a subtle brush of his hand, she saw reassurance in his eyes.

"I will be there, and you will be fine. You are so charming, I cannot imagine anyone would treat you badly," he said. She nodded and sighed in resignation. They were silent the rest of the way, and he left her with a nod at the door of the ladies' wing. Ynith hoped with all of her might that his confidence was justified, but deep down, she had a feeling that Arnsword really had no idea what his family was capable of. It wasn't ignorance or delusion, he simply did not understand the capacity for emotional torture one person could inflict on another. Not when he could not quite grasp the complexities of his own emotions as it was.

Ynith had a sense of foreboding that the trip the Imsgaard would end badly. She wasn't quite sure for whom.

6. Imsgaard

The door latch clicked, and Ynith's hands dropped to her sides. She leaned against the door to her humble apartments, and sighed shakily. Her head was rushing, and she felt the burn of tears in her eyes. With a blink, the pooling of water was pressed into droplets that spilled out onto her cheeks. She tried to straighten herself and managed to move to the chair by the fire, which was lit and cheerfully flickering. There she sat down and took a long, shaking, weary breath.

From the moment of her arrival, it had been a trial. Arnsword's family was comprised of people who were bored and found torturing subordinates a great source of amusement. Arnsword had yet to arrive, and the Lady was kind and sweet, but not at all effective in deflecting the constant scrutiny and condescension focused on Ynith—she was too distracted by the activities of the entourage, and absorbed in whatever they were doing to be aware, or know how Ynith fared.

Ynith was introduced formally to Arnsword's mother, the Queen Consort Evrial. She was a strange, faraway sort of creature who spent the better part of Ynith's first day sitting distanced from others in a small annex to the main parlour defined by a large, open archway. She had two small fluffy black dogs on her lap, and sat by one of the four fires in the room. She barely even fixed her eyes on Ynith when she curtseyed as elegantly as she could before her; more looking through the girl, and nodding blandly without speaking a word. Even the dogs seemed to hold their noses up at her, following her movement with their beady eyes.

It was the younger heirs, two young men and a young lady; all Arnsword's younger siblings, that acknowledged her—but not in a kind way. There were also two very young aristocratic companions present, as well as four cousins to the Princes and Princesses. They sat in three groups. One group was made up of the Queen Consort, the dogs and the very pale and reedy looking second-born Prince—who was slumped in a chair in the annex, paying no heed to anyone, while his mother sat impassively near him. The second group surrounded the Princess, who sat with her two companions and two of her young female cousins at a table where they all partook in a game of cards. The last group was the third-born prince and his two male cousins; they frequently went off together, and when Ynith first arrived were discussing the possibility of taking sport that afternoon. They nodded at her introduction, and then resumed the chat about hunting as if she'd been a servant offering tea.

The Lady, after introducing them all to her shy companion, melted into the soup of young women at the card table, expecting Ynith to fit in comfortably. However, the immediate sign that she was not welcome was that they did not offer her a seat at the table. Instead, she sat on a chaise nearby, half-listening to the idle chatter while she watched the other denizens of this beautifully appointed, cavernous parlor that was also dark and bleak even with the massive, towering windows. Outside the light was bright and cheerful, but it was drearily lit inside. So much so, several candles had been lit and peppered about the room to brighten it.

For a good while, the talk was safely devoid of true substance and remained innocuous and banal. But the eldest cousin, who was called Bina, turned her attention to Ynith, who'd taken up a small book and was quietly reading. "You attend the academy, do you not Miss Ynith?" The other ladies flicked and sorted through their cards, eyes rolling upwards to take in Ynith as they awaited her reply. The Lady was about to answer for her when Ynith decided to respond.

"I do, Miss Bina," Ynith could feel their eyes and their scrutiny. She remained poised and calm, having no expectations of cruelty or snideness. She suspected they would look down on her common clothes and retiring nature to begin with.

"It's unusual for young ladies to attend academy. This academy here is the only one that allows it, is it not?"

"I am not certain," Ynith replied. The Lady interjected:

"Yes, the Darvath is the *only* academy that allows for female attendees. Her presence there is a testament to her worthiness, for only the brightest girls are accepted to study there." Ynith offered the older lady a soft smile.

"Or the girls with no other prospects," the younger cousin blurted, "I don't imply that this is you, Ynith, but I am sure that is a reason why some ladies are there," she added with a mischievous smile. Not a single word of her assurance sounded sincere. In fact, it was imbued with snide maliciousness.

"Now, now, Rhea, you cannot simply admonish Miss Ynith's *classmates*," Ganeen spoke this time, her words perhaps kind, but her expression was one of amusement and sarcasm. She then flashed Ynith a withering glare. She was one of the twin Duchesses.

"What sort of things do you learn at the Academy?" the Princess asked, "Arnsword never speaks of it. We all find his choice to take education there to be completely ludicrous, but you cannot argue with him. He is impossible." Ynith wanted to tell them that it was none of their concern what Arnsword chose to do, nor was it their place to admonish him for it. But she remained politely tightlipped, something the other ladies chose not to do, and they marched on in their polite tearing down of the newcomer. The forced courtesy was fading quickly however, with each additional observation.

"Indeed. What courses of study do you pursue, Miss Ynith?"

"Literature is my favorite; history…"

"How dull," Rhea declared, slapping a card into the central pile.

"Really. Mind-numbing," Bina added.

"I cannot imagine sitting in a class listening to someone droning on and on about history; you poor dear," the Princess mumbled. Ynith forced some cheerfulness into her tone in her reply.

"I quite like it, actually. I like the archive as well. I enjoy transcribing quite a bit, and it puts my skill for drawing to use. I learn a great deal copying texts."

"Intolerable," the Princess interrupted her haughtily. "You must be a very dull, quiet thing, Miss Ynith. I do not think I would find any extended period in your company pleasing at all, I am very sorry to say."

"Your Highness, that is not a kind thing to say," the Lady blurted, her cheeks flushing with anger and embarrassment for the Princess's comportment.

"Well, I'm not sorry for being truthful," she said airily, waving her hand dismissively.

"I certainly don't go about moaning on and on about books. I do have some acumen for general conversation, but I would never presume to be… " Ynith defended herself.

"Well, I for one cannot see how any of this has anything to do with the game. Tally up, Bina." The silent aristocratic girl named Haneen finally pitched into the conversation with yet another rude interruption. She was a twin, but both sisters worked very hard to look as different as possible. One wore a garish teal gown with silver embellishments with matching shoes and ribbons. Her sister Ganeen wore a similarly overly-accessorized gown of a brilliant fuschia with hints of gold and green. Both gowns were made of the finest silks. They were the height of current fashion, enhanced with fine lace ruffs and the loveliest of jewelry. One wore her hair down on her back with the sides pinned up; the other had a large pile of curls on her head interspersed with pearls. They were handsome girls, Ynith could not deny this. But the expression of disdain on their faces, even when staring at their cards, was unmistakable and unattractive.

Ynith pursed her lips after studying each of the twins carefully, and then turned her attention back to her book. The Lady looked mortified, and gave Ynith a conciliatory glance before she dropped her eyes to the text on the page. The ladies remained quiet for a while, and then fell into conversation again, this time giggling madly over a silly story about some hapless creature they met during the spring season they found very amusing. They tore her apart, from her clothing to her mannerisms. Ynith got up to quietly play a small, elegant instrument in the far corner and as she was walking away, she heard Bina say:

"Well, she *was* an unfortunate creature" she said of the girl they'd been lambasting, "yes, but she *could* be an egghead, and that's infinitely worse," which was followed by an explosion of giggles.

"Ladies!" the Lady admonished.

Ynith played quietly, her fingers dancing languidly along the keys, pressing so softly, the sound of the pianoforte was barely audible to the others in the room. She could hear them though. They were criticizing her simple muslin gown, her dark hair, and her drab eyes; questioning her background, never once letting the Lady get a word in edgewise to contradict them or defend Ynith against their suppositions and speculations. They snickered about the cheap leather of her shoes, and her plain clothes and lack of adornments. "Has she no pride, Lady? She is visiting Imsgaard, not some unremarkable landowner. Honestly, dear aunt, I must say I am quite befuddled by your choice of companions, she's so mousy and dull."

As the morning trudged on, the relentless criticisms were starting to wear on Ynith more than she cared to admit. The Princess's censures were often communicated through her cadre so she could appear as innocent as can be. They laughed at her piano-playing, which Ynith found amusing since none of the other girls could play; they would compliment her lavishly on her appearance, her hair and her gown, and then turn and smirk at one another, bursting into giggles without the slightest sense of consideration, discretion or subtlety. They openly mocked her and she tried to withstand it.

When one of the younger brothers of Arnsword referred to Ynith in passing as Lady Ressa's handmaid, she'd had enough. She asked to be shown to her apartment, and locked herself inside, fighting her tears in the chair by the fire. Why she had agreed to come to this place was beyond her, for what?

She took tea alone, and turned the concerned Lady Ressa away. She dreaded the notion of sharing a dining table with her critics. It wasn't until early evening that Arnsword arrived.

His appearance could not be missed. He arrived in a cloud of chaos; even before his coach stopped, two riders clattered ahead to announce him, his horse tethered to one of theirs. His man shouted orders, people scampered about, and then the coach rumbled up. Arnsword unfolded his lanky, tall frame from the carcass of the coach, and stalked down the step onto the gravel where he tugged down the front of his waistcoat and surveyed the front of the house momentarily. He suddenly looked up as if by instinct to see Ynith's pale face far above, on the third floor in the window watching him. She drew away the moment she sensed his eyes on her. She was ashamed of her weakness. Ashamed she was so upset by all the teasing.

"Why is the Lady's guest quartered in the North rooms?" Arnsword barked at his mother, while glaring at his eldest sister. "And why is she not here with the group?" He stamped into the great chamber, and his anger was palpable. He knew the instant he arrived and saw his favourite's sweet, lost face, what his family had done. He had feared it, and had cursed the impediments that made him so late to her side.

"She wished to retire to her rooms," Lady Farnham said, sitting by the Queen Consort. But her eyes betrayed her shame, and Arnsword's eyes darkened.

"Indeed. She chose to leave us," the Queen blurted without a care, flicking open her fan and waving it languidly before her. The Lady Farnham continued:

"I went up after her an hour ago, and she turned me away," she said with some contrition. She'd been sitting quietly by the fire with the Queen Consort, who hunched most inelegantly in her chair, gazing dumbly at her eldest son. Lady Farnham cast her eyes down and then looked accusingly at the offenders, who were still at cards; all the young people clustered about the table.

"This is unacceptable. A guest, specially chosen by me and you treat her so ill she feels compelled to hide; in inferior apartments no less, with no prospect but of the driveway, and hardly any space to move about. She has higher rank than your two ridiculous and wholly useless companions, Adra, this is inexcusable!" he pointed at the duchesses who glanced at one another in astonishment while he directed his ire at his sister.

"Nonsense. Some harmless teasing never hurt anyone. Perhaps if she had shown the fortitude to withstand it, she might have earned some of our respect," Adra declared. Arnsword wanted to slap her.

Adra had been blessed with the beauty and grace both her brothers had been deprived of. She was a patrician creature, through and through, from her refined manners that even her cousins could not match, to the choice of her clothing and the coif of her beautiful deep red hair. She had eyes as green as Arnsword's that seemed to gleam when she flared up at her brother's accusations, and her lips were inordinately red and full. She, however, like her cousins, had an impregnable hardness to her countenance that made her appear quite unapproachable. The set of her chin and the way she peered down her nose at the world seemed to erase the appeal of her physical beauty. One could tell she was, upon first glance, a nasty character, with little compassion or kindness to offer anyone.

"I hardly imagine anything that comes out of your mouth is harmless. I know what you and your harpy friends are capable of. I've seen it before. Do not play innocent with me, Adra, I taught you that game," Arnsword snarled. Adra frowned ominously and then picked a card, placing it on the table.

"She's a simpering fool, and you should be ashamed to be defending her. She does not belong here," Adra muttered, snapping the card down onto the table with vehemence. Her ivory gown was one of immaculate taste, simple but still rich, and unlike her cousins, she kept the frill and frump to a minimum, expressing the richness in the superiority of the textiles and the refinement and unmatchable quality of the lace around her neckline and on her wrists.

"She is a far better person than you could ever hope to be. It's no wonder nobody wants to court you, it's no wonder your suitors flee at first acquaintance; you are a harridan. You tear other young women apart because you envy them for their character. You should be ashamed of yourself. You are working your way towards a life as a loveless lonely old cow. And then everyone will abhor and pity you," he spat. He turned on his heel with a flare of his greatcoat and swaggered out.

"Arnsword, that is utterly unacceptable! You should never speak to your sister like that!" the Queen called out after him.

"I am ashamed to call her my sister," he roared over his shoulder. "I am ashamed of you all!" He charged up the steps two at a time to Ynith's rooms.

Ynith was sitting stiff in her chair, still reeling from being seen by the Prince, when she heard a hard knock on her doors. She stood and padded to it, cracking it open.

"Ynith, I am so very sorry," he pushed the door open more so he could see her face. The sight of her reddened, puffy eyes was enough to send him into a rage, but he bit back his anger, and furrowed his brow.

"I am fine. I simply do not belong here."

"Nonsense. Come with me, we shall go walking." She did not refuse the Prince; she reached for her shawl, and he dotingly wrapped it around her shoulders and arms. He closed the door behind her and then took her hand. He observed her in a very deep grey gown, her hair wound up beautifully on her head without the busy adornments like his cousins and his sister's other stupid companions. She was pale, and wan, but her eyes were wide and she looked comforted by his presence, taking him in with no flicker of doubt, no fear. She trusted him so.

"You look beautiful," he told her.

"You are very kind." She almost started crying again, her voice choking momentarily; and this flustered her admirer.

"I am sorry my sister, her insipid friends, and my brothers were so horrible to you," he grumbled. "I confess I knew it would happen; she's like that with just about everyone. Adra is hateful. She is cruel. And yes, when I am not under your care, so am I; but *I* see your charms, I do not wish that pain and humiliation for you. I tried to get here quickly as to avoid any discomfort for you, but I was not able to get on the road soon enough early this morning."

"I am fine, Arnsword," Ynith assured him. "I've been teased before, I am just tired and perhaps a bit overwhelmed; Imsgaard is very grand, and I feel very small."

"Nonsense." The Everath stopped and looked down at this creature who owned his heart like nothing else in the world. She was bold and leaned forward, laying her cheek and her hand on his chest. It was such an unexpected gesture of affection and trust it caught him completely off guard. He stiffened at first, but then reached up and wrapped his arms around her, relishing the sensation of her being against him, her soft breath, and the vulnerable, fragile nature of her sigh. He could feel her drawing from him; taking some of his strength, and he felt her becoming stronger for it. He was overwhelmed by it; overwhelmed by being so trusted, so needed. He wanted it to last forever, but instead, she rocked back, looking up at him, a bit embarrassed.

"I am not like them," she began.

"No, you are better. And I want you to remember that. Nobody will dare say anything anymore; not when I am here. I have laid them flat, and I purposely directed my anger at the twins; I despise them and always have. They steer my sister very wrong. You should never believe a word out of their mouths. They are ignorant and dull. You are not. You are better." He took her hand and then began to walk again, leading her down the two long, circular flights of stairs that would land them down into the center of the main foyer.

He made a show of walking right through the main parlour where everyone still sat. The Lady smiled gently, pleased by

Arnsword's change of character, bewildered but also happy that he took Ynith so fittingly under his wing. He opened a large window door that led out of the parlour onto a stone patio, and then proceeded down the steps onto a vast rectangle of lawn lined by rows of manicured topiary and roses. At the end of the prospect, a circular lake shimmered; in its center a spray of water arced up into the air and then fell down in a shower of droplets.

"Your rooms should be looking out over this, not the fro…"

"I like my rooms. They're away from everyone else's." He paused, and then frowned.

"Then I shall move to the main house then, so you are not completely alone. There are apartments that are tolerable nearby."

"It is inappropriate for you to…"

"I am the Crown Prince, Ynith. I can do as I like. I asked you here to make this time tolerable for me, and in turn, I must make it tolerable for you. You are the closest thing I have ever had to a friend, and you mean all the more to me. Your presence; it sustains me when nothing else does. They will respect you, or…"

"Arnsword, do not be so angry at them; they are as they have always been. It's not personal to me. They would do the same to anyone else who came along. I just allowed it to affect me when I should not have."

"That is not entirely true. They see you as a legitimate threat, Ynith; someone who could truly capture my heart; someone who *has* captured my heart. Anyone else is not you," he said with a powerful finality. She did not persist. She only smiled at him with her eyes, and then squeezed his hand. She decided then that her strange sense of guard about Arnsword was misplaced. She realized that she had come to care for him, for never in her life had she ever experienced such dedication and concern; nor did anyone appreciate who she was, like he did.

They walked in quiet together, drawing comfort in the presence of the other and enjoying the soft mountain breeze. Imsgaard was an exceptionally beautiful estate set in the finest country. Above the bristling roofline, looming like a frieze were the Havatrai Mountains, massive and ever-white on their summits. Below them, rows of hills covered in conifers washed at the mountains' feet, and then the lake, and before that the circular pond and fountain. It was a view that took Ynith's breath away. To have such a home and only to visit it a few weeks in summer; it seemed almost a crime.

They remained in secluded company for another hour, an act that would normally be frowned upon, for there was no chaperone. But nobody seemed to care—Arnsword had always been singular in what he did—and they would speak ill of Ynith for her impropriety anyway regardless of whether she spent time alone with Arnsword. So they strolled alone, found a nice place to sit and rest in an orchard, and Arnsword picked her a plump pear, which she ate while he talked to her. He spoke of an old wizard who had served his family when he was a child, and how he had inspired Arnsword to appreciate the practice of magic.

A servant came huffing and puffing behind them to notify them that dinner was to be served, and their quiet was no more. Arnsword led his lady back to the house, and they found everyone seated to dine. Ynith had no time to dress for evening, but at this point, she did not care. Arnsword was separated from his companion then, for Ynith was seated at the far end of the table with the youngest heir and the cousins, and he sat up beside his mother.

"Arnsword, it's unseemly for you to be roaming about with an unattached young lady of questionable background; you know how the twins talk. It will be all over Teragaard the moment they chance to write their friends and family," the Queen Consort whispered to him as he settled in.

"I don't care," he replied, "and I would also like to add that she is not of questionable background. She is the orphan of the house of Shalmeen; her status and fortune is likely greater than everyone at this table save for our direct family. You ought to remember that next time my dearest sister and her hunting hounds decide to attack."

"My dear, you are so impassioned by this. It's most unusual." The Queen Consort shook out her large napkin and spread it out on her knees.

"That is none of your concern." The Queen Consort stared at him in utter disbelief.

"It is entirely my concern, Arnsword. Your father would be beside himself if he knew."

"If he knew what mother?" he snapped in a harsh whisper. This discussion was far from discreet, for Arnsword's shoulders had risen into something akin to raised hackles and his usual indifference was prickling with ire, his features sharp, eyes narrowed as he pointed his whispered irritation to his mother. "What objection could he possibly have of her? That she has no parents? What crime is that?" The Queen consort did not answer him for a moment, she merely picked up her fork, which signaled that everyone else was now permitted to do so, and she began to eat. Arnsword sat on his end in a brewing anger.

"She is of the Shalmeen line, Arnsword. A Duchy that has vied to claim legacy to the throne for centuries; it would be unheard of to allow that bloodline to sully ours and use us to gain legitimacy again after four centuries of our line on the throne," she finally said. Arnsword's brow furrowed in bafflement.

"Four centuries? Father carries on a four-hundred-year-old grudge?" he hissed.

"When my sister mentioned bringing her as a guest in her letter, your father was immediately concerned. He explained it all to me, the history of her family and ours," she paused, and put her fork down, pursing her lips and leaning in to whisper very quietly to him.

"The Shalmeen have always claimed their right to the throne, for all these years. Her father was quite vocal about it, and was urging the Consistory to revisit the question of legacy yet again—claiming he had evidence of collusion that led to his line being usurped so many years ago," she said. She then leaned back in her chair and directed her gaze at Ynith at the end of the table before looking again at her son.

"There is a reason her parents no longer live, Arnsword."

The words rung cold when she said them and Arnsword's jaw rippled as he chewed his mandibles. His fury was simmering briskly and quickly turning into a rolling boil.

"Now this Shalmeen daughter drops into our laps so opportunely? I would not fall for that, my dear boy. No, it's entirely too convenient that she appears, and is as devoted to you as she is," she continued, her voice filled with acid towards Ynith. "If you care about her you will cast her back where you found her. If you pull her too close to our circle, she might be *burned*," she said icily.

The darkness seemed to enfold him at those words. His fingers curled into claws on each side of his plate, and he toiled to keep his rage in check. His vision was painted red by his rage, and he fought with everything he had to keep control of it.

This tidbit his mother shared was something new to him. The idea that Ynith's family had been harmed by anyone remotely connected to his was enough fill him with a fury he had never felt before. His eyes rose up balefully, and slowly, panning along the table one face at a time; he painted his black glare down the line, noting with bitter anger the disapproval of his family, overt and passive, that surrounded him. His emerald eyes, glazed in rage, wandered to the end of the table, where Ynith sat, her fork with its tines resting on the plate, staring off towards the center of the table into nowhere. Not a single person was speaking to her.

Without another word he got up and stalked out.

"My apologies, Your Highness, I wasn't expecting a visit so early in the morning," Ynith muttered, clutching her simple dressing-gown closed at the neck. The princess Adra sailed in, already in her finest, in spite of the sun having not yet fully risen. She did not look at Ynith, she instead sank down in a puff of delicate voile in one of the graceful chairs that sat by the brightening windows. "I haven't had a chance to dress."

"Never mind that, please sit, Miss Ynith, I must have a word with you," the princess replied impatiently. Ynith did as she was asked, intimidated. The words were polite, but the tone was cold and brimming with disdain. The young woman's presence was heavy and suffocating. She finally let her narrowed eyes wander to Ynith's face, but she held them there with an air of being almost disgusted by what she saw.

"I've taken the liberty of asking for a coach to be prepared to take you back to your residence at the school. I think it's only fair you understand why, Miss Ynith," she said.

Ynith's stomach went cold. She could not believe what she knew she was about to hear. She'd never given a single one of them reason to think ill of her, but they were sure she was what they had willfully decided her to be. She couldn't escape it. She did not pursue Arnsword, he pursued her. He needed her. She chose to be there because *he* needed her. Because he had nobody else. Because they were all such horrid people, he needed her to keep him grounded; to make him feel like a person in the company of people who seemed utterly incapable of feeling anything except spitefulness. Ynith watched the Princess shift in her seat and turn to look outside, as if she was setting herself up to appear more dramatic for what she was about to say next. Ynith remained tightlipped and poised, and did not stir a mote.

"My brother stands in line to inherit after my father, I am sure *you* are keenly aware of this," she said these last words as an accusation. Ynith's eyes narrowed but she kept a tight bite on her tongue. Adra went on. "He has a great deal at stake, and he has already challenged us all with his behavior and his choices over these past years. But he has been given a certain amount of... tether, so to speak, but those days will soon be over. He must very soon give up his larks, like that school and *other* such things. He *shall* marry a suitable bride and begin the preparations for his eventual ascension to the throne, as is expected of him.

"You must understand that his bride has already been chosen for him. She has been for many years. You must know that any promises he makes to *anyone* else cannot possibly be fulfilled because of his prior obligations. Especially with your family connections, you must understand. He stands to lose his legacy if he pursues the wrong ends. He probably never meant to mislead you in any way, Miss Ynith, I am certain of this. I think your family name might have been part of the reason why he took interest in you, for he knew that a Shalmeen under our roof would irk us all. You mustn't blame him. He merely has a tendency to be a bit unfeeling in toying with a girl's *ambitions*. Especially if it's someone he knows our family would not approve of."

"I *beg* your pardon?" she retorted archly, her spine hackling. "A girl's ambitions? Truly?"

"Do let me finish, Miss Ynith," Adra stopped her.

"I will most certainly not allow you to finish," Ynith blurted, trying her very hardest to keep her countenance about her. She could feel her hands shaking and she gripped them tightly in her lap. "You have delivered your message to me most aptly. With all due respect, Princess, it certainly could have been delivered with many degrees less of spite and maliciousness, without accusing me of ill-intentions towards your brother. He has always been tremendously kind to me, and in turn, I have returned his kindness. Whatever his intentions are towards me; these are his responsibility alone, and none of you have any place dictating this.

"Whatever you and your family have made me to be is utterly misguided, and you ought to be ashamed for treating a friend of your brother so ill. I will leave this place as you all so greatly desire; but I suspect in your driving me away that you have made a grave mistake in thinking it will improve the situation with your brother. But you have chosen your path, and you have chosen to dismiss me without Arnsword's leave, which I am quite certain is the case. I can only comply for I daren't defy the Everai. Now I beg that you would leave me so I can prepare to depart!" Ynith's voice was trembling with emotion, and her eyes shone with tears of defiance. Adra, surprisingly, complied. She got up and walked haltingly out. She did not have a look of victory on her face as she likely hoped she would that morning, but instead, she sported a look of bemusement. Ynith's reaction was one she was not prepared for, and it took away some of the cruel delight she'd hoped to glean from the eviction.

As soon as the door latch clicked, Ynith stormed to the little writing desk and reached for a paper and quill, hastily scratching out a paragraph. She folded it, sealed it quickly and wrote

Arnsword's name on the face. She then gathered up her belongings in haste, threw them without ceremony into the two trunks she'd brought from Gallevin, and dressed rapidly. Two young servant girls appeared only a few moments later at the Princess's behest, and assisted her in a rushed exit.

As Ynith strode towards the door at the heels of the footmen carrying her trunks, she threw her letter right on top of the stack of correspondence already on the salver by the door. She then walked directly out, down the steps and into the coach, so irate and shocked, she thoughtlessly did so without acknowledging the footman's proffered hand.

By the time Arnsword awoke to the news of Ynith's departure, she was halfway back to the Darvath. Ynith was not present to witness what occurred when he discovered she'd been chased away.

Ynith was unsure of what to do when she returned to the archives the morning after she left Imsgaard. The Docent was not present, and so she decided she could simply return to sorting, which was an ongoing need in the archive. She picked up the list for the zoology section, and with a tremulous sigh, set to work. She was glum. She'd spent the entire seven hour voyage from Imsgaard in uncontrollable tears; seven long hours of reflection and uncontrolled sobbing. She could not begin to explain why. She did not understand why she felt so strongly for Arnsword, she still could not find very many appealing qualities about him that justified her hours of blubbering. By the time the coach had come to a stop in front of the girls' dormitory the night before, she was hollow, raw and without a single tear left inside her. She dismounted and led the footmen to her room where they left her trunks right in front of Treen's bed. She waited until they left to push them to the foot of hers. Alone, she flopped down onto the bed, and turned onto her side. Knowing Treen would be returning by the eighth bell, she thought she could sleep off some of her misery before she returned. She did not wake until the next morning.

The Wizard King

Treen had been oddly concerned come morning. She said nothing but she helped her remove her linen traveling gown, which she'd slept in and wrinkled horribly. She then fetched her water for the basin, and wordlessly sat on the edge of her bed and watched Ynith wash her face and freshen up. She finally spoke only a few moments before the breakfast bell.

"Are you going to be all right, Ynith?" Her voice was soft, and her eyes filled with sympathetic caring. The girl nodded in reply and she undressed.

"I won't be attending classes today. I wasn't going to be here anyway, so I'll just go to the archives instead." Treen nodded and let her change into her school gown and robes in order to ready herself for another day in the archives.

* * * *

Dearest Arnsword,

I regret to write this, but I am forced to inform you of my departure this morning. I was asked to leave by your sister, and I have complied as it is my duty. I confess I was not very kind to her, but I must also in my defense say that she was far from kind to me. I have come to realize that our friendship is doomed to be a succession of encounters like these, where your family, in disapproval of my having any part of your life, will strive only to make us both as miserable as possible until they succeed in renting us irrevocably apart. I do not wish to beleaguer you further in any way, as to make your family treat you worse than they already do. Nor do I, selfishly, wish to expose myself to more of this sort of abuse from people who are so wholly unimportant to me. The only reason I would ever suffer through more of this despicable cruelty on their part is for your sake, but the fact that you suffer just as painfully from it, and knowing my departure will end it makes taking leave of you easier than it is, my dear friend. I must state that this is by far the most difficult thing I've ever done, but it is in this departure that I see now with great clarity, how much you have come to mean to me, dear Arnsword. I cannot bear any longer to know that I am the cause of any further unhappiness to you because of the disapproval of your family.

With love, Ynith.

105

Miranda Mayer

7. *Conflagration*

Ynith was in the back of the archives; she was hunched on the floor as she had been that first day she'd met Arnsword, a littering of books all around her. She forced herself to think only of her task. She heard the flutter of heavy hems, and she looked up, her eyes full of hope, but they lost some of their luminosity when she saw the Docent come 'round the book cases.

"There you are, goodness gracious, I've been looking all over for you. You must come at once, my dear, hurry!" The Docent reached out his hand and jutted it out towards her in order to express his sense of urgency. Ynith, confused by his exigency, took his hand and got to her feet, her brow furrowed. The old man clasped her hand and led her away.

"Are you well, Ynith?" he asked, huffing as he led her down deeper into the library.

"I am, Docent. But you do not look well. You look agitated. What is it?" she asked. The docent stopped for a moment and peered at her.

"You do not know?"

"Know what?"

"My dear Ynith, your Arnsword has gone mad. Imsgaard is a ruin, only his father, the King survives. And that is in question now, for there have been great rumblings coming from Amagaard," he rambled.

"Ressa!" Ynith cried out, her eyes immediately filling with tears. The Docent shook his head and patted her hand as he moved.

"My sister is fine. She is at Gallevin as we speak. She is shocked and horrified, but she is fine. She was spared," he assured her.

"Oh thank goodness," Ynith replied, wiping away her tears in relief. Her hands trembled at the idea that Ressa could have been harmed by Arnsword.

"There are wizards coming out of the woodwork, and it is being said that the floors of Wetherly hall are carpeted in bluebells. It is chaos. I heard that there are wizards using this madness caused by Arnsword to practice their own forbidden arts—something has lit their fires, I hope it isn't what I suspect it to be. It is fast-becoming a wizard rebellion, Ynith, and I have reason to believe you could be in danger."

"In danger? From Arnsword?" she asked in puzzlement. "I would imagine I'm the last one in danger of him," she added, her words blunted by her sniffly nose.

"Not from him, no," he admitted, albeit grudgingly. "I wish to shield you from those who seek to harm him—and if it *is* him that is using the forbidden magics," Ynith suspected it could be no other but did not say anything, "...then the hunters could use you to draw him out. We must go to the vaults, Ynith, you will be sheltered there until we can come up with some answers," he huffed. "Come along."

Ynith was moved into a small annex in the caves which they called the vaults. Here, adjacent to the testing chambers, a small set of apartments were set aside for one reason or another. Her things had been gathered from the dorm and she was moved into one of the apartments under the Docent's orders. There were no windows here, only the spare yellow light from the lanterns and candles. She was left there mostly alone for nearly four days while the Docent and two of the powerful Wizard professors went about investigating the incidences that were caused by Arnsword. She was forbidden to exit the premises and told to remain vigilant at all times. They gave her little more information. Not even the person who brought her food and attended to her needs could provide her answers.

The sense of urgency and alarm seemed to fade over those days, and finally, on the evening of the fifth day, she was permitted out of the vaults. The Docent appeared and suggested she go to Gallevin and stay with his sister. He looked haggard.

"You are shielded for now," he told her as he loaded her into the coach in the darkness. "We decided it was a fair price to pay rather than keep you locked up like a bird in a cage. Now, nobody who seeks you using magic can find you. We will come up with a more permanent solution after the lot of us have gotten together to assess the situation," he said. She wondered who 'the lot of us' were.

She nodded and settled back into the gloom of the coach. It set forth into the dark, leaving behind the frail old man. In the pitch of the night, all she could see were the very tips of the leaves of the shrubbery growing by the roadside, highlighted by the swinging lamps on the coach. She stared forward into nothing, unreservedly bewildered.

The Lady was awake to greet her. It was a strained, whispered greeting, and the coach was sent away back to the school in spite of the late hour. Ynith stopped at the base of the steps to the Lady's large home, and the Lady, in an elaborate red silk dressing gown over a flowing gathered night-dress immediately took her hands and led her up the stairs at the heels of the footmen.

"My dear Ynith, you must be so confused," she hissed. "I must begin by apologizing to you in the most humble way, for I failed you miserably when we were last together, and it is partly my doing that this has all transpired."

"How do you come to this conclusion?" Ynith stopped at the top of the steps and gazed intently at the Lady. The candlelight from the entranceway barely reached them. The Lady's face looked pained and gaunt. Her silver hair was down in a single plaited rope on her back, and she, like her brother, looked tired. They entered the house and crossed the foyer to the foot of the stairs leading to the second floor. The Lady paused, a wash of regret passing over her features.

"Had I protected you better, somehow curbed the way the family was treating you, then Arnsword would not have had reason to do what he had done."

"What did he do, Lady Ressa?" Ynith asked. "Nobody seems to be willing to tell me exactly what happened."

"Come, let us go to your rooms, and I'll explain it to you." They climbed the steps and the footmen were leaving the apartments just as they arrived. Lady Ressa shooed the servant girl out and shut the door behind them. She turned and moved to Ynith's trunk, which she opened to search for her night clothes.

"The Princess was presumptuous to do what she had done, but Ynith, I am making no excuses for their behavior; I am only hoping to make you understand their motives better. I don't know..." Lady Ressa sighed, ceasing her rummaging for a moment. Ynith politely moved her aside and she dug out her own night-dress as the Lady continued.

"You are Shalmeen. You know the history, your family's connections to the throne, the imprisonment and subsequent beheading of your ancestor Queen Evemi Shalmeen, the rise of the Emratath bloodline."

"That was several centuries ago," Ynith said, shaking out her nightgown and her dressing gown.

"It doesn't mean that your family members haven't been petitioning their right to rule ever since; even your current relatives have continued to appeal that they have been usurped."

"What does that have to do with me, really?" Ynith said impatiently. "I have no such ambitions, and I know that is what Adra implied." She pulled her delicate muslin gown off over her head and proceeded to shake it out and hang it in the armoire.

"Your name alone was enough. Arnsword might not have seen it; he was so blinded by his feelings for you, that he did not see it. Nor did I, really, until the Queen Consort mentioned it when she read of your connections in my letter when I informed her I was bringing you to Imsgaard. What might seem silly and anecdotal to some might mean something very different to others, especially when they have a legacy to defend." Ynith had removed her petticoat and stays, and was putting them away in the closet.

"I am not connected to anyone. I had to be removed from my birthright and hidden in order to protect me from my own family!" Ynith snapped, her emotions rising up inside her. "I only wanted to be his friend," she started to sob.

"Now they are all dead," the Lady blurted. Ynith's breath caught in her throat and she had to sit. She was wearing only her shift, stockings and still had her little blue slippers on. The Lady went to her and took her hand.

"Arnsword accused his father of murdering your parents, Ynith. He was infuriated by something his mother said at dinner that last evening, and apparently he'd stewed on it all night. He was so angry; angry at the family's treatment of you, and now the possibility that his family could be responsible for your current situation."

"They killed my parents?"

"I do not know, Ynith. What does it matter now? There is nothing left of that family to speak of. Arnsword is the only one left."

"Arnsword..." Ynith said with a gulp. Her tears flowed.

"That morning, you had gone. I got up when I heard the coach, just in time to see you climb into it. I went to see why you'd left without speaking to me when I ran into Arnsword, who was going to your door to see if you had roused for the day." Ynith got back up and started to change into her nightclothes, still sniffling and upset. Lady Ressa went to the sideboard in the other room to pour out two snifters of apple brandy. Ynith, now changed, slipped on her night-slippers and pulled on a simple polished cotton dressing gown of her own, following the Lady out into the sitting room and joining her by the fire. They both sat, and for a moment, there was silence as the Lady prepared to tell the rest of the story.

"We did not assume the worst. Neither of us saw your trunks being loaded; neither of us realized you'd gone for good. We both thought perhaps you'd gone somewhere before breakfast and you would return in time to join everyone. So we went to breakfast. Arnsword was in a black mood to begin with. Everyone gathered but not one person mentioned your whereabouts or even asked. We ate, we spoke of banalities, and then the footman brought the salver with the morning's correspondence and calling cards from the evening before with your letter right on top," Ressa explained. Ynith's hand fell at the base of her throat as she listened, her eyes locked on the flames.

"He read your letter in stony silence. Of course at the time, nobody knew it was from you. His quiet was so heavy and powerful; everyone stopped eating and was looking at him expectantly. Now that I recall, his sister did have a peculiar look about her, as if surprised and irritated—probably realizing what he was reading. I wager she didn't think you'd have time to write anything to him, or perhaps she was surprised the servants didn't merely pass it along to her..."

"I put it in the salver when I was leaving. No servant touched it," Ynith muttered. "I knew that it would be intercepted if I entrusted the letter to any of the house staff," she said bitterly. Lady Ressa sighed and shook her head.

"Of course, I didn't know that letter was from you, nobody did except maybe Adra. Arnsword got up and went upstairs to his room and then returned. By then the rest of the family had moved into the drawing room, and I was just about to follow them. The look on Arnsword's face was chilling. He put this into my hand," she withdrew a small folded parchment from the pocket of her dressing gown, and gave it to Ynith, "he asked me in as polite terms as possible, if I could bring this to you in person; that it was a response to your letter. He also told me it would be in my best interest if I could take leave of Imsgaard immediately to bring it to you. He told me you'd been asked to leave by his sister without being consulted and that he required time alone with his family to sort things out. I will not lie, Ynith, he looked quite otherworldly and frightening. I've never seen him so infuriated; his eyes were almost black with a boiling rage that seemed about to explode at any moment," she said. Ynith clutched her little letter, wanting very much to unfold and read it, but the Lady went on.

"I never knew he'd pursued magic, nobody there did. I knew he was very serious, and I knew I'd failed you on so many levels the day before, so I did exactly as he asked. I went to my apartments and had them pack everything up. The coach was ordered. I took my leave of everyone, in spite of her Highness's protests. As I was leaving the house, I heard them shouting at one another in the drawing room. It was very heated. I could hear the brothers and the Queen. I heard him through the doors shouting about what his mother told him at dinner, something about your parents' untimely death, and then I heard Adra shouting at him. I did not stay. I got into the coach and we set off. Thank goodness we did! As the coach began to move away, great dark clouds began to gather above Imsgaard in the most haunting and unnatural way, churning and boiling into a black mass, making morning into evening; the air seemed to become thinner. I could hardly breathe.

"The horses became so agitated; the coachmen could barely keep them in hand. Suddenly, before we were even well within the park, there was a tremendous conflagration that ballooned out of the house, and the bricks of the house exploded outwards and rained down upon us. The coachman did not need to encourage the horses much to whip them into a mad run; I thought we would surely overturn and as I gazed back from the coach, I saw a great cloud rise up from the autumn palace. It was a luminous teal, with bursts of light shooting through it. It mushroomed up languidly from the ruin that remained of the house."

"What of Arnsword? How do we know he wasn't killed too in that disaster?"

"I do not know of Arnsword, all I know is that the royal guard was dispatched from the main palace five nights ago, and there is a great uproar at Wetherly. My brother met me when I arrived home; somehow he already knew something had gone very wrong, even so soon after the destruction of Imsgaard. He told me then that Arnsword had been studying magic and that he had been among the strongest of the final trials.

"He asked your whereabouts and when I told him you'd gone back to the Darvath, he rushed off to find you; he was determined that you would not be harmed for your connection to Arnsword. He would not allow me to follow him to find you; he assured me he would bring you to me when it was safe to do so. He said something about Arnsword having something terrible in his possession, and he said that this was only the beginning, that everything would soon go very wrong, and everything is about to change for the worse. I've never seen my brother so upset," she rambled. "There is a rumour that Arnsword has murdered the King," Ressa said, her voice hollow. Her eyes were haunted and distant, also gazing at the fire. "I am sorry to burden you with all this after everything you've been through, my dear girl. I hope it won't keep you awake, for I have hardly slept since that day."

"Ressa, I am so sorry, for causing all this... Your sister..."

"Ynith, you were the cause of nothing. You are innocent and your greatest crime was making a madman fall in love with you. You must not believe that I do not grieve for my sister, I do, but we did not grow up together. She was matched as a baby and raised mostly with the court in preparation for her marriage to the King. The time I spent in her company was spent mostly with Adra and her cousins, while my sister slept. My brother knows her even less. I am not heartless, I feel her loss quite deeply, but *you* must not blame yourself for her death, Ynith, and know that I do not feel wronged by you. Arnsword has their blood on his hands, not yours. Pray he forgets you." She stood and put her hand on Ynith's.

"I nearly kept that from you," she gestured towards the letter in Ynith's hand, "but I believe you deserve answers. More than anyone else, ultimately. Try to sleep. I will come and fetch you a bit later in the morning tomorrow so you can rest. Poor dear." Ressa downed the last of her brandy and exited the apartments, leaving Ynith alone with her letter; the familiar standing raven symbol she had seen on Arnsword's ring. She pulled the ribbon aside and unfolded the thick paper. On it, in spidery scrawls was Arnsword's hurried reply.

My beloved Ynith,

I cannot even begin to know what I can do to make up for what my family has done to you. I cannot even begin to apologize enough for the pain they have caused. Knowing that any one of us has caused you pain fills me with more fire than you can possibly imagine. I feel I am not strong enough to contain my sense of injustice and anger, and I know your heart might be changed in its regard for me if you know how much darkness fuels me. I can only see your beautiful face when I close my eyes, and every tear you shed might as well be a dagger cutting through me. I have never loved anyone before you. You are my precious heart. I will protect you from any more pain. Even when you no longer hold regard for me, I remain yours alone, unworthy as I always have been.

Arnsword

Ynith burst into tears and wept openly now that her kind friend Ressa had gone. She folded up the letter and carried it to the bed chamber where she tucked it carefully into her little wooden treasure box. Here she kept some of her humble jewelry pieces and some other family treasures, like miniature oils of her parents on small oval canvases and frames, some of her mother's most treasured jewelry and other sundries. She sat down on the edge of her bed and sighed. Life had been so much simpler before that fateful day in the archive. A part of her wished she could go back to that moment, and wished she had never met Arnsword, for her heartbreak was so complete. But she realized with a depth of heart she hadn't managed to that point, that she would not wish to give up what Arnsword brought into her life; his devotion and his kindness to her, his tenderness and his awkward attempts at romance. She smiled wanly, thinking of his long, angled frame, his sharp features and his green eyes. She thought him handsome when nobody else did. She missed his company; worse, she was bewildered at herself for missing him in spite of what he had done.

She got up and blew out all of the candles and lanterns, and shuffled back to the bed. She drew back the covers and crawled under them. It was several hours before she actually fell asleep.

8. Unwelcome Guests

"Life must go on, I suppose," Ressa had declared in a tired voice, a few days later after informing a shocked Ynith that a party was to arrive at Gallevin for a few days. The unrest at the capitol had not yet quite reached the rural areas, and notwithstanding the now empty throne and unhinged Wizard wreaking havoc in the central region, life around Gallevin hardly seemed affected yet. The sun still rose, the dew still sparkled, and the sky still shone blue.

Lady Ressa received a note from her grandson that he would be passing through on his way north with some friends and hoped to stay at her estate for a few days. Most of the well-to-do that lived in the cities were quietly migrating out to their country estates, and taking refuge from the storm that had yet to fall upon the land. For the moment, the crisis seemed to be restricted to the Ministry's magic bearers, the palace at Teragaard and the governmental complex at Amagaard.

Ressa's grandson was determined to make it out to his own estate, and hoped he and his friends would be able to stop at Gallevin for a few days to rest. He even wanted to set up an assembly to invite local people while he was there. The death of the monarch and his entire family did not seem to dampen the grandson's determination to make as joyous a party as he could and forge forward with his plans.

His note to announce his arrival came with a number of other requests; to hire some musicians for the assembly, and to order food and dispatch some invitations to local people to add to the company. "It is only for six days," Ressa assured Ynith over tea, "I don't think I can bear the noise and revelry of so many young people all at once for any longer than that."

"How many will be staying?"

"Seven total," she said, sounding most irritated. "Oreth is coming up today as well. He sent notice this morning. He should be here any moment."

"Oh, good. I've missed him," Ynith said, sipping her tea. Her cup plinked back into its saucer and she looked at Ressa thoughtfully. "Would it be awfully rude of me to not partake in the party? I just don't have it in me to entertain or be entertained at the moment. In all honesty, I cannot understand how they can be so free to arrange assemblies and have such a merry party while all this is going on."

"I don't understand either, my darling girl. Of *course* you should recuse yourself from any or all demands their society might impose, whenever you please. After the thrashing you got at Imsgaard, it's a wonder you aren't sworn off society for good. I still feel so terrible for not standing up for you more. If I had mayb..."

"No Lady Ressa, I beg you please do not continue to take blame for that. I'm quite convinced because of my name, there is nothing anyone could have done to deflect the teasing. It was a bad idea to go to Imsgaard. That is my burden, and Arnsword's to bear, not yours. I'm just glad I don't have to endure the questions from my classmates. I am grateful to the Docent for taking me away from all that," she blurted. "I am most grateful for your welcoming me into your home as you have." The lady conceded and arose.

"Not at all, my dear. That puts me to mind of what I wanted to remind you of after reading Tureff's letter. You are a resident of Gallevin Hall, my dear—and my grandson and his party are guests. I hope you will remember that when they arrive. Do not let them bully you. This is *your* home," she insisted. She then sighed. "I suppose I ought to meet with the housekeeper and have the rooms prepared and discuss the other impositions this party will bring. I will leave you for a while, dear. Hopefully my brother will be here soon."

Lady Farnham's wishes were granted; for no more than a quarter of an hour after she'd left the room did the Docent arrive looking most drawn. He seemed gratified to set eyes on Ynith and he squeezed her hand when she offered it to him in greeting.

"I am happy to see you are well, my dear. I came with a specific purpose and I wanted to sit with you alone: I see I have the opportunity right now, may we talk?"

"Of course Docent," she replied, lowering her book to her knee. He nodded, his eyes sunken deep into his darkened sockets, the heavy lids folding over the glassy irises that studied her intently. His face was one she'd come to love, and she did not like to see him so tired. He sat down in the Lady's chair, and faced her, perched on the edge of the seat. He hesitated for a moment, seeming to collect his words.

"You do look pale, my dear child. I hope you are bearing well through all this. You know how much we both worry for you," he spoke for himself and his sister.

"I am as well as can be expected, Docent. I will struggle through," she replied, "I have perhaps a burden, but I did not lose a sister, so I cannot even begin to compare my situation with yours." He sighed shakily and wrung his hands. There was a long moment of silence as he turned some thoughts around in his head.

"Have you heard of the Book of Hadris, Ynith?" It was an unexpected question, one she was left confused by. It was out of context with what they had been previously discussing.

"I'm afraid I have not," she replied. It was a little white lie. She had heard of it, seen it mentioned in some of her readings when she was doing her research on forbidden magic. But it was never explained to her exactly what it was. She assumed it was an old fashioned grimoire. Many of the great books had names of their own. She listened intently, curious to have this little mystery solved.

"Well, the Book of Hadris is a grimoire of tremendous power. It was once kept in the vaults at Wetherly, with other books that have proven they require special keeping and a secret, secure location. The Book of Hadris is one of the most ancient books of magic known to man. It teaches a power that is no longer in use by modern Wizards; an ancient power that taps into energies far greater than anything any of our modern fellows know today. Its spells and amulets are most potent. It alone is the reason why we exist in a civilized order today, Ynith. "

Ynith's skin rose up into goose bumps. "It was locked away after the Age of Rains, I venture?" she asked. He nodded.

"Allow me to explain. The last wizard to use the Book of Hadris was a pillar of a man by the name of Ronin. Ronin was one of the first Wizards to employ a code of ethics in his work, and when he imposed it upon himself, some of the other most powerful wizards followed suit. When Wetherly and the others came along, this group of wizards sat down and decided that unrestricted magics were too dangerous to be accessible to just anyone. Too many wizards were using it for personal gain and to terrorize the ordinary people. So, with the help of these other very powerful wizards, Ronin used the magic of this most-ancient grimoire to turn it into a sort of ...eh... a sort of sponge, yes, I suppose that word will do. He did this before he locked it away forever.

"The Book of Hadris greedily absorbs the greater part of the ancient magical energies that are produced from the ethers. In soaking most of it up, it limits the amount of magical energies available for the wizards of the world to use. Ronin and his friends might have hobbled the bad Wizards, but in doing so, they also sacrificed their own access to these same powers. The book in essence, not only holds the secrets of the most ancient magics, but it also controls the very core of it, insuring that even those who practice the forbidden arts can never really have the full potential of their power. It was a precaution taken when the governing body of Magic finally managed to clamp down on the wanton use of the craft. The secret of the spell was written on one of the pages in the book; it was locked, sealed away and protected. Among the higher ranks of magic users, it is commonly known that without the book of Hadris, our world would be very different today. It is the foundation of why we are able to live in relative peace, and the governing body of magic has set into place other means to control those that might abuse the remaining power availed to this world today. But most wizards are completely ignorant of it."

"Wizards can still do great damage in spite of being hobbled, or the hunters would not exist," Ynith reasoned.

"Yes, but with *full* access to magic, the wizards we know of today become something infinitely more powerful."

"May I ask why you are telling me this? I'm almost afraid to ask."

"My dear, our Arnsword has taken the book."

"Oh." Ynith's stomach turned to ice. "That was what I was afraid of. What does that mean?"

"He now possesses what is a doorway to the very core of Magic. He can both break the key, and set loose chaos onto this world it hasn't seen in a millennium, or he can use it to make himself the most powerful creature on this world alone. I suspect he would not share the power he holds. I suspect that our Everath friend, who incidentally is now the rightful King, has ambitions of his own."

"I don't know what to say," she whispered, wringing her hands.

"If he achieves this greater power, things are going to get much, much worse. The fact that the tome is in his possession already raises the stakes tremendously. And you my dear girl are his only true weakness. There will be those who will use you to get at him, namely the denizens of Wetherly. In normal circumstances, these gentlemen of Wetherly would be allies to us. But because of you, they represent a danger, and therefore have become the enemy so to speak. In order to protect you, we must defy the enforcers of the governing body of magic users.

"I've managed to keep you safe from them for now, but it's only a matter of time before someone is able to find the connection between you, and trust me, magic can find anything eventually, even weakened magic."

"What am I to do?" Ynith's alarm made her pale and small.

"I know from your records my dear that you have abilities."

"You mean in magic?"

"Yes."

"I never did very well at it."

"It's in you though," he insisted.

"I suppose. But it's something I never really tapped into since that novice class," she blurted defensively. "It frightens me, Docent. It always has," she admitted. She wasn't sure how he thought he was going to create skill where there was none. The only thing she excelled at in the subject was all the intensive study she'd made of a type of magic nobody was permitted to use. She kept her thoughts to herself.

"Well, my dearest Ynith, this is something you are unfortunately going to have to overcome, because it has been determined by the Academy faculty; namely the magic professors and me, that you will need to be trained at once. You will need to defend yourself. Having a Wizard casting protections over a young lady for no apparent reason will only draw the hunters to you faster."

"Arnsword would never let anyone harm me," she muttered. The Docent gave her a disapproving look and frowned.

"You will not be able to rely on others forever, Ynith. I know you have it in you, and I will not brook excuses. Docent Edwith will be arriving shortly. He will be instructing you, Ynith; in the defenses at least. When we are confident you can defend yourself against those who wish to harm Arnsword, then we may start talking about ways of using your abilities to draw Arnsword out."

"I beg your pardon?" Ynith snapped. "I will have no hand in that! With all due respect, Docent, I could never..."

"He murdered his family!" the Docent barked, quite loudly. "He murdered our sister!" Ynith's mouth snapped shut and her eyes filled with tears. "It doesn't matter how horrid they were to him and to you, Ynith, they did not deserve to be burnt up like so much straw."

"No, they did not," she snapped, standing. She moved around her chair, her hands clamped on the back of it, "nor did my parents deserve to be murdered. I will not align my heart against Arnsword for his actions, no matter how awful they were. His rage was fueled by *them*. He did it because he had learned what they had done, and because he loves me. I do not excuse him of his crimes, but I will not be his judge or his betrayer," she sobbed. The Docent's hackles seemed to drop at the sight of her tears and confusion, and he sighed wearily.

"Will you at least agree to learn the defenses? Please," he begged her. "I ask you because I have grown to care deeply for you, Ynith. You are an innocent soul, dragged into a situation you should not have been. You and Arnsword should have been allowed to be who you are, and to love one another, and to marry and to be happy. But it did not happen. Arnsword lost control of a power that was already quite measurable according to his professors. He was one of the strongest of the magic students from the beginning. His impassive nature never really raised any concern, until the trials. He tapped into something bottomless and made all his peers look like amateurs. There was passion there, fire, and I think it's there because of you."

"He may surprise you, Docent. He may surprise everyone. You all think the worst, that he will abuse the book of Hadris and use it to his advantage; but I think he is capable of better," she whispered, dabbing her eyes with a kerchief she'd tugged from her stays.

"I will learn defenses if I am capable. I make no guarantees that I have the ability. But I will try." The Docent sighed in relief and finally leaned back into the chair. He looked less burdened just from her small concession.

"Good, good, good," he said, smiling again. "Where's Ressa?"

"Working with the housekeeper to prepare for your grand-nephew's arrival," Ynith replied.

"Oh, blast! I cannot stomach that child. Such overindulged idiocy I've never seen in all my days. When is *he* coming?"

"I believe tomorrow afternoon. He comes with a party."

"The world is crumbling and as usual, Tureff is worried only about parties and cards. How long will they be imposing upon us?"

"Six days," she said. The Docent sighed irritably and groaned.

"Well, never mind. We'll find somewhere for Docent Edwith to stay while he works with you. The house is big enough." He went off to find his banyan and a fresh periodical so he could hide in the library and ruminate.

The following afternoon, just after the three had taken lunch, the party arrived with a great clamour. Ynith was not permitted to flee until they made introductions and so she remained in the drawing room while the seven of them came in. Four men, three girls, all somewhat near Ynith's age, entered the room in a titter. They were quite amused by something, for they laughed and laughed, making whispered jokes and laughing some more. They quieted down as they approached the three others. Ressa took on an immediate air of irritation, the Docent didn't bother to get up or lower his periodical, and Ynith looked quite stricken by the whole crowd.

Ynith had never been in society, she had never had a circle of friends with which to travel about and follow the seasonal circuits. The sight of all these young women and young men all together was jarring. Their ease was off-putting. She sat up rigidly, and clasped her hands, staring wide-eyed at them as they gathered near Lady Ressa.

"Grandmother!" a reasonably handsome fair-haired young man declared. "How are you? Well, I hope. I've been very much looking forward to seeing you, and Eminy here has been simply aching to meet you since I told her what a grand lady you are," he pointed to a little waif of a thing with a thin little frame and huge brown eyes. She smiled at Ressa only briefly, instead fixing her wide and curious gaze on Ynith, studying her prettiness with care—gauging potential competition.

"This here is Eminy's sister Vee, and her husband Lord Grey. This cad here is Mr. Baran Ock, my closest chum, and this strapping fellow is Mr. Mardro Evrin. The young lady hiding behind them here is Miss Phrinn, Eminy's closest friend."

"Pleased, Tureff, I am glad to meet your friends. This is my brother Docent Oreth, and this is my companion Miss Ynith." Everyone bowed and curtsied as was required and there was an awkward moment. Ressa smiled warmly. "You should make yourself at home; I do hope you all will. I'm sure Mrs. Urneet will take good care of you." There was a consensus of nods and the group broke up into mostly pairs and filtered about the large space, finding other areas to sit. Eminy's sister Vee decided she would play the piano. Mrs. Urneet then arrived and announced she would show everyone to their apartments, and the whole group vacated, leaving the room quiet for a spell.

"I do hope they won't expect me to follow them about," Ynith muttered a bit bitterly. Lady Ressa shook her head and picked up her book.

"I would think you are the mistress of your own fate in this house; you are not obligated to do anything you would not like to do. I would not hold it against you to stay hiding in your room when that is probably what I will do for the duration. You are a resident here now, not just a guest, Ynith. They are the guests. Remember that." Ynith nodded and smiled.

The quiet, pleasant ambience of the house immediately changed with the arrival of the party. There was noise none of the residents cared for; young men shouting, out shooting, horses trampling the driveway into muck, ladies twittering and all manner of other noises that all three wished would go away. The arrival of the new Docent went unnoticed by the party; they were too busy making arrangements for their assembly. Docent Edwith arrived just after the Tureff's party. He was a man of perhaps thirty, with a youthful face and body but eyes as wise as the Docent's.

Ynith was charged with seeing to the Docent's comfort. The Lady, Oreth and Ynith occupied the south wing of the house, which was quiet, overlooking the sea through a scrim of trees. Ynith put the Docent in the apartments near theirs, away from the north wing where the party was housed. When he arrived, the footmen brought in his trunks, and Ynith greeted him.

He was a well-looking fellow; she'd never met him before, in spite of all her years at the academy. He reached out and took her proffered hand and squeezed it. "Miss Ynith, I've been worried for you. I'm glad to see you are well—although if I may say so, you do look a bit careworn." He had kind eyes of a deep milky brown that she found assuring.

"You must be hungry. I ordered some light refreshments for you to tide you over until supper, Docent. If you'll follow me, I'll show you where you are to stay. I've taken the liberty of putting you on our side of the house, where we can enjoy the quiet away from the Lady's visiting grandson and his party," she said while walking. The Docent followed, glancing about the place as they climbed the main stairway and left the main hall for the south wing, entering a windowed corridor. "We have our own drawing room there where we enjoy the peace, and the library, so we will hardly see much of them during the day except during meals. The Docent thought it was what you would prefer as well."

"Oh, yes. I have no patience for such silliness. I do hope you are prepared to meet with me first thing in the morning, Miss Ynith. We have much work to do." He looked at her with an expression of concern.

"I'm afraid I cannot do anything tomorrow morning. I'm to help with the arrangements for the assembly that is happening tomorrow night. I will however be ready the morning after, I promise. I am resigned to do what the Docent thinks is best," she sighed. "However I cannot imagine I will glean enough skill to defend myself against the masters that might seek to harm me," she muttered. The Docent stopped and she did likewise, turning to peer at him in puzzlement.

"I will do what I can, Miss Ynith. The Docent and the rest of the faculty are determined to keep you safe. The entire magic department is contributing to the shield that protects you now. Your family has a strong line of the magically inclined, and I will teach you some very old tricks that are not common anymore," he assured her. She shook her head in bewilderment and pursed her lips. *How could they know of her family's history of magical use?* With a sigh, she lifted her hand to direct him on. He began walking again.

"The Docent tells me you have not dabbled very much in the magic arts," he ventured. She nodded and sighed once more, tucking one of her side-curls behind her ear.

"I did not do very well in the novice class. I was unable to consistently hold the source energies as the others could. If and when I could wrest them, it was difficult for me to control the effect of connecting with them and almost always lost control. I could feel the connection, always, once I found the energies, I could see and feel them almost to the source, but it was always fleeting and unstable. My castings are always far too wild and impossible to tame." The Docent nodded knowingly and smiled.

"That does not imply a lack of ability at all, Miss Ynith. I'm surprised your professor didn't recognize it, but I have a feeling that your sex might have had something to do with why he did not bother further investigating why you had difficulties. It has been a continuing challenge to convince the older faculty that ladies are quite capable of the same things as the young men. Many ladies have been given up on too quickly because they simply needed to be shown another approach than the standard one. Women are different. You are intuitive creatures. You reach the energies differently to begin with. The connections that you made using the standard methods were not unstable because of your lacking, that I can assure you. And your wild castings as you call them might be interpreted by some as loss of control, but others may see it quite the opposite."

"The professors always made me drop the strands and shut the portals the moment they would start flailing," Ynith said. "I was a danger to myself. They knew it, I knew it. I heard the stories, like that of Alsparath, who was consumed by his own casting because he did not keep his strands in check; of the young man whose strands lashed out and cut the arm off of his friend," Ynith rambled, her eyes locked ahead.

"Those were symptoms of bad technique from erroneous instruction, Ynith, not of their lack of skill or magical ineptitude," he assured her. He sighed. She wondered why, if he and other magic bearers knew of these failings, that the tragedies were allowed to occur. But she did not speak. He continued. "We failed you terribly, it seems, the magic department. Had I known these were your symptoms, I would have been able to encourage you on; in fact, what you describe tells me that you have a strong natural skill for connecting to the magic, my dear. Quite strong. It's a matter of helping you find your connections in less ordinary ways. You're sensing the source and you have lively strands; that is a good sign, Miss Ynith. An excellent sign."

* * * *

Ynith melted into the grouping of people that lingered by the table of refreshments. She couldn't find a place to go where there weren't people pressed up against her. She backed up towards the wall; the back of her knees came up against the edge of a chair and she sat down.

It was insufferably hot, and the bustle of people and bodies around her was making her head spin. The noise was mind-numbing, the music, the people talking over it, some of the more boorish characters shouting to get the attention of their friends. This was supposed to be a small assembly, but it was comparable to the crush of a ball in the center of the Teragaard city. From where all of these people had come was a mystery to Ynith; it seemed the entire county's society had come to this assembly, some from many miles away.

There was a celebratory air; however there was also a bizarre undercurrent that felt like a desperate grasp at normality. The conversations around Ynith seemed forced and strained, as if everyone was willfully avoiding the heavy matter that hung perilously over them all.

It was too much for Ynith to bear. She sat against the wall in the chair, obscured by people, her knees being brushed by lush silks as the crowd pressed around her. She drew her elegantly gloved hand up against her temple and dropped her head a bit.

She thought she was going to faint; she couldn't manage to breathe deeply enough and felt lightheaded. A hand carefully cupped her elbow and she looked up. "Are you unwell Miss?" It was a handsome man of about thirty, with an earnest expression of concern on his face. "I think perhaps you need some fresh air. Come," he reached out his left white-gloved hand and Ynith took it gratefully. The gentleman put his right shoulder forward and ploughed his way through the crush, creating a path and a wake that made for a quick escape out onto the patio, where the warm night hummed with grasshopper song. Inside, an ebullient, vigorous dance was being woven on the instruments of the band, and the noise level increased. She was grateful for her rescuer.

The open air immediately made her feel better. She let go of the man's glove, adjusted her shawl to cover her arms and walked to the stone railing, sitting on it, and taking in long breaths, getting her senses back as best she could. The gentleman had followed her and stood nearby. She looked up and smiled wanly at him.

"Thank you for the kind rescue. I'm not certain how much longer I could have endured being caught up in the crush," she said softly. He turned and looked at her squarely.

"I'm afraid I am overstepping. We have not been properly introduced. But since this is such a mad occasion with so many people, who could say we weren't? My name is Keffrin Zeath," he extended his hand, and Ynith put hers in it.

"I'm Ynith," she said in almost a whisper.

"I know," he confessed with a smile. "I asked a mutual acquaintance who you were."

"I am hesitant to ask why you needed to know who I was..."

"You are a beautiful young woman, who wouldn't want to know who you are?" he asked with a feigned innocence. Ynith squirmed a bit and then stood.

"That's very kind of you, Mr. Leath,"

"Zeath," he corrected her with a smile.

"Mr. Zeath. I thank you for your thoughtfulness," she curtsied quickly and scurried off towards another set of doors to the great house, where she thought there would be fewer people. She squeezed in before he could catch up. It was just as crowded if not more, but she locked her eyes on the archway to the entry hall and headed towards it, biting her lower lip and wending through the crowd as best she could.

She was angry with herself for coming to this so-called assembly. She should have stayed safely ensconced in the relative quiet of her apartments in the other wing. Why she agreed with Eminy to participate, she did not know. She thought herself stupid to think she could tolerate this sort of thing. With resolve, she pressed forward, occasionally having to rudely push past people who could not hear her soft 'pardon me'.

Suddenly a hand grasped her wrist, and she was spun around to come face to face with Arnsword. He didn't look like the normal Arnsword; he'd cast some sort of glamour to disguise himself, but she knew his eyes at once, and a gasp escaped her lips. He led her back into the crowds, back to the door of the office which had been tightly locked for this ball. It opened for Arnsword, and they slid into the room unnoticed, locking the din out behind them. As soon as he was inside, he cast away the spell, and he was himself.

He was dressed for a ball; white breeches, white stockings, a white waistcoat and a black frock coat. His cravat was folded to perfection. His slippers shone. Ynith trembled at the sight of him, but when he stepped forward, she found herself doing the same, and they met only inches apart, she straining up to his face, he leaning down and cupping her chin in his hands. He searched her eyes for judgment, for dislike or fear, but he found only the regard of a girl filled with concern and questions. His tense shoulders relaxed a shade and he sighed gently. He wordlessly kissed her, and to his joy, she kissed him. She then threw her arms around him and hugged herself to him, her eyes filling with tears. He did not expect her to react like this, after all that he'd done. He was more grateful than he could have ever hoped. He quelled the surge of emotion he felt upon seeing her, and his expression grew very grave.

"You've been marked," he said. "I came to warn you." She stepped back and he kissed her again, unable to resist her gaze peering up at him.

"What do you mean, marked?"

"They're watching you. The hunters. They're trying to insinuate themselves into your life, so that you will lead them to me."

"Are you not endangering yourself, Arnsword, speaking to me now?" He smiled at her, in a cool, loving way.

"I am fine," he said almost laughingly, but then became quite serious again. "They are of no threat to me. To you, however, they represent a terrible threat. One was in pursuit of you; I had to draw you aside quickly.

"Mr. Zeath," she concluded. He nodded, and she pursed her lips. "He was inexcusably flirtatious with me." The Everath frowned darkly and hugged her closely.

"I have missed you. I have wished to see you since..." his voice fell still and she hugged him again, her eyes wide and faraway. They stood in an embrace for a moment, lingering in silence. "I cannot stay for long; the Hunters will begin to sense me eventually. I just wanted to see you, and to tell you to be wary of strangers."

"Do you think they wish to harm me?"

"I have no idea what they are capable of, dearest Ynith, but in the effort to capture me, they might be willing to do the unthinkable. I will do my best to shield you from harm, my beloved one—but your diligence is required. I see that the old man has brought in one of the magic instructors from the Darvath. That means you will be receiving some private instruction in magical defenses. That was a wise choice. I must go," he said. To Ynith, he looked the same as he always had; the tall, lanky, awkward character she'd first seen only a few seemingly short weeks ago. It was hard to imagine him to be the evil the world was painting him to be. Impossible. He looked so dashing in his lovely ball clothes. She reached up and adjusted his stiff cravat, her eyes glassy.

"I love you so very much Arnsword. I'm not sure how I can in spite of what you've done, but I do," she choked. His hand reached up and he clasped her hand, kissing her gloved palm.

"My love for you is the only thing that keeps me sane. If anything were to happen to you, I am not sure what I would do. It frightens me. I beg you be wise and safe, and I will watch over you as best I can. Stay safe." She nodded, receiving one last soft, yielding kiss, her lips spiced with the salt of her tears.

And with a wisp and a small gust of air, she was kissing nothing. He was gone, and with him the light he had apparently been casting to brighten the darkened room.

Ynith stayed in the office for the rest of the evening. She lit some candles and sat down on the heavily padded chair, removing her gloves, kicking off her slippers and drawing up her feet underneath her. She leaned back into the corner of the chair, threw her shawl over her knees and fell asleep in spite of the noise.

She did not leave until the guests had all gone away, and the party of visitors and the Lady had gone to bed. She opened the door carefully and peered out. It had unlocked when she approached it. The servants were preoccupied on the other end of the room, gathering up glass goblets and sweeping up the mess. Her dainty emerald green slippers in hand, she tiptoed out, and closed the door behind her, hearing it lock without any assistance from her.

She padded gingerly in her stockinged feet through the archway, dashing across the floor of the entrance hall, and up the steps in unfeminine sprints two steps at a time. She ran down the broad corridor towards her rooms, rounding a corner and finding herself face to face with Mr. Zeath. He stood there holding a three-light candelabra which had burnt down to near stubs. He seemed quite unsurprised at her hasty appearance. She threw her shawl onto her shoulders and wrapped herself up into it, looking at him in puzzlement.

"What on earth are you still doing here Mr. Zeath, it's late and everyone has gone home."

"I was concerned. Nobody else seemed to be."

"Because they know I am well-capable of taking care of myself," she whispered loudly.

"You have been missing all evening. Since I pulled you away from the crowd."

"I took refuge in the library for the rest of the evening. I did not wish to be found."

"You did not see anyone during your absence? Meet with any male visitors perhaps," he speculated quite brazenly. Ynith froze, and glared at Mr. Zeath. He *was* a hunter.

"What could you possibly mean, Mr. Zeath? Do you believe me capable of such impropriety?"

"If it was someone dear and familiar to you, perhaps so. I do not know you well enough to know what you are capable of, Miss Ynith."

"If you had even the most remote familiarity with my behavior, you would know that I am not the sort of person to do such a thing. If you would excuse me, I'm quite fatigued and wish to sleep," she circumvented him and dashed down the corridor, giving him a stern glare and a wide berth. When she looked back, she saw him turn and leave. She slid into her apartments and closed the door, her heart racing. She would have to ask the Docent if there was a way of identifying these busybodies. She took a deep breath and unfastened the front of her gown. Exhausted, she threw her clothes onto a chair and crawled into the bed in just her shift. She reclined into the softness, her hands clutching the top of the blanket, eyes wide.

Miranda Mayer

9. *Enlightened*

Ynith's fatigue made her a less than enthusiastic pupil the next morning. After breakfasting in her room, she put on a simple, unadorned day gown with a light chemisette with a ruffed collar and some false sleeves. Over that she donned a grey linen pelisse with some broad tambour-work scrolling on the hem and sleeves. She made her way to the library where she was to meet Docent Edwith. He was up and looking bright-eyed and bushy tailed. He was an attractive man, although he had an unkemptness that was common to the faculty; a sort of carelessness about his appearance. His beard stubble was coming in; obviously he hadn't shaved, and his hair was askew and the front was standing up, bits pointing in different directions. His frock was wrinkled, and he had a stain on the cuff of his white shirt. He was not in robes, but in simple day clothes; a brown-linen frock coat with an old-fashioned cutaway front, a plain black waistcoat and some black breeches and worn stockings. His cravat was limp and tied loosely.

"Good morning, Docent," she said with little enthusiasm. "I will have to call you Docent Edwith from now on in mixed company, for I have two docents now to address." He nodded and gestured for her to sit at the work table where he had lit the two reflection lamps and distributed a number of small objects on the table in the pools of light cast from them. She glanced at them in turn, her brow furrowed in curiosity. He did not say anything and instead poured her some tea and dolloped in some cream and a little lump of sugar and handed it to her, which she took and stirred absentmindedly while she observed the objects he'd laid out for her. She sipped, her eyes locked on Docent Edwith. He merely sat down across from her and watched her until she put her cup down.

"I believe I may have met a hunter last night," she finally said. He pursed his lips, but did not look surprised.

"There *are* ways of knowing for certain."

"I thought so," she replied, sipping again from her tea. "How do you suppose I could in this short time, amass the same level of skill in magic as these hunters have? They, like Arnsword, are products of years of training, and had to pass the trials. I could possibly lift small things like these, or open some brief windows, to hide things but how likely would it be that I could somehow shield myself from being taken by them, or being harmed in earnest?"

"You are looking at it the wrong way," he replied, his normally quiet voice had elevated in strength and volume, his bearing becoming bolder. "What they learned in the Academy, those are prosaic skills," he waved his hand dismissively. "Yes, there's some power there, but it's nothing really useful in the end. No match against *real* power. I'm not going to teach you what they learned. I am going to teach you what they do *not* know."

"And what is that, exactly?" her brow arched up and she reached for her tea again for a quick sip.

"The Ancient Arts. And one does not need years of schooling to master those, only the ability to connect to the energies with broad portals—and I'm quite sure I can show you how to do that. Going by your descriptions, I believe you are uniquely suited for it, actually, which is perfect. The trick will be to build up your tolerance for the drain the practice of the ancient arts will take upon your body."

"I cannot believe you are speaking of teaching me forbidden magics," she blurted in astonishment her teacup clanking into the saucer loudly; some of the tea sloshed into the saucer. With a flick of his finger she watched the liquid pool together like quicksilver and rise up into globules, plopping back into the cup, leaving not a droplet of moisture behind. Ynith's eyes rolled up to observe him. He was looking out the window, pinching his stubbly chin. She could hear the rasp of the hairs as they brushed his fingertips.

"The hunters that would be a danger are already after you; perhaps for different reasons but they represent the same danger either way. Wetherly is already awash in bluebells, you have nothing to lose learning these skills now, Miss Ynith," he said admonishingly, unable to contain a certain joy in knowing that this was the case. "And besides, you don't need any formal training to speak of to do instinctive things, not like you do to wield the weaker magics that require more energy of the wielder to control. There are tricks you can learn, yes, spells to help shape your will; but all in good time." Ynith was intrigued but did not say so. She glanced down at her hands and bit her lip. What he was saying she had read before. That the forbidden arts were instinct more than skill. That they tapped into one's subconscious will rather than requiring conscious direction. She bit back her questions and rolled her eyes up at him.

"And you know these arts? In spite of them being forbidden?"

"Every generation someone is identified by the ministry to carry the skills forward so they are not lost forever. That is why you never met me at the Academy for I was not there to teach; I was there to learn and to be a keeper of the ancient skills."

"For what purpose would they keep these arts alive if they are forbidden and dangerous?"

"Because there would surely come a time when they would be needed again. The ancient masters knew that the balance would not hold forever, and they needed to have people with good sense in place to fight the fight when that time comes," Docent Edwith stood and clasped his hands in front of his hips, looking down at her. "These parlour magicians the school produces can look into the near future and a bit into the past, they can focus enough of their will to set something ablaze, they can compel people, they can levitate objects, clean up spilled tea," he gestured to her cup and saucer, "they can create mirroring glamours, but they are nothing next to the ancient magicians, Miss Ynith. Absolutely nothing!" His chest swelled with passion as he spoke, lifting his hand and jabbing his finger into the air dramatically.

"Arnsword looked half dead after the trials. It couldn't have been that much of a lark, if it taxed him so greatly."

"It can be when we demand that the students perform tasks that are specifically made to be painful and challenging. The Academy wants only the very skilled to pass, dear girl; only the very best. Normally the tasks also help weed out the sort of person that would be prone to abuse their abilities, but in this case, it didn't work with Arnsword," he mumbled, seeming disappointed. "Anyhow, the tasks often require more than is commonly possible with the amount of magic available to the modern wizard these days. But some have that extra spark, that little inlet to the ancient sources they aren't even aware of. Your friend Arnsword especially."

He pointed at her, shaking his finger to punctuate his words. "Your friend Arnsword; what he did at the Imsgaard estate, that was *ancient* magic. Nothing of that power had been used for hundreds of years!" The docent dropped his hands onto the edge of the table and leaned towards her, and then rocked back and threw up his arms. "A great explosion of magic, that wasn't taught to him at the Academy, you mark my words. *They* don't open portals any bigger than a coin. The portal needed to create that explosion must have been colossal. That was accomplished by his using the forbidden magics. He must have found something, some instruction somewhere to teach him to tap into them. The way everyone is taught today steers them deliberately away from using magic in any way that can be truly powerful!" He laughed gently and shook his head, his eyes wide and filled with wonder. "It took years for the founders of the ministry to unteach the world the skills that Arnsword has learned on his own. Decades, it took, to erase from society's collective memory the powers that could be had even with the access to the ethers restricted by the book of Hadris.

"That's most intriguing, about your friend Arnsword; how powerful the magic is he casts, even weakened by the book of Hadris. You can only imagine how potent these forbidden arts *could* potentially be if the book of Hadris no longer stood as a restrictor between the ethers and our world. With the book of Hadris in his hands, there is no telling the destruction he can wreak." Docent Edwith's words were infused with a barely restrained excitement.

"And *you* are an appointed keeper of forbidden skills? The one appointed to fight this darkness?" she asked, still incredulous. He seemed more admiring of Arnsword than against him.

"I am the newest one, yes. Your friend the Docent Oreth is the one that precedes me." Ynith's brows shot up in surprise.

"He has some lessons yet to teach me before his work is done. But that little dodderer is quite the skilled Wizard, and you would be surprised to see what he is capable of," he said with a proud smile. "He would have gladly instructed you, but he thought it would be appropriate for me to try my hand at instruction," he added. Ynith didn't really hear his last few words; her eyes were cast elsewhere, into a question that popped into her mind while he rambled. She looked at the Docent who'd just ceased speaking.

"Where would Arnsword have found something to show him the dark arts? I thought the governing wizards held all books and talismans left of the Age of Rains in great secrecy, and the Docent told me Arnsword only got the Hadris book because he'd already learned the dark arts and knew how to get it," she blabbered. The younger docent listened and then sighed. Ynith was most familiar with how difficult it was to find any texts from the Age of Rains, describing the use of now forbidden magic. It was her favorite pastime, after all, one she hadn't been able to pursue since her position at the archive began.

"He is... was Prince, Miss Ynith. The Throne has its own vaults, its own archives, and its own ancient libraries that it has maintained for many hundreds of years with access allowed only to select few. All doors are open to the Prince. We could not hope to think we were able to find every little object, every bit of writing, every token that came from the Age of Rains. He could have found something if he were looking. He could have found something that nobody else was looking for. That was true. Ynith knew first hand there were still lingering artifacts and documents from that period peppered all about the Darvath, she had seen and read many of them. She suspected there were more to find, but she knew they would be more secure than the little tidbits she had discovered over the years.

"The governing body has expended tremendous efforts to de-emphasize the use of magic, to trivialize it in many ways, as to draw interest away from it. And to an extent, it worked, for hundreds of years. But chaos is chaos, and things are going to happen, and Arnswords are an inevitability that the governing body is afraid of, but irrevocably prepared for," he sighed. "It is why we, Oreth and I, have purpose."

"You do not seem too put out by the developments with Arnsword and the bluebells at Wetherly," Ynith observed. He saw her eyes, the look of accusation on her face. She was keen on his wonder about the whole matter, and she saw him realize this. His puff and excitement deflated a bit, and a sort of meekishness overcame him. He leaned towards her across the table and in a conspiratorial whisper, he said:

"I confess I have much wished to once see the dark arts in full form. To breathe in all the theory, to memorize all the practices and to never be permitted to use it, or see it in use; it has been something all appointed keepers quietly wish for," he admitted. Ynith, inside her head, agreed whole-heartedly. It was her wish too.

He sat down again, clutching his hands before him on the table. Ynith saw a little bit of the irrational in this man, a harmless kind of gentle madness that she found somewhat charming.

He leaned in, his voice still a whisper, but louder this time. "I have never been allowed to even test the theories beyond the minor practices because there are of course those who would be alerted of my transgressions. Although Wetherly and the Ministry are one, we Keepers are something of a secret facet of the Ministry's workings, and not everyone knows of our true purpose, perceiving us mostly as magic scholars rather than preservers of old, forbidden arts.

"When I heard that the floors of Wetherly were blue in blossoms, I admit that I felt a surge of satisfaction. Do not take me to be evil, Miss Ynith, I do not wish anyone harm, but this subject I've been marinating in for two decades," he left the rest unfinished. Ynith merely nodded in complete understanding.

"I took the liberty of playing a little bit with the material I've been studying, at last. It was like," he breathed out loudly and broke a radiant, passionate smile. He then shook himself back to the moment falling into an awkward silence.

"You certainly know that not *all* Wizards in the Age of Rains were bad, not all of them used their powers to create chaos or elevate themselves. If they had all been so, there would be no Wetherly Hall or governing power over magic today," he argued. "There *are* those who can touch these powers and respect them; honour them."

"I understand," Ynith reassured him. He straightened. He'd been leaning over the table towards her again. He tugged down the front of his waistcoat and then sighed out loudly.

"Now, I will pass some of what I know onto you, Miss Ynith. This is a great, great honour. In these new times, it will be imperative that you know them. Imperative. And what you said, of your feeling the source, your wild castings; that is a fortunate, fortunate thing. You *could* be a powerful wielder, my dear. You could be more powerful than me, or Oreth, or even your friend Arnsword—only time and trials will tell. Now with that said, it's time to get started."

He glanced at the objects strewn about the table. There were two small ceramic figurines, a small brass box, a snuff spoon, an odd pearl earring, and a pair of tiny scissors made to hang from a chatelaine. They were particularly attractive little scissors, and she reached out and picked them up. They were designed to look like a heron, with little leafed feathers etched into the handles and the blades were the beak.

"I want you to take all these things and I want you to transform them into a single object," he said with the decisiveness of a teacher. Her brow arched up immediately and she put the scissors down. "It's one of the simplest of tasks. Not a lot of mass to work with; a child could do it given the right understanding; it doesn't require alarming amounts of power to do, but the way you do it is what's important." Ynith was confused. She hadn't even mastered the ability to summon the magics to begin with, how did he expect her to complete the task?

"Do you think perhaps I ought to focus on trying to summon the connections and holding them rather than just jumping right to transformations?" she asked, appalled. The Docent crossed his arms.

"This is different, Ynith. You do not summon with the dark magics like you do with modern techniques. With the dark magics, the connections come to you, to your will, but you must be able to receive them. You must learn how to attract them. I know you can do it already. Your past efforts revealed that capacity. You just need to develop a sense of trust to let the connections establish themselves in their own way, and stop trying to control them as they teach at the Academy."

"And how do you suppose I do that?"

"Start by doing it the way you know; but when you feel like you are losing control, don't let go. Go with it. Once you do that, we'll start from there," he said, scooting his chair closer to the table in front of her.

"The strands will fly quickly out of control if I try to sustain them. They become almost impossible to hold in place. It feels like I'm trying to stop a running horse by clutching its leg."

"Just trust me; I will guide you through it. The only way you can learn to cast using the ancient methods is to start by using the modern ones—once you have a good understanding of how one can become the other, you will forget everything those professors taught you, and you will find you will cast with greater ease. But you must let me guide you and trust me not to lead you astray."

Ynith sighed and drained her tea-cup, setting it aside genteelly. She then patted down the front of her skirts, shifted about in her chair and focused on the objects in front of her.

The one thing she did accomplish with aplomb in the novice class she attended was the summoning, no matter how unstable and fleeting it was. She knew she could at least get that spark of connection. She just had to remember how. She hadn't even tried since she was eleven or twelve.

For a moment, before she cleared her mind, she saw Arnsword's face, then the shape of his lanky body silhouetted against a bright window, as it had been when she first saw him at the Lady's house the first time after their chance encounter. It seemed so long ago. With a sigh she focused. Not on the objects, but on the space somewhere between them and herself. She took a deep, cleansing breath. She felt the familiar sting of her powers coming to life inside the front of her head. She closed her eyes, thought everything away, and then opened them again.

Like little pinholes, she had opened portals just like that; only three; each tiny dots of golden yellow light floating above the objects directly before her eyes. It was a strange feeling to see them, to feel that buzz inside her brain as she managed to cut through the veil of her world into the ethers. It was from there the energies came that could shape her will, if she was capable of controlling them.

She concentrated on the three tiny dots of light before her. She chewed on her lower lip and gripped her fists, and the dots pulsated and drew themselves out lengthwise by a bit, forming short worms that wriggled as the power spiraled around from inside the pinholes, writhing like vortexes. With a narrowing of her eyes the strands lurched into a larger size, perhaps as long as earthworms, undulating in a serpentine fashion before her, the narrow heads poised before her face, hovering over the tabletop. Several small beads of sweat formed on her upper lip, which distracted her. It felt most improper, but she kept hold of her portals, as instructed.

It was at this stage where she always felt the first instability that would eventually cause her to lose grip of them. Usually, they would shrink rapidly in a wild, whipping tangle, and then vanish. She could never sustain them or grow them beyond that point. When she did have them open, even for a brief time, she could feel the connection quite strongly. She never understood why she had such a hard time controlling the powers that emanated from them if the connection to her portals was so bright and clear.

But the energies were so strong and pressing it was difficult to bear, difficult to keep hold of, like trying to hold onto a wild animal, as she described it to Edwith. Ynith could not imagine how anyone could widen those holes, broadening the strands, and actually manipulate them. In her class, she recalled seeing students summon them up in tens, each one a perfectly, unfrayed slender strand that they could weave together, to spread into mists that would flow over their task and enact their will. They would eventually learn to summon these portals rapidly, with such ease and skill, that they would appear and vanish so quickly that they would be unseen to the eye; just as Edwith had done when he had lifted the dollop of tea back into her cup.

Ynith could feel her newly conjured strands losing stability as usual. They undulated more and more wildly, one occasionally sending off charges in little spidery arms out to another. This was the sign of collapse. She felt herself losing control of the little vortexes and began to waver.

"NO! You must persist. Let them charge, do not follow the old rules. Let them do as they will, and you will not have to work so hard to sustain them. They will open *for* you," the Docent snapped.

"It will consume me if it gets out of control!" she muttered fearfully.

"Nonsense. Do as I tell you, Ynith! I would not lead you to do anything that would endanger you. You must trust I know what I'm doing." She nodded nervously, her strands wavering a bit as her doubt solidified into acquiescence. She had never held them for this long before. Her studies of the ancient methods never mentioned the summoning process. This part terrified her. A magic professor normally would be shouting at her at this point to drop them. As the strands began to curl and twist like dying serpents, whipping about and lashing out at one another; charges leapt from one to the next in their delicate webbed tendrils with a sizzling noise—she knew by conventional standards this whole scenario was wrong. She could not control her power, they would tell her—if she persisted it would consume her they would warn her, their voices edging on panic the longer she tried. She must learn to control them or stop at once, she would have been commanded. She would release them and they would vanish. It had always been this struggle. Allowing them to fly wildly made them impossible to control. That's what she was told. Now the Docent told her the opposite.

She did as he instructed and firmed her resolve, casting aside the ideas impressed upon her by the professors of magic. Instead, she focused on keeping the portals open, and tried not to pay attention to the lashing arms of energy threaded through them. As she did, the arms spread out, growing longer and thinner, still shooting out sizzling connecting fingers to one another, but now in greater numbers and thinner webs, connecting and shooting out even thinner tendrils in dense branches, sustaining the connections longer.

"Good, Ynith! *Very* good!" the Docent exclaimed. She could see his face through this luminous tangle of light, and he was absolutely delighted.

A few of the arcing fingers that jumped from one string to the next began to leave connected pathways in their wake. The connections began to pulse, still arcing and wiggling, but remaining fastly connected to another strand. The three strands were growing brighter, in spite of their longer, thinner size. The more they connected, the brighter they glowed. The tendrils were shooting out in sprays now, as thin as spider's webs, bright and white, merging with other arcs and strands in flares of light. The light began to resolve between the connections, like pools of water blending together. The noise was growing almost unbearable, an electric snapping and fizzing that hurt her ears.

In an abrupt, jarringly unexpected pulse, the strands resolved into a single ball of light, and the noise suddenly ceased. The ball of light was the size of a large dinner plate. It floated silently above the table now, illuminating everything with its brightness. Ynith realized that what she was looking at was one large portal, not the peppering of small portals she was used to. She wasn't doing anything extraordinary, it was effortless. She saw the Docent's smiling face leaning out around it so he could look at her.

"You have officially cast a portal of the forbidden kind, Ynith. See?"

"Why isn't it consuming me?" she whispered, bewildered.

"That's a lie they tell. Do you think any magic user today would know what to do with a portal *this* large? With a strand of energy *this* broad? I think not. This little ball, my dear is just the beginning. This little ball is nothing. You see how little difficulty it took for you to conjure it. You will learn in time to summon them so quickly, you won't even see the formation anymore, or hear the crackling but for a fleeting second. It's important you know how the large portals are formed, and that they can be formed safely. And instead of needing to work to keep it open, look, it remains awaiting you. Now, lead it with your gut, my dear. Tell it what it must do. It is a manifestation of your very will, and it can do what your body cannot. Do not be extreme in your requests; this is but a small summoning."

Ynith had barely even had an opportunity to learn to control these strands. She had never really been able to control them well enough to keep them stable. But she focused anyway, and stared at this thing that just hovered there, remaining open and stable with very little effort on her part. She realized how little she was actually doing to keep it there. It was no more than keeping herself conscious of its presence with the back of her mind. Even the buzzing in her head that working magic usually produced had gone away. She reached up and pulled a kerchief from her cuff, daintily dabbing away the perspiration from her lip and brow, tucking it back into her sleeve.

Her eyes dropped to the items, and she thought of what he wanted her to do to them. *To merge them into one thing.* She tried to visualize what they should become, and she pursed one side of her lips, making a strange half-frown, all the while keeping her power open and alive before her.

As her eyes wandered up, she saw the shape of a brass hart affixed to the base of the reflecting lamp, and admired it for a moment. It was a handsome sculpture of a fully grown buck, with large antlers and a strong, sloped back. She studied the second lamp, which showed another hart in a different pose, this one peering up with its ears perked towards some unknown sound. She thought, *if only I could make a shape like that.* Before she could even bring her eyes onto the objects again, the sphere of light softened, flared up in brightness and then spread out, washing over them—much like the smaller portals did in class for other students; but this mist was luminous and vibrant, unlike the much lighter version she'd seen before.

The glow had become soft enough to see through, and she could still perceive the objects, each one blurred by the cloud of light enveloping it. She was able to watch each item as they began to disintegrate, the matter falling away like ash, swirling and blowing all towards one spot in the center of the light slightly above the table. The cloud drew the very elements that made up each object out in delicate drifts, like sand being carried by water, and in the center, a shape was being amassed from those elements as Ynith's will took everything apart and then put them back together in the shape she apparently desired.

It felt as if Ynith were merely picturing this, inside her head. It was so easy. For a moment a brightness of understanding and enlightenment filled her soul. She'd finally figured out how to do this; she was indeed capable! She was for a fleeting second proud of this, watching her deer take shape before her. *It's so easy!* Then she realized what that could mean and the idea unexpectedly filled her with a cold fright, and the stark realization made her lose control, the portal closed and the light vanished. There was a loud clank and crash as the half-formed object fell on top of the partially disintegrated figurine of porcelain, shattering what remained of it into tiny pieces. The rest of the objects looked like artifacts worn by centuries under the sea, their details gone, their shapes blunted and shrunken, even the tiny scissors; the sharp blades were now as narrow as sewing needles and as thin as a sheet of fine paper.

"What happened?" the Docent asked, looking at her incredulously. "You were doing so extraordinarily well."

"I was distracted by a horrifying thought," she replied, standing. She looked pale.

"..And?"

"It's just too easy. Much too easy," her eyes were wide in horror.

"Ynith, it's easy to play with little toys; a task like this, done so slowly as you did, that is a trifle. It's the big things that are hard, my dear, and those are also exceedingly taxing. How Arnsword managed that explosion he summoned, I do not know; the energy it must have taken to will it must have been vast. His passion and rage perhaps fed it, I suspect. I personally do not have experience with spells so grand first-hand, so it is impossible to know. The small tasks," he pursed his lips and waved his hands dismissively and that's how he completed his thought.

"It's the things that will be required to keep you safe that won't be easy. It's best you sit down and practice the easy things, learn to manage the physical demands and build a tolerance for them—because you'll need as much strength as you can muster to keep those hunters at bay." Ynith gazed at him impassively for a second, mouth open as if trying to formulate a reply, wavering on her feet.

"Go on, sit." She clapped her mouth shut. She plopped down into her chair and looked at the mess before her. He waved his finger over it, and said: "finish what you started then. I'll refill your tea while you do." He reached for her cup and saucer and pulled them towards his side of the table, clasping the pot. He looked at her expectantly as he lifted the teapot. "Go on," he insisted. With a sigh and a look of annoyance at the young Docent, she looked down at her handiwork.

She delicately put her hands into her lap and gripped her fists, willing three new dots into existence.

10. Learning Curve

"Oh Ynith, this is lovely, where did you get it?" The Lady was delighted with the gift. Ynith had joined her only a moment before after her long morning locked in the library with the Docent. The elder Docent was sitting in his chair reading when his sister's exclamation claimed his attention. He looked up just in time to see the Lady taking a statue from Ynith's hand.

"I made it. By casting magic."

"It's a doe, how lovely." The Lady turned it in her hands, admiring the work.

"The reflecting lamps in the library have similar deer on the bases. I thought I'd make a third, to put between them to match. I made her lifting her foreleg, and looking back, as if about to take flight from a hunter," Ynith explained only realizing the depth of what she said after it came out of her mouth. She'd conjured a facsimile of herself. The Lady, oblivious to Ynith's realization, turned the doe in her hands, admiring her artistry.

"You even managed to patinate it to match the lamps, bravo."

"Bravo doesn't even begin to describe my feelings towards it," Edwith exclaimed with pride, striding in shortly after Ynith. "This is a product of her *first* session of instruction. This bodes very well, does it not, Docent?" Oreth nodded and stood, walking over to examine the artifact more closely.

"The detail is astonishing," he declared. "Skill in magic and in art."

"Well, if hunters can be deterred by detailed statuary, I am in good shape, I'd say," Ynith said with a half smile. Everyone chuckled and Oreth reached out and patted her hand.

"All in good time, dear girl. All in good time." All Ynith could think of at that moment was that Arnsword would be very proud of her too. She flushed at her own thoughts. She was startled from her reverie by a loud bang, and then another.

"Ugh they're out shooting again?" the Lady intoned. "I wish they would just go away!" She stood up and rushed to the window to peer out at her grandson and his gentlemen friends, who had taken up shooting clay pigeons on the lawn. They were naturally facing away from the house, and were too far to hear the Lady's furious tapping on the window. She threw down her hands in frustration, and huffed to the wall where she yanked hard on the summoning cord.

"The impertinence of that child is beyond measure. This is *my* house, and he treats it as if it is his own!"

The butler appeared from the summons, a man by the name of Kennock; a meticulously combed and trimmed silver-haired character. He wore some moderately outdated fashions, and a frock-coat far too elaborate to be worn by anyone of consequence today. The old man seemed a bit winded when he approached and bowed shallowly to his mistress.

"My Lady?" he asked breathily.

"Send one of the footmen out there to tell my grandson and his friends that I will tolerate no more noise and shooting so near the house." Just to punctuate her angry words, two more rifle-shots sounded off outside to which she winced each time. The butler nodded and backed out of the room.

Ynith moved to the table by the window to observe this, and was shocked to see that among the young men out taking sport was Mr. Zeath. As if he sensed her watching him, he turned around and looked at the house for a moment, but turned back to the shooting as they prepared another round.

"I wonder what he's still doing here." Ynith whispered to nobody in particular. He was in riding dress, so he must have come on horse from wherever he was lodging. He seemed quite amicable with the other young men, and took hold of another man's rifle to shoot the next round of pigeons.

Just as they shot a young footman came running from the house, and went to the other fellow who was operating the device that flung the clay targets. With a few words from the footman, the operator straightened, and Tureff approached to see what the problem was. When those words were shared, the rifles were lowered and the young grandson, looking markedly upset, marched towards the house. Ynith did not want to see Mr. Zeath, nor be part of the bickering to come. She returned to the chair where the lady now sat looking most put out, and picked up the doe that was on the table by her arm.

"I'll put this in the library," Ynith told the lady. Lady Ressa was so irritated by the noise and the situation with her visitors, she didn't hear her. Ynith did not wait for an acknowledgement though, and took her deer and exited the room in a rustle of skirts, carrying it back to the library, where she put the deer on the table between the two lamps. She sat down in her chair and stared at it.

The younger docent had followed her, and stood in the doorway for a moment, gazing at her. Ynith sighed, sensing his presence behind her. She twisted in her chair and looked at him, and then at her doe.

"I just came to the realization that this doe is a depiction of me," she muttered, pointing her finger listlessly at the frightened, backward looking deer.

"The statue is a product of your will, Miss Ynith. It will inevitably reflect your heart and your fears. It will always be painted by your experience, no matter what it is you are doing."

"I don't *want* to be a terrified flight animal," she snapped, jumping to her feet in a fit of temper. "I don't want to be afraid and always looking over my shoulder!" She could not believe she was losing her composure but it was impossible to contain any longer.

"Then we must stay the course for as long as we can, and *you* must learn to become the hunter." He approached her, coming within arm's length, his gaze locked on her eyes with an intensity that froze her. She recognized his expression, the warmth of his eyes, the way his mouth curled into a soft smile. It was the same look Arnsword got when he was near her. She wended her way around the chair and brushed past him, leaving in a hurry. As she crossed the hall to climb the stairs, she could hear shouting going on in the drawing room bleeding through the doors; the Lady's angry voice, intermingling with Tureff's.

It came to Ynith as she closed the doors to her apartments behind her that being passive was simply not the answer. Relying on the efforts of others to keep her safe was indeed not an option. Being a retiring, frightened doe would not do! With her lips pursed in determination, she moved about the room collecting some objects, putting them on her round work-table by the window. She had taken a faceted but chipped glass goblet, the frame of her old bonnet from which she was salvaging the trim, and a large silken dahlia she now hated that had once lived on that bonnet.

She decided to clear the table of projects to make room for her conjuring, and picked up the lace-making pillow Lady Ressa had gotten her that was sitting on the work table. She carried it to the bed, the spindles rattling together as they dangled from the front. The piece of lace she'd started had a small completed end hanging down from the bristle of pins outlining the delicate pattern pinned to the surface of the pillow underneath the lacework. She paused after she put it on the bed, and stared at it. Picking it up again, she carried it back to the table and swiped the other objects aside, putting it before her.

She sat down and gazed at her lace pillow. There was nothing meaningful about lace; nothing that could hide unconscious messages to upset her. It was a design, tied into tiny knots, the thread woven around spindles that hung in a cluster in front of the pillow, dangling. She looked past the pins bristling from the pattern, to the lines she'd traced from a book of patterns. Part of the pattern was covered in carefully woven and knotted threads, the rest waiting to be surrounded by the webbing of string that now was wound around the spindles. What she saw sitting on the table before her was potential.

With a determined breath, she leaned back and focused. Before her, five tiny pinpricks opened up into the ethers. She stretched them out as quickly as possible, now utterly unafraid of their immediate flailing and crackling as they collided and reached out with spidery limbs to connect. Her ball resolved itself in a quarter of the time it had taken her previously, and it washed over her table and lace pillow. She watched the three items she'd collected begin to shrink as their matter was taken. She concentrated on speed, stripping them down as quickly as she could. As she got a feel for the way her will was being fulfilled by this energy, she guided it subtly with her mind and the objects shrank even more quickly.

The spindles fell from the thread onto the floor. The thread was severed and lifted into the air in waving tendrils. The matter streamed to the ends of the threads, and while this happened, it wove in and round itself. She realized that the magics were finding more sources for matter, consuming the pins themselves, and then the paper from the pattern, soaking it all up like a rag soaking up water; blending them into the lace as it wove itself. When the pins and the objects were gone, the strings knotted themselves neatly. The pillow and spindles were a gift, she would not use them.

The magic dissipated, her portal retracted and then vanished, and before her lay the round pillow upon which she made the lace, the velvety fabric a deep burgundy, and against it, pristine and delicate beyond anything she'd seen made by hand, a skein of lace lay across it, long enough to trim a neckline.

She didn't even feel slightly spent. She picked up the lace and looked at it; woven by magic, it was as delicate as air. The part she'd started by hand hung heavily from it like a clumsy facsimile. She furrowed her brow and conjured another set of portals in an even shorter time, and she poured herself into refining the portion of lace she'd woven by hand, replicating the design without the pattern, taking the extra matter from the thicker, denser piece to edge the whole thing in a delicate scallop. When she was done, she was looking at the most beautiful piece of lace she'd ever seen. A soft smile crossed her lips.

She got up excitedly and went to her sewing box, and took a needle and a card of thread. She then went to the armoire and took her white gown down from its peg; the one from her first visit to Gallevin, the one she loved best. She sat down, and with great care and quiet concentration, she stitched the lace to the neckline. There was just enough left to trim the cuffs of her sleeves as well. Conveniently, it was a perfect fit.

Ynith spent the rest of the afternoon making things to enhance her dress, learning to draw mass from the dust in the air and on the furniture at first, but then she discovered she could pull mass through from the ethers, just as the books she'd studied had suggested. She felt triumphant that she was able to figure out how.

Enhancing a gown might have seemed a trite activity to use to practice one's arts, but it was harmless enough to teach her to resolve her magic portals increasingly quickly; to better understand how she controlled the portals, and how she could get what she needed from the ethers if required. It had been a good exercise to teach her to begin and it didn't take her long to create things without having to destroy someone's objects. Her obsession with the subject made it all the easier to understand in practice, and to finally know with certainty what all the theory she had absorbed actually meant. She reveled in how simple it was.

She spent the time unchecked, unsupervised and unthinking, and by the time she was called for supper, she barely had the energy to dress and was thankful for the help from the young girl assigned to assist her. She walked down the steps feeling light-headed. When she entered the dining room, everyone was seated and they all looked upon her at once. Edwith jumped to his feet and immediately came to her side.

"You have been casting!" he hissed in a whisper, his brow furrowed. "You look so pale, you almost look dead." He was quite upset. He guided her to her chair and everyone looked upon her with concern; even Tureff, Mr. Zeath and the other guests, who all had a sheepish, contrite appearance as a group, were wrinkling their brows in curiosity.

"Are you unwell, Ynith?" the senior Docent asked. He was seated beside her and he reached for her hand. She squeezed his dry, wrinkled fingers. She shook her head but could not reply for Edwith replied in her stead.

"She's a bit overcome from the exercises we did this morning. I suspect she might have been practicing some trickery, and overworked herself. I did not give you any assignments, Ynith. You should not have done anything without my guidance," he admonished. He had saved her from explaining herself and implied before Mr. Zeath and the others that he was merely tutoring her in silly trickeries. She liked how he'd painted her as so delicate that even the smallest tricks would weaken her.

She frowned, and looked at the empty plate before her. Just as she did, a gloved hand deposited a shallow bowl of soup on top of it. Her stomach roared the moment she set eyes upon it.

She ignored the chatter about her frail, weakened state, and picked up her spoon and began to eat. The effect was nearly immediate—the more she ate, the stronger she began to feel again. The colour came back to her cheeks and she began to feel more engaged, looking up and listening intently to the talk, occasionally piping in if she had a thought to share.

"That's a lovely gown, Ynith. I do not recall that being among the new ones," Lady Ressa observed, after the soup bowls had been removed and a plate of roast mutton was put before her. Lady Ressa produced her eyeglass, and pointed it at Ynith. She dug in, taking a big bite so she could ruminate on a reply while having the excuse of a full mouth.

"It's my old gown," she finally replied. "I merely added a few pieces of trim."

"That lace is remarkable," Ressa said, her brow wrinkling and her eye squinting as she peered through her eyeglass at the delicate ruffle of thread-thin lace that decorated her neck and cuffs. Ynith did not like inventing lies, but she did not want to create a complicated lie for the sake of lace trim.

"It's my mother's lace. I've been keeping it for some time. I decided I ought to use it."

"Well, I'm not surprised at all that your mother would own such fine lace. I don't recall ever seeing such beautiful, delicate lace before. I imagine a Duchess could afford something so beautiful and elegant." Lady Ressa rambled. "I'm glad you decided to take it out and to share it, but it seems awfully delicate and rare to put onto such a simple muslin gown."

Ynith looked down at the ultra-fine muslin that hung like spider's silk over the soft, light petticoat. She'd applied a new lace border over the hem of the dress, and made some very subtle, delicate decorative trim for the bodice. Lady Ressa could not see all the detail, only the very delicate, gauzy lace hovering over Ynith's pale skin around her neck.

"Simple dresses are the fashion," she replied levelly. Lady Ressa did not argue. In fact, Miss Eminy offered her opinion:

"Yes, gowns have gotten quite plain next to the fashions of a year ago, there's truth in that, but your gown is not *so* simple, it's difficult to see from where you sit, Lady Ressa, but she has some very lovely lace sewn over the top of the gown, and she has some trim as well, but it is all white. One must be closer to appreciate the intricate gown. I covet it!" Miss Eminy declared. "I try to keep myself fully abreast of the most current of fashions out of Teragaard, and the Princess is always a trend setter and of late she has been weari…" Eminy stopped the moment she realized what she was saying. "S… sorry," she muttered.

The elder Docent was staring at the girl with a look of overt disgust. He then rested his eyes on Ynith, and he smiled gently. The table fell silent for a spell, processing that moment of reality that had broken into their dinner. But the quiet didn't last long. Tureff asked his friend something, and the buzz resumed. Ynith was glad. She could focus on eating.

Ynith was feeling a sight better after having eaten. She'd never felt this voracious before, and she cleaned her plate before serving herself from the cheese platter and then partook greedily of the sweets. The only person who noticed her increased appetite was Docent Edwith. Everyone else was engaged in their own conversations on the most part. Once the discussion of her gown was over, the young people broke into their own discourse, Tureff noticeably ignoring his grandmother. Lady Ressa and her brother were quiet and thoughtful, occasionally speaking in low voices to one another. Edwith sat across from Ynith, watching the colour return to her cheeks.

After dinner, the younger crowd retired to another drawing room in their wing, leaving Ynith, Lady Ressa, Oreth and Edwith to take up happily in quiet pursuits in their own space in their own wing. Ynith was glad for it. But the moment everyone was settled in, the younger Docent sat down next to her and gave her a stern glare.

"What have you been doing?" She looked at him wide-eyed and innocent.

"I was practicing what you taught me this morning, nothing more."

"Be honest with me, Miss Ynith. You were conjuring. That lace, I suspect. But you were conjuring things without balance objects, weren't you?"

"I didn't know I could do it," she outright lied. Her studies had told her otherwise, but she did not want anyone to know of her interest in the forbidden arts. Even Edwith, who shared a similar obsession. "I had underestimated the mass of what I was taking from in order to complete what I was making, but I sensed that the ethers had what I needed, and my will drew it out without even knowing."

"You're putting the cart before the horse, Ynith. I understand you feel compelled to learn quickly now that you have a grasp of the portal, but pushing yourself too much could result in disaster. I told you it could be taxing. When you take from the ethers, it exacts a cost. Luckily you were only making lace. You must learn to balance the costs, to give back what you take without giving too much from your own body, Ynith. You did not know that with every bit of mass you take from the ethers, it takes an equal

157

amount from you; your life force itself." Ynith did not know *that*. It was ill-advised for her to press forward doing things she didn't wholly understand; but she was afraid. She wanted to take her own fate into her own hands as soon as possible. The texts she had studied had given her just enough knowledge to make herself dangerous.

She paused and then nodded in agreement. Edwith looked relieved.

"And Mr. Zeath?" she asked him.

"Yes, a hunter, without a doubt. He has been scrutinizing me as well as you. I have ways to keep myself above suspicion, but your weakened state could have given him clue."

"What am I supposed to do? I'm practicing forbidden arts with a hunter in the house!"

"He will have no reason to return after Tureff leaves tomorrow morning," Lady Ressa blurted out loudly. She was apparently listening. "I've convinced him not to stay the full six days as he had planned. I impressed upon him the importance of seeking protection considering the situation with his royal cousin, and told him it would be advisable as a relative of Arnsword to keep a low profile. It seemed to work. He has rallied up his friends and they are leaving tomorrow." Oreth sighed in relief and added:

"I've been playing about a little bit with Zeath's perceptions as well, so Ynith may not be in any danger at the moment. It all depends on the depth of his skill as a magic bearer. I suspect he is a run-of-the-mill product of the academies, and nothing to worry about. At least I am mostly confident of that. Those types can be shrouded of truth with marginal ease, if done correctly. With luck, he will leave here tomorrow and not return."

Ynith smiled wanly. They would all be gone in the morning.

"It won't be long before the sword drops, my dear child, so I suggest you concentrate on your work with Edwith, but also refrain from overstepping your capabilities for right now. The effect of the collapse of the government hasn't made it out to the country yet, but it's coming like a storm. Arnsword is not gone, I am sure of it, his feelings for you are too strong to simply leave you be." Ynith blushed, thankfully unobserved by the elder

Docent—but noticed by the younger Docent, whose eyes narrowed at Ynith's reaction. He kept his thoughts to himself for Ynith's sake, but the look he gave her told her they would be revisiting the subject when in private company. Ynith merely dismissed his reaction and sipped nervously on her sherry.

It had been a day mixed with both wonders and challenges. She was exhausted. With a quiet exclamation of her fatigue, she got up and went to her room. Her gown on its peg, she sat in her shift and stockings on the edge of her bed, staring at the floor. Tomorrow, Mr. Zeath would be gone. Tomorrow she would learn new lessons. Tomorrow she would begin to do whatever she must to escape this insufferable purgatory. All she really wished for was to go back. To return to the uncomplicated life she had before Arnsword. To return to the transcribing room, to the stacks, to the tea with Oreth in his dusty office.

True to Oreth's words, the sword *would* drop. It would do so only after Tureff's group piled into their coaches and rumbled north in search of less oppressive pastures where they could shoot and pretend nothing was amiss to their hearts' delight. Ynith stood at the window on the mezzanine over the foyer, looking out as they all left. Mr. Zeath made his appearance first thing to accompany them, how far, nobody knew. He sat on his horse as they fussed about the coaches, occasionally glancing up at the window where Ynith looked on unapologetically. She caught his gaze and did not shrink from it, standing her ground and letting her gray eyes grow hard with resolve. He finally looked away as the coach was finally loaded. The first coachman whistled and snapped the reins, and the two assemblages and two riders moved forward and in a crunch of crushed shells. He left with a backwards glance, and Ynith almost believed she saw a challenge in his eyes as they drew away.

She frowned darkly and turned on her heel, storming towards the library where Edwith patiently awaited her with a new array of much larger objects arranged on the table. With a stern look of resolve, she plopped down into her chair, accepted the cup of tea Edwith gently offered, and set to work.

Miranda Mayer

11. Caught

By the time afternoon tea was served, Ynith was exhausted, but gladly, further enlightened. Edwith was an attentive and excellent teacher, and he was showing her how to expand her portals, control the flow of energies that passed through them, and to 'pay the tax' as he called it, in an economic and intelligent way that didn't take too much out of her. Edwith was also, in essence, learning with her. Although he knew the theory, this was his first foray into the practical application, and he often found himself astonished at the way certain energies reacted, or the colour of the light; things he never knew about because nobody had written about it.

He was impressed at how quickly Ynith was grasping what he taught her and how aptly she took his lessons and put them into application. He told her she was natural-born for magic, and he confessed he was quite confident she would become proficient enough very soon to ward off any potential danger from conventional magic use, requiring only minor assistance from him or Oreth. Privately, he wished for more time. He feared she would be unready if they came for her too soon.

He praised her as they walked towards the drawing room where tea was being served. She was so tired, and she was voracious. She barely noticed his kind words. Nor did she notice how well Edwith looked, his chin freshly shaved, his hair combed forward fashionably, his clothing neat and pressed, if not a bit unfashionable and shabby from use. But he had obviously made an effort that Ynith did not quite acknowledge. He cupped her elbow as she made her way down the steps and led her into the room where her benefactress and brother were just settling in after being given fresh cups of tea. Ynith sat, accepted her cup from the servant, but put it aside onto the small table at her arm, and instead fixed her eyes on the tiered platter being carried by another servant, which contained a variety of cakes, sandwiches and other foodstuffs.

Ynith filled her plate greedily and ate. Oreth chuckled, "seems magic has given you a man's appetite, my dear." She blushed and slowed herself down, pacing herself as to not appear a savage. She was embarrassed.

"I confess, I've never felt this hungry in my entire life."

"It's not unusual for anyone who has been using magic of any kind for a prolonged period to find their appetite to increase by tenfold until they've put back into their bodies the energy they'd spent," the elder Docent explained, his eyes smiling at her. "You go ahead and eat your fill my dear girl, don't be ashamed of your hunger. We two understand, and by extension, her Ladyship does as well." Ressa nodded in confirmation and daintily picked up one of the cakes from the platter, which the servant had left on the low table set between the four of them.

It was only after Ynith had slaked the immediate hunger that she took notice of things around her. Her determination and resolve from the morning had melted into ease. Because of this, she began to see things she'd initially glazed over before. It was at that moment she realized that Edwith was remarkably handsomer than she'd ever noticed before, and she finally observed that he'd taken special care in his toilet that day, most likely for her benefit.

She was in the middle of eating a small tasty smoked fish pâté sandwich when she grasped this, and stopped mid-chew and stared at him, not realizing what she was doing. His response was to smile broadly at her, and she choked a bit on her sandwich, dropping her hand holding the other half while she collected herself.

She swallowed, and put the other half of the sandwich down on her plate and stood; pardoning herself she exited in a hurry, breaking into a run across the hall and up the stairs. She did not want Edwith to admire her, she thought frantically.

Her mind was thus occupied when she rounded the corner of the corridor only to collide right into the chest of a strange man. She fell back onto her posterior and tried to scream out, but instead made a small croak of a noise to her mortification.

"You must be the infamous Ynith," the man said, in deep bass voice. "How convenient that you come when you do," he said. He was broad of shoulder and solidly built, like a draught horse. He had a thick pelt of mahogany hair, part of which was tied back into a tail, the front coiled up into three side-curls on each temple. His clothing was that of a rich man, but his bearing was not. He had a broad platter of a face with two glassy eyes set into deep folds, and a pair of thick eyebrows which were at present, slanted into the expression of anger. His great meaty hand reached down and grasped Ynith by the trunk of her arm, and yanked her to her feet as if she were made of straw.

"You are to come with me, young lady," he said. "There are some gentlemen who wish to see you." He started to drag her back into the depths of the house. She shook her head and opened her mouth to cry out for help, but a force of some kind smacked her mouth shut and made her bite her tongue. "Neh eh-eh, young lady, there will be no shouting, we need to leave this place," he continued to pull her along; her resistance was doing very little to hinder him.

She collected her wits about her, and yanked hard on her arm, digging her heels into the rug on the floor. She still could not speak, but she did not need to speak. She closed her eyes and concentrated just long enough to open a small spray of pinhole portals, which expanded, softened and spread into a perfect sphere around them with astonishing speed.

All around them, where the sphere had come to being, the walls and floor, the ceiling and furniture decorating the broad corridor began to crumble into dust; streams of the material arcing out in tentacles, flying towards her assailant. As quickly as dry sand being poured from a vessel, the dust sifted onto him and clung to his body, quickly hardening into a mold around his shape. His hand released Ynith as soon as this happened, and he crumpled to a shapeless form on the ground. The floor was being undermined underneath him, reduced to dust that in part melded onto the thick carapace that was building on the man's body.

The floor, weakening and thinning at the very bottom of the sphere, finally gave way and the man fell down through into the corridor below-floors. The choking shell that had been forming around him smashed like porcelain into a thousand pieces, leaving the man lying unconscious but groaning on the carpet below; surrounded by shards of a strange ceramic-like substance.

The crash and noise of this fall alerted Edwith and Oreth, and they hurried into the corridor from the drawing room, the lady cautiously at their heels. They found the man there. Their eyes then wandered up in bewilderment to the hole in the ceiling. Ynith was kneeling by the edge of the hole, her pale, tear-streaked face peering down at them.

Edwith's cheeks and ears turned a searing scarlet and he turned on his heel to the hall, vaulting up the steps to Ynith's side. As he approached her small, hunched form kneeling inside a flawlessly curved concavity in the floor, the joists poking out like ribs at her knees, he was astonished by what he saw. His eyes took in the destruction around her. The corridor had been bitten into by the magic; the areas eaten away were rounded, leaving an eroded-water-smoothened appearance to the remaining surfaces. The sphere had cut into the box-beams of the ceiling, exposing a small saucer-sized hole into the third floor, and cut out two concave impressions on each side of the corridor, one deeper than the other, but neither so much that they eroded through the wall—only eating away part of an oil painting and a tapestry.

There was a wooden settle that had been cut into as well, part of the back and arm simply gone, the legs thinned but not breached. The wood was smoothened as if someone had sanded it. Ynith looked tiny amid the mess, still gazing down at the man on the floor below. She looked up when Edwith's footfall on the thinned floor of the concavity creaked. He reached out and put his hand gently on her shoulder.

Her eyes were filled with horror, and he realized she thought the man below had been killed. She could not verbalize her fears, but he knew this was what she expressed so plaintively with her beautiful eyes.

"He's not dead, only unconscious. He was groaning softly when I came up to him. Come, the floor isn't safe here," he said. Ynith stood shakily and took his hand, looking back down once more to see Oreth stooping by the man and the lady gliding closer, before following Edwith. He clutched her fragile, cool, trembling hand and looked once more at the hole she made in the house; and could not keep his skin from rising into little bumps.

"She cannot speak. She can only write. The spell will wear off at length, but she is most distressed," Edwith explained. "She writes her regret for the damage she caused to your house, my Lady." He held a parchment where there were various patches of writing scrawled upon it. They'd been using it to glean exactly what happened from Ynith.

"Nonsense. She is safe. That is all that matters. What of that man?" The Lady had stayed until Rofrick, her strapping stable-man, along with the groundskeeper Hennik dragged the limp bodied trespasser away.

"He is recovering. We have him locked in the tack room, but I can't imagine he will remain there for long. He's from Wetherly," Oreth muttered. "I confess I am at a loss to what I should do next. To restrain him with magic would be against the laws, and put both of us in danger of arrest as well, which would be disastrous for Ynith."

"I can take Ynith back to the Darvath, to the shielded room," Edwith suggested. They spoke of her as if she weren't there. She sat, calmer now, hands folded gently in her lap. Docent Oreth studied her for a moment while he mulled his options. But he was distracted by what she'd accomplished. She'd taken a basic lesson of accretion magic, and had used it to defend herself. He was almost afraid to imagine what she would do when they taught her to summon the arms lightning, or the fire columns. He hadn't seen anyone cast this sort of power in so many years; he almost forgot the strength of that kind of magic. He shuddered to envision what she could do if the book of Hadris wasn't meting out her source power. Moreover, he found it even more troubling how rosy and fit she looked in spite her expending such tremendous power. It hardly taxed her at all; even after a morning of taxing herself. He did not understand.

"I must say, Ynith, bravo for quick thinking," he admitted. "You took a basic stepping-stone lesson and turned it into a viable defense. I don't know if I could have thought of it in such dire circumstances," he praised her. She looked up at the Docent, and her eyes began to mist over again, and she dropped her chin in shame. He took her hand and patted it, sitting next to her on the long backless bench. "Now, now, Ynith, don't fret. You did what you had to. You had no way of knowing who he was and what he planned to do with you," he assured her.

"Now we must decide what to do with her. They surely will come looking for the intruder," Edwith insisted, losing his veneer of calm and patience. The Docent nodded.

"I think that's the only practical option. Ynith, I am sorry to have to do this to you yet again."

"Oreth, brother, is it truly necessary to uproot her *again?*" Lady Ressa exclaimed. She stood and walked behind Ynith, placing her hands on her shoulders protectively. "She's been dragged to and fro enough as it is."

"She is most noticeably unsafe here, if strangers can appear from the depths of the house. Who is to say there aren't more people lurking about as we speak? This brazen assault is only the beginning. She needs to be protected. Someone knows she's here."

"I do not wish her to depart. There must be another way," Lady Ressa said, her voice markedly troubled. "How can we watch over her if she leaves us?"

"There are other Wizards at the Darvath to watch over her. Here, we are isolated, and it is evident our shielding spells have been ineffective," Oreth replied. There was a pall as the four of them thought it through. A good minute or two of silence elapsed. With finality, the elder Docent stood, still holding Ynith's hand.

"I'm very sorry Ynith, but we must leave here at once."

"That would be most inconvenient, seeing as we've only just arrived," another voice chimed in. The four occupants of the room turned to look upon the intruders. Once more, people had entered the house without leave. It was Mr. Zeath in the company of two more gentlemen. They all looked upon Ynith with narrowed eyes.

"Good day, Miss Ynith. Seems you've been a bit busy since I departed this morning," Mr. Zeath said, tugging off his gloves and stuffing them into the pocket of his elegant black wool greatcoat. "Clever little thing, using the dark magics when with all the rampant use of forbidden magic, you could easily go unnoticed. But I noticed, Ynith," he said, his dark eyes upon her.

"A most efficient use of it to boot," another of the gentlemen uttered, "taxing your victim instead of yourself; most unusual." Oreth's brows rose and he glanced at Ynith, his grip tightening on her hand. He felt her grip constrict on his in return.

"You do not speak, Miss Ynith? I would think you would wish to have a say."

"She was struck by a silencing spell by her attacker," Edwith snapped.

"Attacker?" Zeath interrupted, his face incredulous, his eyebrows arching in surprise. "Indeed? If I am not mistaken, Miss Ynith is not the injured party. Miss Ynith was not suffocated and drained. I am quite certain the attacker in this situation is sitting right here before me, not being loaded unconscious into a coach, to receive the care of physicians at Wetherly. No, sir, her silence is a consequence of self-defense if anything."

"This dear girl would never attack anyone unprovoked! She had to defend herself. He was trying to take her away!" Lady Ressa blurted, her hands still on Ynith's shoulders.

"He was arresting her," Mr. Zeath snorted, "on *suspicion* of using forbidden magics; however she is beyond suspicion now. She must leave with us now, there is an inquest prepared for her at Wetherly. She, among some other violators of the laws will be questioned."

"Is it usual to arrest someone by entering a home uninvited? Manhandling a defenseless young woman?" Ressa persisted.

"This girl has proven she is far from defenseless!" Mr. Zeath laughed merrily. Ynith's brows furrowed and her gaze blackened. "I'm half-inclined to take you two in as well; because I'm quite certain you've had a hand in her making as a caster. If you continue to obstruct me, I will, mark my words." Neither of the Docents spoke. They knew they were better help to Ynith as free men than detained as she would be.

The three gentlemen suddenly froze and they all three trained their gazes at Ynith in unison. "Miss Ynith, are you really trying to cast again? Here? What could you possibly expect to do with three wizards in the room with you? Wizards trained to suppress the forbidden magics, and to prevent the use of it, no less. You are an unapologetic little creature, aren't you?" he almost sounded impressed. He then laughed. "Do you think we would allow that? Heffrey might have been unprepared for what you are capable of, but we are not. If you persist we *will* incapacitate you for transport," he warned her darkly. "Now, you must come with us to Wetherly."

Ynith's anger flickered through her wide eyes and she unclenched her jaw, slipping her hand from Oreth's. She stood, and turned to Lady Ressa, taking both her hands. She offered her a long, poignant look of gratitude. She then did the same for Oreth, assuring him she would be fine with but a glance. She smiled wanly at Edwith, whose eyes were wet with emotion and his jaw rippling in anger. She shook her head at him and tried to comfort him in her silence, but his angst was most unmistakable. She turned to her accusers.

Mr. Zeath merely lifted the trunk of his arm. Ynith approached, reached out, clasped it, and walked to his side. They exited the room to the front of the house, where in perfect timing, a coach rumbled to a stop. No trunks, not even a bonnet or a shawl, Ynith was handed into the carriage by her captor. She caught a final glimpse of her benefactors gazing out the window helplessly as the assemblage rumbled away.

Miranda Mayer

12. Wetherly

Mr. Zeath chose not to ride his horse as is companions did, and instead idled with Ynith in the coach, making no effort to hide his admiration of Ynith's beauty. His gaze was so overt, it was making her squirm. She could not verbalize her irritation, and locked her hard glare out the window, watching the landscape roll by.

"You are a conundrum, my lovely Miss Ynith. A titled lady, no less. But so seemingly shy and reserved. Profoundly beautiful, no mistaking that—yet drawn to a man who is neither handsome nor redeemable by any means. He murdered his family, yet you protect him," he said, smiling at the look on her face realizing she could not debate him. She turned and gave him a sardonic arch of the brow, knowing full well Arnsword needed no protection from her; he was quite capable of taking care of himself.

"If you knew the devastation he has inflicted so far, perhaps your regard for him would not be so steadfast." He shifted on his bench, and crossed his leg over the other, the sleek black of his top boots catching a shine from the greyish day. He wagged his foot as he mused. He then lowered his leg and leaned forward, scooting to sit on the very edge of his seat. It was uncomfortably close to Ynith. She leaned away as best she could.

"There was nothing left of the king but a charred husk. His mother, his sister, his brothers, his cousins, but piles of ash," he told her. "Their bodies held their shape until someone touched one. The bonds that held them together were so fragile; the touch of a finger caused them to disintegrate into heaps." His hot breath did not have to travel far to wash on her face.

Her voice came back to her that moment, but only in the form of a whimper as she fought tears, she twisted her face away from his and pressed herself into the back of her bench, her hand cupping over her mouth. The sobs were difficult to control, and the longer he remained close to her, the less she could keep them from happening. Her weeping caused him to withdraw a shade, and he studied her closely. Her voice was returning with her sobs.

"I do not understand you. You should fear him. You should be doing whatever you can to help us stop him, but instead you hide, and you let those amateurs teach you to defend yourself against the likes of us," he said in wonder.

"They believed I was in danger," she croaked between sobs, her voice hoarse and broken from the spell.

"From who? Us?" She nodded, her eyes flickering into his from a sidelong glance. He sat back and crossed his leg again, watching her try to compose herself. With an impatient sigh he reached into the breast of his waistcoat and withdrew a handkerchief, offering it to her. She took it and swabbed her eyes and nose with it, still sniffling.

"Why would they think we would harm you?"

"Because of my connection to Arnsword," she replied bitterly, sobbing again.

"And so now you are under arrest for practicing forbidden magic," he said. She rolled her eyes and sniffed again.

"Do not lie to me, Mr. Zeath; you hope having me in custody will draw him out. My magic use is secondary, if anything at all." He sat up and chewed his mandibles for a moment before shrugging and sighing.

"Naturally, we did consider that this could be the case if we took you in. However, you did commit a crime," he said.

"What if I hadn't retaliated out of fear for my own safety? What reason would you have given me to arrest me today? As far as you knew I had not done anything wrong, yet that man appeared and took me by the arm," she rubbed her upper arm, which was bruising in the shape of Heffrey's ham-hand. "Why, other than to use me as bait?"

Mr. Zeath did not answer, because he did not have one. "You would have arrested me under the supposition of my use of forbidden magic, perhaps?" she said acidly. "You want Arnsword and you think by taking me to Wetherly, you will capture him." He shrugged his brows and pursed his lips, his fingers thrumming on his hand.

"He won't come for me," she said with finality.

"I very much doubt that," Mr. Zeath said, sitting up straight, locking his eyes onto hers intensely. "I know the Everath's history, Miss Ynith. He has cared for nothing in all his life. Except you; he cares for you. He will most certainly come for you. And if he believes you are in imminent danger, I am quite sure he will come to your aid."

Ynith looked out the window and suspired heavily, her throat choked still from the force of her sorrow. She clutched the kerchief to her lips and tried her hardest to ignore the burn of Zeath's gaze. She was fairly sure Arnsword would not come. Unless he thought she was in danger. What frightened Ynith was that she believed that Zeath was capable of doing the unthinkable to capture this powerful, out of control Wizard King.

Wetherly was an ancient edifice, built before the Age of Rains; its architecture grave and heavy, the masonry streaked in black and mottled with lichens of gold and burnt red. The whole thing was built in the middle of a lake. The compound itself was built as a simple bastion castle, with four curtain walls of equal length; a drum tower at each corner, and the main building and some peripheral buildings built on a rise within. Even after all these many years, the masonry was sharp, the corners hard, and the angles severe.

Over the years the wizards of Wetherly had added on and performed some restorations that added more modern touches; glass windows in the stone mullions, a sloping bugle-shaped roof on each drum tower and an elaborate arched bridge of much more refined design leading over the water and into the archway through the ancient portcullis.

The coaches and accompanying riders took no time in crossing the mirror-still body of water in which the old castle sat. The water reflected the grey walls to perfection, with nary a ripple to mar the facsimile. The rumbling wheels of the coach echoed as they passed through the curtain wall and out into the broad bailey that surrounded the buildings within. The coach went right up to the front of Wetherly Hall and drew to a stop. Ynith disembarked; her eyes puffy, her mind spent. They'd traveled through the afternoon, night and morning, with only two stops to change horses and refresh themselves, eat and rest for a brief moment. She had barely slept at all; and what sleep she did get was interrupted and rife with discomfort. There was one small addition to her comfort. She had been given a threadbare shawl to wear by the owner of the first waystation where they'd changed horses. The kind-eyed woman was concerned when she saw Ynith shivering in her short-sleeved, wispy muslin day gown. It was already well into night when they'd stopped, and it was a chilly evening. The woman gave it to her wordlessly, only her eyes smiling at Ynith. She thanked her, and offered her a grateful smile in return.

She now hugged that shawl around her shoulders, wrapping her upper body and gazed about in the light of the late morning. It was a beautiful, if not austere place, this Wetherly. They'd taken special efforts to soften up the area inside the walls with planters and a garden to one end. There was a perimeter of smaller buildings, possibly residences all along the inside edge of the parapet. A few random souls were walking about the bailey, and a couple of old men stood by a wall fountain with little cups and drank, talking all the while.

"Come, Miss Ynith," Mr. Zeath grunted. The other two men dismounted and handed their horses off to a young boy who'd appeared with three other stable-hands. The guards went to extricate their wounded friend from the second coach. Ynith followed Mr. Zeath up the broad steps and to the massive door, which was opened the moment he set foot on the landing.

A silver-haired, sharp-faced woman let them into the atrium, and closed the door behind them. It was warmer inside, but not much. To Ynith's astonishment, the moment she stepped inside, she was knee-deep in bluebells. It was as if she'd stepped into a bluebell wood. The vibrant blue, perhaps dimmed slightly by the darkened interior was oddly cheerful.

Paths were worn through the thick carpet of spring flowers, but they were slowly repairing themselves, new plants sprouting up where the crushed ones were. One path led from the entrance to a large set of double doors which were closed at present, and another leading to the stairway that led to a mezzanine dripping with more flowers. It was a bizarre occurrence to say the least. The woman who'd let them in took a worn path to another door off under the stairway without a word or a backward glance, and Mr. Zeath cupped Ynith's elbow and guided her towards the double doors.

The bluebells inside the room were flattened when the door opened, but some languidly righted themselves and put out fresh arcs of blue flowers the moment the door was nested in its frame again. The room would have been commodious and comfortable if it weren't for the bluebells, which rose higher than the seats of the chairs and benches that littered the space.

It looked like a ballroom in many respects. The walls were paneled in modern style, painted a soft robin's egg blue and hung with frowning portrait after frowning portrait of the great wizards that had dwelt here before. The furniture, that which could be seen, was lovely and well-appointed with rich damasks and silks. The ceiling was stunning; a vaulted space with wooden trusses and beams criss-crossing the arched space in the most pleasing manner. Ynith liked this room, even with its thick growth of bluebells.

Ynith sensed something here. It was something she'd gotten a taste of when Edwith cast a quick spell to demonstrate something for her. It was the scent of magic. It permeated the place. Portals were opened and closed with such frequency here, the area buzzed with the energies. The scent of it reminded her of the air after a thunderstorm, when the world still seemed prickly in the wake of the lightning that had spidered along the bottom of the clouds and lit up the sky. She felt it kiss her skin like morning mist, and her skin rose up into little goose bumps. Her fatigue seemed to melt away. She was so lost in the sensation, she didn't immediately notice the four old men in the room. They were garbed in black from head to toe, save for the shock of a white shirt and cravat and the thin edges of their cuffs. Their faces were also made quite pale by their dark clothing. They all four stood when Ynith entered, and they waited for Mr. Zeath to lead her to the place by the fire where they were situated, sharing two of the three large sofas that faced the fire in a low arch.

One man reached into his waistcoat pocket and took out a small eyeglass attached to his fob, which he lifted up to his eye to study Ynith more closely as she approached. All four of them seemed quite incredulous at the sight of her.

"This little thing can cast a great-portal?" one of them uttered; his voice gravely and filled with doubt.

"Oh yes. She performed one of the biggest accretion spells I've ever seen. It invested Heffrey in ceramic like a mold. He might have suffocated had it not been for luck," Mr. Zeath replied, his voice grave.

"Indeed!" the one with the eyeglass said, bringing it away from his eye. The lens magnified his eye several times as he did this, and Ynith could scarce keep from snickering. He tucked away the glass and opened his hand flat, gesturing for her to sit. "Come young lady, do come and sit by the fire. You look like you could use some warmth." Ynith trod tentatively forward, thrashing through the plant growth and circled 'round the back of the long center chair. The old men stepped back when she entered their little space, and all remained standing until she'd sunk down into the chair and settled her shawl around her shoulders. The fire did feel good. The bluebells tickled her stockinged legs.

"You may go Mr. Zeath," the most rickety, bony of the four said. Mr. Zeath did not appear pleased by this command, but he obeyed, albeit grudgingly.

"Mind her, Masters, she could be prone to cast if you're not vigilant."

"Thank you Mr. Zeath," another of them muttered, more insistently. The younger man nodded and turned shoulder, wading through the bluebells to the door.

The old men settled in and pondered things for a few minutes, allowing Ynith a moment's peace. But it did not last.

"The crown prince, I beg your pardon, the king has been causing all manner of trouble for us, Miss Ynith. Of course you know this. Everybody knows this."

"I don't think everyone really has a true understanding of what sort of trouble Arnsword has created; I think most people have some inkling something is amiss," she said forwardly, "but life has been going on as normal on the most part, seeing how things were on my voyage here."

"So you acknowledge that the prince must be stopped."

"I am not sure he can be stopped for one. Nor do I have any evidence he's doing anything horrid at the moment. Anything that requires stopping, that is," she said.

"He murdered his family, is that not evidence enough?"

"With all due respect, that's a separate issue, sir. What Arnsword did there was a personal matter. What you fear he could be doing now is not defined at all. What 'trouble' do you speak of, besides using the forbidden magics?"

"And possessing the book of Hadris..."

"...which he hasn't used in any discernible way as of yet. He may use it to supplement his own power, that would be possible, but I can't imagine he would give anyone else equal footing with him, it would defeat the purpose."

"And then what? We all live in harmony with an evil Wizard ruling over us?" one of the younger of the old men asked.

"I don't know what, gentlemen, I don't have those answers. What I do know is that there is a great deal of panic over something that hasn't happened yet and likely will not. I know Arnsword may not seem so, but he is very much a passionate person. He represses it, as everyone does, but especially him. He loves me. He truly loves me, and at the idea that his family might have done something that might have had an adverse effect on me, well that made him go mad for a spell. Yes, he did something horrid, Mr. Zeath was very apt to make certain that I knew exactly how horrifying it was, but it has nothing to do with what's happening now. That chapter is past. What it is you fear now is beyond my knowledge—and I do not believe it will help you get closer to him by having me here."

"We must get the Book of Hadris back where it belongs," the eldest grumbled. "This issue must be settled, and the practice of the ancient arts must never be used again, by him or anyone else, including you, Miss Ynith. Mr. Zeath's message stated you are quite powerful, even in your fledgling stage. You can only be more dangerous if you continue."

"I was defending myself against a man that assaulted me," she said archly. "I am capable of controlling myself."

"Everybody says that in the beginning. Then they get a taste for the extent of their powers, and everything changes," another of the old men grunted. "It's in our nature." Ynith could scarce keep herself from rolling her eyes, but she did.

"Somehow, some people managed to control their power enough to end the Age of Rains. This very great edifice is evidence of man's capacity for self-restraint. With all due respect, gentlemen, I seriously doubt *everyone* that uses the forbidden magic will be tempted to abuse their power," she snapped a bit too acidly. She was chilly, hungry and tired. They hadn't even asked her if she cared for a cup of tea.

They sat in an awkward silence until one of them sighed. "Well, you are here; I can't see why we can't get you settled in for the duration."

"How long do you plan to keep me here?" Ynith asked. Her shy, reticent veneer was peeling away, and she was becoming more caustic with each additional interaction with these old men.

"As long as it takes," one of them muttered. "And after we secure the prince, we will address the matter of your magic use." This was not the reply she expected to hear from the elders. The eight eyes rested upon her with stern, castigating expressions.

"Arnsword is the King now," she corrected the speaker archly. "He is no longer prince." The old man gave her a scowl, and then shook his head in annoyance. Ynith was then guided out of the room by a manservant who appeared without being summoned, and led into the back of the edifice to a room that opened out into a small courtyard. She was left there without another word.

The room was not uncomfortable, it was however, compact and there was little to do but stand in the middle of it in confusion. There was a small writing desk in the corner next to the large window doors, with elegant cabriole legs with an equally pretty chair to match. The bed was narrow, shoved up against the wall on one long side. It still managed to appear large because of the heavy frame built around it. The dark paneled wood covered the exposed side, and the headboard and footboard were identical, stylish mirror-image curves shaped vaguely like an S. The coverlet was thick, old-style brocade and there were several pillows and bolsters lined along the wall-side as to make the bed appear to be like an old-fashioned settle.

An armoire hunched beside the bed, and there was one rather narrow but comfortable wingback chair sitting by the tiniest fireplace Ynith had ever seen. The small hearth had a lively fire in it, still snapping and popping from having fresh wood placed on top of the kindling quite recently. Next to the chair stood a tiny round table that rose up to the arm of the chair.

She stood, wavering for a moment and then sat down in the chair. Still in her clothes from the day before, no reprieve from her stays, she was at a loss as to what to do next. Curiosity got the better of her and she stood and walked the few steps to the armoire, opening the door. Inside were clothes. New clothes; several gowns hanging from pegs, folded shawls, fresh undergarments, even a freshly sewn set of stays. She frowned darkly and closed the armoire, returning to her chair. There she sat for several hours.

She was woken from an uncomfortable sleep by the sound of knocking. It was a soft knock, but loud enough to snap her out of the nap she'd slipped into while sitting in the chair. Her head had lolled over onto the side of the wingback, making her neck quite sore. She startled into awareness, and then groaned out a quick 'enter,' before straightening herself out and trying to cast off her grogginess with little success.

A young woman entered carrying a tray of food for her. She had no idea what time it was, but the day had wore into afternoon. The girl did not make eye-contact. Instead she put the tray down on the small table and asked Ynith in a small voice if she normally required assistance disrobing for bed. Ynith shook her head and the girl turned to exit.

"Does anyone dine at a common table? Am I to dine here?" Ynith asked.

"You are not permitted to leave this room, Miss," the girl told her, her voice fearful. She then turned and slipped out of the door, the latch clicking behind her. Ynith rose and walked to the door, gripping the latch, only to find that it would not budge. She yanked on the door, unable to even shake it in its frame. She turned to the large divided-light window and tried to open that as well, only to find that it too was snug in its frame and the latch immovable. She roared out in frustration and tears filled her eyes.

With intense focus she pointed all of her ire into one spot, and a tiny portal no larger than a firefly, one single portal managed to squeeze itself into existence. It would, however, have taken as much of her energy to sustain it as it had to perform the accretion on the intruder and she had no source here for the energy except herself, and she was already so tired.

She released the tiny dot into oblivion and rubbed her face. With a sigh of resignation, she closed the curtains to the courtyard and turned to the armoire. If she was to be held prisoner here, she would at least be comfortable. She rummaged and found what she hoped she would, a lovely nightgown and a dressing gown. She stripped off her gown, which was wrinkled seemingly beyond salvaging, and then her undergarments. She pulled on the night gown and the dressing gown and sighed in relief, placing her soiled clothing into the small basket by the armoire. She then sat down and finally looked at the food they'd given her. It was a simple but good meal; some roasted chicken, medallions of casseroled potato and a salad of julienned vegetables and greens, and on another diminutive plate, a modest square of cake with some sort of cream icing. She tucked in, understanding she was famished but not quite aware of exactly how famished she was until she cleaned her plate and gobbled up the cake.

She felt drained. More drained than she'd ever felt before, and it came to her that perhaps this was how they took away her ability to cast magic; they drained her. She ate with the same voracity and greediness that she had that first evening after casting the lace for her gown. But she hadn't done any magic since Mr. Zeath had returned, except to cast the unsuccessful portal moments before. This revelation made her angry again. Weakened and fatigued, she crawled into the undersized bed shortly after eating and fell into a deep sleep.

The morning came at length, and the arrival of the young lady drew Ynith out of bed. She brought Ynith a towel, washbowl and a decanter of steaming water, which she placed on the table by the chair. She left Ynith to do her toilet as best she could, considering the circumstances. She longed for a bath. Ynith stood listlessly while the girl helped her into her clothes for the day, grateful for the warm wool stockings and the thick peppin-wool shawl taken from the armoire. She sat placidly while the girl put her hair up into a loose heap on the back of her head.

She was then left to eat the large breakfast that was brought to her, which she again devoured, leaving nary a crumb. She still felt depleted and tired, and even the anger she felt because of this had no fire behind it; they'd taken her passion as well. After an hour of staring emptily at the fire which the girl kept alive, she was summoned from her room by the servant girl and led down the corridor into another chamber.

The blossoms of bluebells did not reach this place or her room. There were several old men seated in this library, the floor scattered with four separate sitting areas. None of them were the same elders from her arrival. Six of the old wizards were present here, all seated in the central sitting area, one chair was deliberately left empty. They looked at her the moment she entered. Their silence was expectant. She bit down on her anger and stepped forward, sitting in the chair, facing another inquisition.

As she sat there, she felt something unusual. Her ears began to thrum from her heartbeat and a fire grew in her chest. Her skin tingled and she felt some of her vitality returning to her. She looked up at each of them in curiosity, all the while feeling the warmth of colour returning to her cheeks. She was bemused by these new developments.

There was one gentleman wearing an elaborate gold and silver livery collar with the Wetherly wolf medallion hanging from it. He leaned towards her, twisting his body so that one shoulder jutted forward, his knee bent, his other hand clutching the arm of his chair.

"Before you go off half-cocked casting ways to escape us, Miss Ynith, be aware that we still control your ability, and we are only giving you some of your power back so we can gauge exactly how adept you are at casting."

"My experience is laughable, gentlemen, there's little to show. I learned only to make objects using the mass of others. I might have become proficient at it, enough so to invest Mr. Heffrey into a shell, but there isn't much more than that. I have no understanding of other spells or incantations."

"Well, then show us what you're good at, Miss Ynith. I would like you to do to that chair what you did to Mr. Heffrey." A long arm rose up and the fingers, draped to the knuckles with a white cuff, curled into the hand, a single long finger left pointed towards one of the other sitting areas. She glanced over at it briefly and shook her head.

"It made a hole in Lady Ressa's house, sirs. I imagine you do not wish this pretty room to be damaged," Ynith did not bother to hide the sarcasm in her voice. All pretense of true gentility had melted away in her irritation with the situation, and the blatant and unapologetic manipulation of her powers from these meddling old dodderers. She did not feel like a doe any longer; she felt like a chained beast.

"Let us worry about the damage, Miss Ynith. Please, indulge us." Ynith sighed and looked at the chair he'd pointed out. It was a tall throne-like thing, upholstered in a ruddy green fabric that was worn and threadbare. It sat across the room amid a grouping of other chairs by a bookshelf.

With a little concentration, and faster than the eye could detect, she opened portals, merged them and cast the energies over the chair. It was only a few seconds before matter began to stream from objects around the chair, glomming onto it; investing it layer by layer until it became a strange amorphous blob with the texture of gritty stone on the continually expanding outer shell.

The elder in the livery collar stopped Ynith, or she would have continued making the chair larger and larger. She scoured any object within the area of its constituents. When the nearest objects were depleted the area gradually grew larger and larger. The sphere was at least twice the size of her first, if not thrice. It was growing closer and closer to their location in the room.

Ynith was putting everything she had into this casting; she could feel her strength slipping away at incredible speed. To her relief, she felt a hand on her arm, and she let go and the remaining mass that hung in the air fell like sand. She turned to the man with the collar, and wavered. Her face was unnaturally gaunt and wan, her eyes sunken. She was faint. His brows rose in astonishment as he saw her eyes cloud over. She swooned and fell forward, crumpling onto the floor at the feet of the old men.

Miranda Mayer

13. The Cavalry

Edwith had yet to perfect his ability to turn theory into practice. However, he had the basics well rehearsed, and ever since Arnsword had started what seemed would be the inevitable downfall of the magistrate's control, he was able to play with the magics he had always hoped to try. Seeing Ynith take to it like a fish to water did make him feel slightly envious of her natural skill, but it also fueled his passion for the ancient magics, and his desire to make good use of them while he could.

His first course of action was to do what he knew he must. He knew he had to go to Wetherly as soon as Ynith was taken away. He and Oreth discussed the matter, which turned into a debate. But in the end, Oreth concurred that the Wetherly wizards were not going to be kind to their girl, and it was deemed imperative that she be freed from their clutches at first chance—even if that meant working against the very ministry that supported the Docents both. It was only by someone's good graces that neither of these men was held accountable for Ynith's breaches, and they had only been lucky not to have been called to the carpet over their own dabbling in forbidden magic. Edwith thought Ynith was worth the gambit—and he planned to move forward with somehow helping her.

News from Teragaard arrived just before Edwith departed for Wetherly; the Wizard King had made eleven Wetherly wizards disappear. To where, nobody knew, but they entered the palace in hopes of subduing the King and did not return. This was a declaration of war against the institution, and Oreth was immediately concerned for Ynith. At that moment, Edwith's reckless plan to go to Wetherly after her became quite reasonable to the older Docent. That morning at breakfast, when Edwith entered in his riding clothes, the elder Docent addressed him.

"You must get her out of there before he destroys Wetherly!" he told Edwith. Now he was allowed to be concerned, and in his largess, he was concerned not only for Ynith but for the brethren at Wetherly who were now most evidently vulnerable as well. "Get her out so he won't level the place!" Ressa nodded emphatically in agreement, wringing her hands anxiously. She had done nothing but worry for Ynith since they took her away. He suspected that Ressa wasn't all too concerned about the brotherhood of wizards as she was about Ynith. Edwith insisted he would do his best, and left them with the assurance that he would keep them apprised of the situation.

"Be careful. Get her back," Ressa said to him as they saw him off. Edwith nodded, swinging up into the saddle. With his brow set into a grim line, he bade Oreth and his sister farewell and took to the road at a flying gallop in hopes of arriving there in time to save her—still utterly without clue about how he would go about doing so. He entertained the idea of exercising those forbidden arts that he had so long coveted and studied. He knew it was a great risk, with the doubtless horde of magic-bearers he would be up against. He decided he would suss it all out when he got there. He could not plan on speculation, and he had no idea what to expect and what awaited him when he arrived. He recklessly charged towards the old fortification, his lips tight and his mandibles rippling. In his mind, he saw the sweet, temperate, shy Ynith he'd come to adore, vulnerable and alone. That alone fueled his courage to keep moving forward.

14. She Alone

When Ynith awoke she found herself lying in bed. It was sometime in the evening and she was still in her clothing from that morning. She'd been laid gently on top of the coverlet. She was sore, every muscle. She barely had the energy to sit up. When she did, her head spun, and she felt her gorge rising. At the same moment, she was so hungry she thought she was going to faint again. She stood, wavering for a moment, and walked to the side table where a decanter of water had been placed, still chilled. She poured some of it into a glass, and drank it down in only a few gulps.

She then walked unsteadily to the door, testing it. To her surprise, the latch opened and she was able to walk out into the corridor. She moved towards the sound of voices. She wanted food.

"...see to it she gets some broth or such. Some sort of sustenance she can take in her state; don't give her too much, her strength should remain moderately controlled. We don't want to quicken her awakening needlessly."

"She *should* have been weaker than that. I am *sure* we did not drain her enough. She managed to not only open a great-portal but broaden the flow of the energies even while I tapped her."

"You could have killed her Iverin. It was unwise to take that much from her while she was casting."

"It made no difference, so why are you rebuking me about it? She has a depth of power that I confess it was... gratifying to steal. But she had plenty left to create that atrocity over there. She doesn't need that kind of power; she shouldn't be using the forbidden magics, it's as simple as that, and I will stop at nothing to get to the bottom of her capabilities and to hobble her if I must. It is unnatural for anyone to have that sort of power, and even more so for a young lady. It is simply unheard of and should be stopped."

Ynith, weak and shaken, stomach roaring, stood by the wall near the door-frame of a chamber not five doors down the corridor from where she was roomed. She had heard them as she approached, but realizing it was the wizards and not the servants, she slowed, treading gently on the carpeted floors, wondering what they could be doing. There were four or five distinct voices from what she could hear, a few grumbles of assent or disagreement interspersed the terse discussion.

"Iverin, I understand your prejudices against her use of the forbidden arts, but she is still a young lady, and we should not do anything to harm her. The purpose of the test was to see how strong she was, and we could have easily tested that without draining her as much as you did. The amount you took from her was excessive; it made her faint and she looks wan and close to death. It will likely be that she does not come out of it for a long time, if at all, and then what? We need her. It was unwise for you to push the test as you did, very unwise."

"Think of the dangers if *he* was to find out what you've done? He killed his family for merely insulting her, we have no way of knowing what he would do to this place and to us if he finds out you harmed her," another voice intoned.

"I will not live in fear of that tyrant!" someone with a gravelly voice intoned. The Iverin fellow interrupted.

"She will be up and about in a day or two," this Iverin said dismissively. "She was not harmed. She managed to sustain her magic well beyond the point where I was sure she would have lost her grip on it. But she is fallible, as you saw for yourself—and what I did proved as such. It also proves what a danger she could potentially be, and should warrant more stringent controls on her."

"I've summoned the healer. I'm hoping he can do something to bring her back to some measure of health," another wizard said with irritation.

"When she wakes up..."

"*If,* Iverin. *If* she wakes up, let's be clear. She was spent beyond anything I've ever seen before. She will be unconscious for days at best, indefinitely worst case scenario. Of this I am certain. I've seen bearers use themselves up to this point before. She could die if we are not attentive." There was a brief pause in the discussion.

"*If* she wakes up then, we will have to have something in place to tap her powers in increasing amounts. It might have kept her from casting when she first arrived, but it's losing its effect on her as time goes on. We had only released her a little bit when she performed her spell, and her power was remarkable. I shudder to imagine what she could do without our controls in place. If she realizes this we are all in danger of her."

"She's a young woman with no ill intentions; of that I do believe. But if we breach her trust, or we do something to make her change her mind about us, we may lose the only power we have against the King. We should be working to gain her assistance, not abusing her or making her ill. And she is not subject to your whim, Iverin, even if you disapprove so greatly of her audacity to cast anything besides mere trickeries as most ladies do. She is not here for you to experiment upon and to drain of her powers to bolster your own."

"She will grow resistant to that as well, as you know with *these types*. She is an abomination. I should tap her clean," Iverin snarled. There was a stretch of icy silence.

"Iverin, I believe you overestimate the girl. She is young, she only knows one spell, we are fortunate in that. Her instructor, which I strongly suspect to be the King himself and not the young fellow from the Academy as Zeath claims… whomever it was, knew the forbidden arts well enough to give her a strong foundation in a short time—but she has a foundation and nothing more. I think she was given just enough so she could protect herself. We must operate on the assumption that this is what she thinks and doesn't know differently.

"But truth be told, it could be the case that she's been practicing just shy of detection for years in secret, or reading some unknown texts for all we know too. Perhaps it was their mutual interest in the forbidden magic that brought them together to begin with. I don't think that is the case, but it's difficult to tell. I won't discount it.

"I *do* believe her when she says she only knows what she's shown us. Her sincerity is strong. But that doesn't mean she isn't capable of more—and this is where we must tread carefully. If you know anything of the ancient magic and I know few of you do, it is that it is instinctive and anyone with even a respectable capacity for it could develop an understanding of it to do more than just minor things. She already casts super-portals. That is all she needs. That and intuition," the speaker paused; "and more so—motivation.

"We must hope she doesn't come up with any of these things on her own. She probably could, if we give her reason enough, motivation enough to fuel her resentment, and spark her creative intuition. She will learn to improvise while casting portals larger than any of you could even begin to cast. Then there is no limit. So I warn you Iverin, do not push her.

"If we lose control of her, and lose her, there will be nothing in the way of her beloved, who stands to destroy everything Wetherly has stood for all these centuries. I beg you to rein in your prejudice and behave or I shall have to impugn you and you will forfeit your place among the elders." There was a pensive silence; Iverin had chosen not to respond. Then there was the sound of them moving about.

Ynith's brow furrowed, and she turned, padding away before anyone exited the room. She slid into her little chamber and closed the latch silently, breathing heavily from the effort. She sat on the edge of the bed and quietly processed what she had heard. The idea of what they were doing infuriated her.

The door opened and the young servant girl stepped in, looking startled to see Ynith sitting on the edge of the bed. "My goodness, you're awake! The gentlemen did not expect you would awake so soon, Miss. I will return in a moment."

Ynith wasn't sure how to know where her capabilities were at this moment. She closed her eyes, letting herself feel on the most basic, physical level, what her body was telling her. She was fatigued. She was voraciously hungry. But she was awake long before they expected she would be. She had fainted, but only after expending great power while being bled of her strength. Was she indeed above their control? And if they could drain her powers and infuse them into their own, could she do the same? She took pause on this. It's what Zeath claimed she did with the intruder. She wasn't sure what that meant before, but now she was closer to a conclusion upon hearing the discussion between the elders. She wouldn't even know how to do that, she thought. But she already had. She was so terrified; she didn't recall ever being conscious of it. She mulled these things over as she sat there; her anger fueled her. It almost felt like it was giving her some strength back.

The door opened again, startling her eyes open, and in it stood two of the elder wizards, both looking pale and astonished at the sight of Ynith sitting up on her bed. "My goodness, Miss Ynith, you are full of surprises, aren't you?" The voice was the same as the one who had chastised the Iverin fellow. He concluded his words with an uncomfortable chuckle, and wrung his hands.

Ynith looked at him expectantly. She tried to be conscious as best she could of what was going on in the undercurrents. They *were* doing something... trying something, she could feel the effect on her physical being, a bristle of the hair on her arms, a tingle inside the back of her head. Her gaze blackened and she glared at them.

"I've had enough of your tinkering," she snapped. "Stop whatever you're doing at once!" Her growing anger was a surprising fount of strength—and it piqued her other instincts, firing them up. She remained perfectly still and poised, her hands folded delicately in her lap; only her eyes were directed at the two men in the door. She felt again the strange unidentifiable sensation, and she realized that the other man had to be Iverin, and he was trying to drain her of her power again.

"Stop," she said through gritted teeth, her eyes sliding and locking onto Iverin. The man, a short, pudgy fellow with red splotchy cheeks and beady eyes, glowered at her, his gaze darkening as well. Ynith glared balefully at him. She could feel it now that she knew it was him, drawing from her body like lifeblood itself the very strength that fed her power. It was a stream her eyes could not see, but as she focused on it, her mind could sense it. She followed it, this invisible flow, being drawn from her head across the room, and merging into the center of his chest. She could almost see it in her mind, like a soft, orange mist glowing inside him, growing brighter and denser. She crept along this pathway with her mind, across the room, and into his body, and found her awareness surrounded by her own power; her essence was swimming in it. He was filled with Ynith's power.

What enraged her more was that he was not only stealing her strength and power, but using it to summon more from her. Her anger flowed like heat through her veins, and washed over her mind, rushing across the space between them to where she was lingering. All this occurred in but a few seconds in the physical world. Without really understanding how, she summoned her power back. But not in a slow trickle as he took it from her, but in a single, forceful rush that yanked him forward to stumble into her room, a look of astonishment on his face.

"Oh dear," the other man muttered, his eyes broadening to platters. Ynith had done as he had feared. She'd allowed her intuition to lead her powers. He stepped away one pace, watching her warily.

Ynith felt the current pour back into the rightful body, filling her to her fingertips, swelling her weakened frame, flushing her cheeks and quickening her heart. She felt utterly renewed. She stood; her bearing ladylike. Iverin got to his feet. In his stumble, he'd upset the small table and the decanter of water, smashing it to bits on the floor. He now looked frail and weak, drawn and gaunt; he now was emptied of his power as she had been. Ynith smiled gently at him.

"That will hopefully teach you not to take what does not belong to you. And for what you took from me when I first arrived, I've reimbursed myself, of sorts, from your power. I do hope it does not inconvenience you," she said, the rage in her voice barely controlled. The other wizard merely gaped at her, wide-eyed and incredulous.

"I will take my leave of this place now," she declared. She reached for the shawl that was given to her on her journey to Wetherly, and draped it gracefully over her arms. "I would like someone to provide me with transportation back to Gallevin House, please."

"I'm very sorry, Miss Ynith but we cannot allow you to leave the premises," the other wizard said, the fear quite evident in his tight voice. He stood in the doorway, preventing her from moving forward. But his face was filled with trepidation. He wavered, watching her closely.

"I beg to differ. I don't think you could stop me if you wished. I think however, that you should not attempt to stop me, but should instead be gentlemanly enough to do as I ask, and take me back to my current home from where I was most unjustly taken. I believe this would be the prudent choice," she said with a soft warning.

"Miss Ynith, I alone cannot stop you, this is true, but all of us here at Wetherly are able to. I would hope you would not force us to bind you, Miss Ynith."

Ynith did not fear binding. She suddenly realized she did not have to worry about it. If she could do what she'd done to Iverin, there wasn't a single magic-bearing soul who she could not empty of his power, and use it to do whatever she liked. They could not know what she could do. She could take it from them before they could even suspect it. It was a humbling realization, and she had to ponder it for a moment. How awful she felt suddenly, how cruel she would have to become. She resented them for making her this way.

As she reflected this briefly, a silent summons had brought forth the sound of many footfalls clattering down the corridor towards her, and a great force surrounded her. She felt as if a great hand had reached down from the heavens and gripped her. Her breath rushed from her body and she staggered a bit under the crushing weight.

Her politeness dissipated at once, and with a palpable rage, Ynith screamed out, and cast forth a spell torn right out of her unconscious. A sphere of destruction exploded from her chest and in a strange glass-like ripple, radiated outwards, rending everything in its path into dust. It blew out the doorway and the wall, the wall across the corridor and exposed the room behind it. The ceiling clattered down.

The arriving wizards scattered and leapt quickly aside. The one in the doorway and Iverin had been blown back from her; Iverin thrown through the window behind her into the courtyard. With a lurch backwards and her beautiful face turning dour and baleful, she hunched forward and lifted her arms, curling them inwards, making a motion that implied she was drawing something in.

The wizards began to crumple to the ground in writhing heaps, one to the next. She seemed to swell as this happened, her eyes narrowing, her shoulders straightening until she looked like she could contain no more.

Ynith then threw out her arms and screamed, and the building shattered around her, the shards blowing outwards, and then breaking into dust. The wizards, weakened to a state where they could no longer fight her, cowered away from her, recoiling under their robes to hide their eyes from the sudden and blinding light she generated.

Ynith stumbled forward a step, her feet knocking into the shards of ceramic from the broken decanter. She felt weaker, but not so much that she could not walk. She took a moment to compose herself. Like a pale lily, she stood for a moment amongst the wreckage, the wind throwing her skirts against her. Only a few corner walls of this particular building remained intact. Everything around her had been utterly decimated. The direction of the destruction was like a sunburst, radiating out from where she stood. All around her, figures lay hunched under robes, some groaning, others silent and still.

She stumbled inelegantly forward through the wreckage, her strength beginning to fail her. She feared she would not escape the compound, and she would not make it far enough from these wizards that they would let her be. She stumbled over rubble and flattened bluebells, gripped pieces of fallen timber to lean on whenever she could. Her breathing was ragged.

She made it out of the ruined building into the bailey of the fortification, where some of the few denizens that remained standing, lingered, fearful of this wispy creature that made her way unsteadily towards the exit; unsure of what had happened. The area outside of the main building was mostly intact. It took Ynith most of her strength to cross the broad space. She wasn't sure if she was going to make it.

But to her relief, as she approached the gatehouse, she saw none other than Edwith riding through the portcullis, his eyes wide in horror at the scene of destruction behind her. When he noticed Ynith his attention focused entirely on her from that moment on. He drew up on his horse just in time to see her fall with little grace onto the cobbles while murmuring his name.

Miranda Mayer

15. Respite

Ynith awoke and rolled her head, which was resting on a soft pillow, to the side. She was tucked into a large bed in a room that was not familiar to her. It was the morning judging by the colour of the light filtering through the tall, leaded windows that dominated the left wall of this room. They were dressed in sheer white fabric that undulated under the power of the breeze coming through one of the open panes. It was extremely still.

She sat up, and found herself clothed in a neat little white nightgown and her hair was down and plaited into a rope that was resting over her right shoulder. She shoved the heavy covers aside, and scooted to the edge of the bed. The flag floor was cold on her bare feet, but she braved them to walk to a chair where a dressing gown was elegantly draped over the back. She pulled it on. It was a bit large and heavy; something old-fashioned made of striped and leafy brocade. It was pleated off the high yoke on the back and flared out into a modest train that hissed on the floor as she strode about. The sleeves were long, and covered the knuckles of her fingers. It was warm, which she appreciated because the room was a bit crisp; the breeze still carried the freshness of the night.

She stood for a moment, observing the space. It was a dated room, but not unattractive. It had character. The furniture was very old, some pieces remarkably so; weighty and densely built, the fabrics worn in places, other pieces reupholstered in newer styles of fabric, but still dated nonetheless. There were some oils on the wall. There were some depicting scenes from myth, others held portraits of unknown women, one portrait depicting a lady in moderately recent styles, perhaps a couple of decades back, sitting with two young children, a young boy by the looks of his skeleton suit, and a cherubic infant with dark mahogany locks, in a white gown and red shoes; the sex indeterminate.

She glided about the room, studying the variety of decorative objects, curious to whom all this belonged. It did not appear to be part of Wetherly. She peered out the window when she passed one of them, and saw only a span of green lawn with two sheep on it, and then a wall of trees not a hundred steps from the house. That was it. She circled the space. When she reached the door, she put her hand on the latch and with consternation, tried it. It wasn't locked. This was a good sign. It lifted, and she pulled the door open. It opened into a darkened corridor. There was some light cast in from open doorways, making brightened puddles of sunlight on the long runner, and more light was generated from a broader space at the end of the corridor on the left. She exited, treading softly on her bare toes. There were rooms with open doors, private sitting rooms, a library, an office. There were more bedchambers with sheets of white enrobing the furniture. It was too quiet, for a great house such as this would normally be bustling with servants—unless closed for the season, perhaps, if the resident family was elsewhere. As she neared the source of light at the end of the corridor she found herself on a landing connected to a mezzanine. A few steps up were offset to the right, and a flight of stairs also descended to her left. The mezzanine simply crossed over a broad, vaulted gallery below, and led to another landing stairway like this one, mirrored on the other side, serving a corridor directly across, which was dark.

She turned left and went down the stairs. The floor was marble here, and it was worn and yellowed with age; the shine of newness had been worn into a matted finish that gave the marble the appearance of transparency and depth. It was oddly warmer for her feet. At the base of the stairs, she listened. She heard nothing. With quick look about she called out: "hello?"

There was no reply. She stepped forward and looked to the first door she could see, directly on her left. She opened it, and slipped into the room. It was a much warmer room, with a lively fire crackling in the hearth. It was dark, and it felt like the fire was the only thing keeping the damp at bay. Outside the tall, stone-mullioned windows, a bright morning seemed a world away; the sun's increasing warmth unable to affect the stony, cavernous home that surrounded her. At first she thought the room was empty, but then she heard a brief snort, and turned to look at a chair behind her, where Edwith slept fitfully, snoring now, softly, his fingers interlaced over his tummy, his head listed what looked uncomfortably to the right, his chin resting on his shoulder.

She walked to him, and rested her hand on his, and he started from his sleep, looking disoriented and confused for a brief moment before the recognition washed over him. "Miss Ynith," he muttered, reaching up to rub his eyes with the hand that Ynith was not touching, straightening his neck with a wince. "I worried you would not awaken. I was anxious you would be too ill to come to at all."

"I feel well now."

"You must have seen the King, but how could he have left you in that rubble? Has he no heart?" he asked. Ynith was confused by this for a moment, but then she realized that Edwith was assuming that it was Arnsword who'd leveled Wetherly, and not she. She dropped her hand so it fell listlessly against her hip, and mulled it over for a moment.

"I don't know if he saw me," she replied vaguely. She stepped back and turned away so Edwith would not see any clue that she was withholding truth from him. She feared he would be alarmed by what had happened if he knew it was she who had done the damage. She herself was shaken by the ease to which the power came to her, and how horrible it was that she'd tapped the wizards themselves to source the destruction of their venerable old hall. She was awake and alert because of this. The act of destruction had taken surprisingly little tax from her in the end. She walked carefully to a nearby chair and sank down into it slowly, her eyes cast away from the fire and Edwith.

"I brought you here because I was certain it was the safest place for you. Nobody connects you to me aside from my instruction, and this is my family home."

"Were they dead?" she asked hollowly, her hands clasping tightly in her lap.

"Who?"

"The Wizards of Wetherly? Were they dead?" Her eyes were wide and inquiring, her face waxen, even her normally flushed lips were pale.

"No. They were in mean state, however. They'd spent all their power fighting the King, it seems. It will be a long time for them to recover. The youngest will be as old men for some time, weakened and frail. The old men will likely sleep until their strength returns. He is most powerful, this new King of ours," he said groggily. "I did not stay long, I was most concerned for your wellbeing and I did not wish to linger for others to see me take you away. I sent a message to Oreth to alert the lower houses so they could address the situation at Wetherly. Oreth is the one that told me how the wizards fared."

Ynith blanched, but she was already so pale, it was unnoticeable. Had none of the wizards told the docents she was the one who had been culpable of the destruction? Why had they not shared this? Did they fear retribution from the King, perhaps?

She shifted in her chair, uncomfortable to be less than truthful with someone as guileless and kind as Edwith. He stared at her through his tired eyes with a look of concerned affection. He sat up when he realized he was drooping in his chair, and tried to compose himself. Ynith thought he must have slept in that chair through the night. Someone had stoked the fire for him, at least, and a small throw blanket was resting over his knees.

"You must be very hungry," he said. She nodded blandly, averting her eyes. She kept forgetting it was early morning; it was so dark inside this room. "Lady Ressa will send your trunks here as soon as she receives the message I sent yesterday. But in the meantime, Mrs. Annees will assist you in finding something to wear for the day. I am certain there are some things about the house that would fit you. If not from my mother's things, than perhaps she will find you something from those of Miss Ives, my mother's companion. Both are away, gone west to Ignam to stay with my uncle. Mother was concerned by the rumours of unrest at Teragaard and thought it was too close to home. I am happy, to be honest, that she is not here." Edwith rose and rang the summoning cord by the mantel, moving to stand beside Ynith and offering her his hand.

Ynith paused and looked out at the bright morning that performed like a theatre piece outside the windows, another world seemingly, going on without them. She wondered idly what Arnsword was up to. He did not come for her when she needed him. This concerned her. Was something amiss? She internalized her concerns, and stood, taking Edwith's hand. He led her to the door where a woman of about fifty years of age entered just before they reached it.

"Mrs. Annees, I would like to formally introduce you to Miss Ynith, now that she is awake. We must find her something to wear."

"I have already found some clothing, and have it ready for her. I have since yesterday, sir," the woman boldly interrupted. "I will also see to it she gets some breakfast. She must be famished," she said. She gestured for Ynith to follow her and they both left Edwith behind. Ynith followed her back up the stairs to her room, and stood quietly by while she helped her into a beautiful morning gown with a good sized train on it, slightly old-fashioned but still very pretty. It was thankfully one of the older styles that tightened to the body by drawstrings, so it fit her quite comfortably.

Ynith was then ushered to a morning room downstairs; a pleasant, cozy space with broad windows, one of which was opened to admit the fresh breeze off the grounds. She was seated at a small table by the window, and served a breakfast which she ate voraciously. She'd forgotten how hungry she was. She ate alone, and then was left pretty much to her own devices after breakfast, given broad directions to where the library was, and other places where she might find idle occupation while she waited for the world to end.

* * * *

Arnsword apparently had his own fish to fry in the days in which Ynith had been taken to Wetherly, and Ynith was learning of these things in small bits and pieces from discussions she partook in, or overheard when Oreth and Ressa arrived. Oreth, having made contact with the Wizard Brotherhood, was instantly made aware of the goings-on at Teragaard, and he was most shaken by the rumours. Still, none of them mentioned any rumours regarding her involvement in the destruction of the Wetherly building. She feared it would come out sooner or later and expose her for not being completely honest with her benefactors. She was afraid.

Ressa had decided to accompany Ynith's trunks along with Oreth; they left at night, and under a guise spell so nobody would follow, and made it to Bairesedge undetected so far as anyone could tell. They arrived in the darkness of late night and Ressa insisted on being taken immediately to Ynith, who was in her room at the time, her legs curled up in a chair, her eyes cast to the black window in contemplation. The arrival of Ressa startled her, but she could not say she was not glad to see the familiar face.

Everyone was quite astonished that Arnsword managed to find the time to rescue Ynith from Wetherly, considering the challenges he apparently faced. But nobody questioned whether he really did rescue Ynith or not. They seemed quite convinced she had been spared imprisonment by her obsessed suitor. Ynith did not make any effort to tell them the truth. She knew deep down that the docents would not take the news of her capabilities lightly. She had yet to even touch her powers again since, and remained quite happily away from the use of magic as much as she could, stricken perhaps by her own abilities. She was also without a doubt disgusted with herself. Her caustic anger that had fueled her through it all, her violent response; these were things that were not her nature. She did not like it.

Ressa told her first that Arnsword had secured the throne with little resistance, and that the family's servants and advisors were serving him without question. They said that rumours were seeping out of Teragaard that implied that Arnsword did indeed have the book of Hadris, and that he was known to be spending a good deal of time with his nose between the pages.

But Ressa then said that a group from the brotherhood of Wizards had organized in a fashion, and had planned a rather large assault on the palace in hopes of deposing the new King and hobbling him. She said that Arnsword had done something to the men that had gone to the palace. They had simply disappeared. It was done in such a way that it was quick and effortless, and it was shocking to the magical community. She could not elaborate, for she had no more information than that.

The Wetherly wizards retreated to regroup and plan. Ressa said meanwhile, there was a growing faction of wizards who supported what Arnsword stood for; the release of the forbidden powers, and the freedom to use them. When Arnsword had begun this whole ordeal, the wizards, many like Edwith, who secretly knew of the secrets of the forbidden arts, and who surreptitiously desired to use them, began to practice them the moment Arnsword set Wetherly blue with flower, and were now willing to stand against the Wetherly governance to prevent them from imposing any limitations on them again. They were the ones, among others, that were happy to call Arnsword the new King.

Arnsword was gaining support, and the faction of 'Dark Wizards' as Ressa called them were gathering at Teragaard in preparation for what she was convinced would be a great wizardly war. They hoped to protect Arnsword so the forbidden magics could continue to be used with impunity, and with the hope that the King would someday free the energies from the book of Hadris again.

Ynith was not surprised Arnsword had supporters among the magical. She imagined many wizards had harboured the same dark passions as Edwith, but did not cling to any ideals as Edwith did that made them wish to hold onto the restrictions that bound them. She knew that the docents assigned to keep the knowledge of the forbidden magics were surely not the only ones who knew of them, or understood them. Even she, in her small, limited world, had been able to find some knowledge about the forbidden arts in spite of her lack of full understanding of it. Had she been properly trained in magic earlier, she might have understood it better, and been much like Edwith or Arnsword, or any Wizard, curious to apply the practice instead of admiring the theory. She found it strange, ultimately, that Edwith was not more open to Arnsword, more supportive. She listened without prejudice as Ressa explained all these things in a hurried, breathy voice, fatigued from her travels but too keyed-up to save all this talk for the morning.

Ressa also told Ynith that a call for the hunters and also a call for the Edredgemin of Deleth had been made by the sister houses of Wetherly just before its destruction. Ynith did not know much about the Edredgemin of Deleth except that they were extremely powerful magic bearers from the southlands, and that they would be brought to Teragaard to assist in opposing the Wizard King. Arnsword and his ilk, in the meantime had been tasked with fighting the constant efforts to restrict their powers, wall after wall of dampening magic was being cast from the sister-houses, to little effect, ultimately, but it kept them all quite busy and preoccupied. It explained why Arnsword had not been present.

Just before Ressa finally decided to go to bed, she did reveal something to Ynith that brought her a touch of satisfaction. She said that when Wetherly was destroyed, rumours from Teragaard said that the entire city experienced a wash of pleasure. Of course, Ressa said, "nobody knew it coincided with the destruction of Wetherly until later, but it was like a wave of sensation was cast from the palace outwards, and it washed over the people and sent everyone into shudders of delight that rendered them all senseless for a good while. It was only after, when word of the fall of

Wetherly arrived, that the people of Teragaard realized it could be connected. They had no idea the Wizard King had left the palace, but apparently when he returned his pleasure was so great, it infected the entire city of Teragaard."

He knows. Ynith fought back the soft curve of a smile that was irrevocably fighting to form on her lips. *He knows it was me.* She watched Ressa bustle away and when the latch closed she was free to sigh out and smile. He knew and it had pleased him greatly. She was awash in a strange, freeing happiness, for knowing his pleasure was so great confirmed that he still loved her, and confirmed that he was thinking of her. She slept deeply for the first time in weeks.

Miranda Mayer

16. *Declaration*

Ynith sat on the grass out in the gardens, just on the edge of the shade created by a large weeping willow. In her fingers, she twirled a buttercup. She was feeling a great deal better this day, now that she somehow felt connected more closely to her distant Arnsword. She was quietly and furtively exploring her connection with the ethers, trying to suss out a way on her own, how to communicate to Arnsword directly. The wizards of Wetherly had communicated several times in silence, so she knew it could be done. She did not have the knowledge of the spells as did the docents, and there was no source to seek the answers from that she knew of without having to ask them. She understood how to use her accretion spell and reverse it to create the sunburst, but she did not know anything beyond that. To take power from the wizards, well, that was instinctive. The thing she sought to do didn't come to her as intuitive or instinctive like those spells. But she worked on this in quietude, investigating what she could from a detached state of awareness, under her tree, her fingers still twirling the stem of the small golden flower. She was startled by the arrival of Edwith.

The younger docent had been mostly remote for the past few days as Ynith was allowed to 'recover' from her ordeal at Wetherly, and to work through the trauma of the events, or at least so they thought. It was the first she'd seen of him for more than a brief moment since that first morning at Bairesedge when she awoke. He looked well, remarkably so. He'd tended carefully to his toilet and once again, made himself as attractive as he could. He wore a pair of ferruginous breeches, white stockings, an ivory waistcoat and a rust-coloured frock coat to match his broadfalls. He did indeed look well dressed.He was attractive to Ynith; she could not lie to herself and disallow this. His deep, brooding brown eyes and look of obvious affection could not be denied. When he said her name, she dropped her flower and twisted around to discover him there in the shade of the willow by the trunk, smiling gently at her.

"I would ask what you are pondering so deeply, but I imagine you have much on your mind of late," he said. She smiled wanly, and brushed her hands together, her fingertips tinted yellow from the buttercups she'd been toying with. She did not reply, she only dropped her gaze and her smile faded.

"You look quite lovely in the sun, Miss Ynith. I don't recall ever seeing you outdoors like this before," he said. "This light does your beauty great advantage." She blushed and turned her face demurely away. He admired her. She was in a gown the colour of tulip stems, the skirts crumpled elegantly around her legs which were curled to her side. Her dainty feet, bound in black leather slippers and raven ribbon ties 'round her ankles over white stockings, peeked out from the hem, one foot crossed over the other. Her dark locks were bound up on the back of her head in a mass of wild curls, some dangling like pennants onto the back of her neck and on the sides of her face, a ribbon of a light pink wound through the locks. Her shawl, a solid deep forest green was twisted and rumpled around her as well.

He moved boldly to her side and sank down onto the grass beside her, looking squarely at her, in spite of her keeping her eyes deliberately averted and her face turned away. He reached up and pressed one of her loose side-curls back behind her ear, and she was startled by this. She reached up as if to block his hand from repeating it, her fingers curled by the side of her face.

"Miss Ynith, I am deeply concerned for you," he began. She dropped her hand, her dark brow furrowing, her lips, now flushed pink once again, pursed and tight.

"There is no need for you to be worried, Docent," she said formally.

"You needn't spare me your distress. You needn't spare any of us of it. We are here for you, all of us." Ynith had a powerful longing to go back to the transcription room, to be drinking Oreth's tea and wearing her ink-stained apron. For Arnsword to still be hapless and innocent; for things to still be simple. She knew what Edwith was about to do. She was terrified of it, but she knew she could not reveal her depth of feelings for Arnsword, to say her heart belonged to him.

Edwith, kind, and besotted, was also predictable. And he bowed his head, reaching out to pick up her discarded buttercup and pinching the stem between his fingers, he looked at the golden face of the small blossom.

"Miss Ynith, I declare in all my days at the Darvath, my thoughts never strayed from my work; I was never distracted by what I thought were frivolous things, never tempted to the allurements of romance. I did not interact with the ladies of the academy, I did not spend much time away from the Darvath, and if I did it was here, with my mother, and her spinster companion. I never thought I would ever meet anyone who would take ownership of my heart and make it her own," he said. Ynith squirmed a bit, but remained exactly in the same pose, her legs folded to her side, her body and shoulders twisted partly away from Edwith, leaning on her hand, her face directed towards the garden so he could only see her cheekbone and her ear, and the tips of her long lashes.

"I confess, in these past days in your presence, teaching you, watching you, I have become quite attached... no, not just attached, I dare say, I find myself thinking of you more than seems natural, more than seems right for only benign feelings. I have been pondering this for some days now, and have concluded that my feelings for you are far from benign, and that your mere presence lifts my spirit to heights I've never experienced before. I believe that I have come to love you Miss Ynith," he declared. "I am almost certain of it."

"Almost?" she asked, bowing her head, her lashes flickering, her face still pointed away from him. "If there is doubt then it can only be infatuation, Docent, you must be mistaken." He shook his head, she could sense it. Her hands, both now flat on the grass, clutched and curled around the blades of greenery.

"I am in no doubt of your effect on me, Miss Ynith; the only thing I doubt is my understanding of my own feelings. Chalk it up to inexperience, I suppose. But I know how I feel when I am near you; I am only unsure on what to do with it."

"Indeed, Docent, I am flattered, but I have only been so recently the object of someone else's affections, only to discover that he…"

"Yes, of course, of course, lovely Ynith, I have this on the top of my mind as well; do not worry that I make this declaration for any other reason than…" he paused, as if unable to put what he wanted to say in words. He shifted, lifting up a leg so his knee was steepled before him, his wrist resting over it, the flower twirling between his fingers. "I say this because I wish you to understand that my devotion to you is more than just obligation. I wish you to know that no matter how difficult things may become from this point forward that I am here to protect you; to love you. I know in these circumstances how selfish it is of me to make this admission to you; understanding what you have endured only so recently." She felt the hot sting of tears filling the brim of her eyes, and she kept her gaze averted. The tightening of her brow and jaw however gave him clue that she was overcome. He straightened, and shook his head.

"Ynith, I am so very sorry, I never had any intentions of upsetting you, what a fool I am to think this a good time to say such things," he said with great concern.

"Docent, I am the sorry one," she replied, sniffing. She reached into her sleeve and removed a kerchief, which she used to dab her eyes and nose. She then gathered her limbs about her and gave him the briefest of apologetic glances before standing, gathering her rumpled shawl about her shoulders, and scurrying away in a rustle of skirts.

In spite of his upsetting Ynith, the younger docent seemed intent on solidifying his feelings for Ynith, and did not withdraw after that. He was attentive and kind, sweet and doting, so much so Oreth felt it necessary to pull him aside and warn him to check his feelings for this was no time to be distracted by such things. But the longer Ynith remained in his care, and the more time he spent near Ynith, much to her great discomfort, the more attached Edwith grew.

She'd taken to spending more and more time in Oreth's company as a sort of defense against Edwith's growing regard for her. The old man seemed happy to shelter her from the hovering younger man, and welcomed her whenever she came to sit with him.

During this time, the peace that had surrounded Teragaard was beginning to fray. Some skirmishes between the Wetherly wizards and the dark wizards were spreading out from the great city, and news of this began to trickle outwards to the countryside and smaller cities. Various local militia groups were being dispatched by the surrounding nobility, and in some cases there were stories that even minor magic-bearers were being rounded up in some meager effort to control them before they could potentially become a problem; this upset Oreth very much. He was storming about the house when he heard this news, barking out his anger.

"Now begins the unrest and fear of all magic bearers. Now begins the distrust," he shouted in the sitting room, which he shared only with Ynith. Ressa was sleeping off a terrible migraine and Edwith was somewhere else as he often was when Ynith sought the company of the elder docent. "It can only end badly now. Even with the hunters and governance fighting the bad elements, it won't matter anymore. The people will distrust *all* the magic bearers and will continue to do so for years after this madness resolves itself, if it ever does," he spat. Ynith poured him some tea and stepped into his path, halting him with a gentle press of the hand on his arm.

He looked up at her as if forgetting himself for a moment, but then he gratefully accepted the tea, gripping the edge of the saucer, and staring down at the amber liquid in the delicate china bowl. He sat down and sipped the soothing concoction, staring pensively at the tree outside the window that was chockablock with hundreds of starlings. Their clamour of calls and shrieks was striking, even behind the closed windows. The boughs of the tree itself bent under their collective weight. He observed this quietly, and Ynith's eyes followed his.

"I imagine a great deal is going to change, Docent. A great deal," Ynith quietly concurred. He looked at her squarely.

"I'm quite surprised your Arnsword hasn't released the lock on the magics from the book of Hadris yet, to be honest. I can't imagine why, but again, even with the limitations, he is remarkably more powerful than any other wizard. Why do you think he's sitting on that power?"

"I haven't the slightest idea, Docent," Ynith said, with some difficulty as the birds outside grew even more raucous and she could barely be heard. She stood and walked to the window. She threw it open, and the sound of the collective taking wing at once was like a great percussive burst that Ynith actually felt in her skin. She watched the blob of birds take to the sky in an undulating cloud, casting themselves eastward. It was mesmerizing. "I imagine he too must have the collective in mind," she said while still staring out the window. "He must be aware of the potential for chaos, if everyone had access to the vast resource of powers they've never had before. I imagine he would remain exceptionally skilled, superior even then, with the ethers unchecked, so I don't think he would be threatened, but perhaps he desires to continue to restrict the others. Perhaps he took the book of Hadris not to use it ill, but to insure that it would not wind up in the hands of someone else who would—who now employing forbidden magic, could loose the power of the book onto the world," she speculated. It was nice to speak freely of this with the old man, and to see his eyes wandering as he pondered what she said. There was no disapproval in his expression.

"I would like to think this were true. That the King has not entirely selfish motivations," he murmured.

"Arnsword is perhaps not as terrible as everyone thinks."

"You still have bias towards him, my dear; is this why you spurn the admittedly ill-timed advances of my colleague?"

"I still harbour affectionate feelings for Arnsword; I will not fib to you, Docent. He was kind and good to me. The young Docent Edwith is a worthy man, but it is far too soon."

"I suppose this is the truth. Arnsword has been nothing but honourable to you. In spite of what he's done, he has protected you. I won't hide the fact that his protectiveness hasn't come at a great cost; but his intentions towards you have always been well meant, if not misguided in his method," he sighed. "Poor hapless boy," the Docent muttered. "I blame his upbringing. Such a cold and unrelenting environment for the development of a young mind. My dearest sister, she was a wretched, indifferent mother to him. His father, well, his priority was rule, and the children were not to be bothered with. Not his responsibility," the old man lamented. Ynith poured him some more tea, and he studied her as she did, his watery eyes taking in the lovely, seemingly calm creature as she gracefully lifted the teapot away.

"You don't speak of Wetherly. I understand it must have been traumatic, but I confess I am quite curious about what happened when they brought you through the doors." Ynith glanced up briefly in her task of pouring herself a fresh cup of tea, set the pot down on the service table, put the cozy back on it, and picked up her saucer and cup, moving to her chair to sit.

Only when she was settled in did she deign to reply. She'd given herself a few moments to think about it.

"Well, the first thing I noticed was how lovely the old fortification was. Then the bluebells of course, so strange. They were fresh and crisp as they would be in the forest, carpeting the ground, and releasing a scent whenever crushed beneath the feet of passers-by. Then new ones would simply sprout up in their place. They grew almost everywhere in the halls; save a few rooms here and there."

The old man sipped his tea and listened intently.

"I was led by the hateful Mr. Zeath to a chamber where a group of the elder wizards wished to speak to me. I felt," she paused, and drank some tea, glancing up at Oreth with her large eyes, unable to think of the words for a moment. "I felt... infused at first, by the power of the place. As if it was steeping in magic and filtering into me. But then they began to drain me. At the time, I did not know this is what they were doing. Mr. Zeath had offered me no comforts on the way to Wetherly, and I was already fatigued and frightened.

"They provided me a tiny room and locked me in it. I was only removed once to be *assessed*," she paused again, this time her face betrayed her distress. "They had me do an accretion spell on a chair. It was draining as it was, but to boot, one of the wizards was tapping me as I cast, and I collapsed. When I awoke..." She did not want to lie to Oreth, but she did not wish to tell the truth either, so she left it at that, shaking her head and grasping her tea-cup to indicate her unwillingness to speak further. Oreth took it as shock, and nodded understandingly.

"Yes, I see how it must have been; to awake to such destruction. Edwith said the main building was all but flattened, and the debris had damaged many of the parapet buildings. He said wizards were lying about everywhere groaning." Ynith nodded vaguely and sipped again, her eyes elsewhere.

"Well, I am glad you are well, and you escaped that situation marginally intact. I hope that no more of this madness comes to you, Miss Ynith. I hope the Wetherly wizards are too preoccupied with Arnsword to bother with you anymore."

Fat chance, thought Ynith. They now know her capabilities; they will come after her as surely as they continue to come after Arnsword. However now, it was no longer just because they wanted to use her to draw the King out. Now it would be because she posed a significant threat to the entire brotherhood, now that they knew she could use their power to supplement her own.

Arnsword knew how to cast tremendous spells without the need to borrow from others; but somehow, she thought she was more destructive than he, capable of much greater damage if the cost had to be paid by the life-force of others.

She tried to hide her alarm, as she realized this. She got up and excused herself hurriedly, and retreated to her rooms, careful to avoid running into Edwith. There she remained, contemplating what she could possibly do next.

The next morning came grim news. Oreth and Edwith were in the library discussing the matter, and were greatly alarmed. Ynith went to find Oreth after she breakfasted; Lady Farnham came to find her and told her that something bad had happened and that she should go and find her brother at once. She did not seem to know what it was, or perhaps she preferred her brother to relay the news.

Ynith lifted the hem of her morning gown and flittered down the stairway to the main hall. She lifted her hand to the door latch when a bedraggled man swung the door open from inside and they startled each other for a moment. He smelled of horse-sweat, and his skin was covered in road grime. His boots had mud splatter on them. From the grey great-coat and signature red gloves, this was a relay rider. His exhausted slouch straightened at the sight of the young woman, and he bowed his head in acknowledgement of Ynith. She stepped aside to allow him to pass, and he did, pausing to bow shallowly again.

"Miss, I beg your pardon," he said. He then swaggered across the lobby and exited without ado. Ynith entered the drawing room, and crossed to the door to the small corridor that connected the drawing room to the library. She passed through the darkness and grasped the handle of the library door, emerging in a rather modest library with many shelves that were mostly bereft of books and crammed instead with decorative objects as if being stored here for another time. Against one wall, two stacks of portraits and paintings were lined up against one-another. Furniture was also stacked in clusters here and there. It was cluttered in here, as if being used as storage for items the family wanted to keep but did not want to display. Ynith would have thought that Edwith would have had a resplendent library, and was surprised at the disarray when she saw it the first time days ago. Now she'd gotten used to it, and used to the little corner that had been carved out of the space to be used as libraries ought to be used. It was here she found the Docents. They were here often—one, the other or both.

"Miss Ynith," Edwith said, the moment he saw her pale face appear in the doorway. She closed it, the door blending into the paneled wall. There was a larger, more formal doorway across the way, but it was blocked by a few old-fashioned pieces of furniture stacked one atop the other. She wended her way across the clutter of items to the space where they sat, and nodded her greeting to Edwith, and then to Oreth.

They were sitting at the work table, their backs to the modest fire, looking contemplative. "I saw the relay messenger. Ressa indicated that I should find you."

"Yes. Sit, Miss Ynith," Oreth muttered. He glanced at Edwith and then back to her. "The King has released the power of the book of Hadris, but it is not accessible to all."

"I don't understand," Ynith uttered, her brow furrowing as she wound around a chair and fell into it, sitting across from the two men.

"We heard from another Docent at the academy that the King has performed an Ogrein summoning. This is a spell that requires nearly impossible amounts of power; powers that are simply no longer available even to the King anymore—unless he released the book's hold on the energies. But to see for ourselves, we cast a Bringing, and it came to no use. We could not open a portal large enough to allow the amount of power needed to pass."

"Ogrein Summoning? Bringing?" Ynith asked, her eyes riddled with confusion.

"The Ogrein have been summoned to Teragaard, to be restored."

"I don't understand," She insisted.

"He needs an army, we suspect, to keep the Wetherly brotherhood at bay. His supporters are many, but not enough. So he has summoned up the Ogrein to help. Word is that Teragaard is crawling with them, and they are wandering outwards. It takes great, great power to do what he has done. Far beyond what anyone, even he can do without the full powers."

"How could he influence these Ogrein to his ends? From all that I know of the ogrein, they are free-willed creatures, are they not?"

"They are, Ynith, but you are talking about a people whose very immortality rests on the flow of magic to sustain it. When the Wetherly governance restricted magic, they reduced the ogrein to what we know them to be; pale, withered, sallow creatures, hunkering in the shadows, weakened by light, sunken-eyed and gaunt, feeding on the forces of mortal beings in order to prolong their lives. To win their fealty, all Arnsword has to do is to give them back their strength, to fill their bodies with the magic that essentially sustains them. They need no more to feed off of the lifeblood of mortals to merely continue their pathetic existence; their limited strength once limited their capacity for death and destruction. Now, Ynith, now they have their essential sustenance. The hunt for mortals will again become great sport for these detestable things, as it used to be," Oreth reached for a cut glass goblet in front of him filled with deep scarlet sherry. He took a big gulp of it and plunked it down.

"Arnsword controls the magic, he controls the ogrein. One good thing is he has not loosed that magic to all, we are clear on that now. But has given the ogrein back their connection to the ethers; enough to return them to their former strength. Word is they are back to how the historic texts describe them to be. No more shriveled, reclusive ogrein, no. These are the harbingers of myth; lean, willowy, powerful casters, pale and dark-eyed, stalking about the darkness of night with boldness, magic streaming from their long fingers with such power few could stand against it, filling their hollowness with the terror of those they consume for no reason other than to delight in the act of killing," Oreth finished. Ynith was horrified. She had no idea of this history of these mysterious creatures, that they were something other than what she knew them to be today. She leaned back into her chair, her lips parted in wonder, her eyes wide.

"Arnsword summoned them from all corners, and they continue to go to Teragaard to be given back their powers. Once they've been given this dark gift from the King, they go back out, and they have been quickly moving towards other cities, focusing mostly on the Brotherhood and its governing body, but the relay spoke of horrifying things that have happened already. Destructive, violent things, I do not wish to share with you, Miss Ynith," Edwith added.

"What did you mean by a Bringing?" she asked him. Edwith sipped from his own sherry and looked squarely at her.

"There are many incantations that can only be performed when the flow is free between the ethers and our world. Some spells are just too great to manifest on the trickle that remains in our world today. One of those spells is called the Bringing. It is a seemingly simple spell, to draw a Sayer from the ethers to foreshadow things to come. This isn't the paltry parlour tricks of the modern magician, Ynith. A Sayer is a powerful spirit that exists in the ethers; it lives in the very depths of the magic that fills that mystifying place. To summon it requires great power, and to keep it here in our world long enough to ask it to tell us what is to come, even more so. These are no vague prophesies; the Sayer speaks in specifics—relating what it knows of what is to come of the caster himself, and is never wrong. But gaining its favour is a great task. Oreth and I, we both attempted to bring it forth this morning, before the relay arrived. We were not successful. We have been testing the flow for days and days, since the King took the book of Hadris, and we have yet to touch the true magics. He keeps them at bay; for now."

Ynith held her breath and bit her lip. Locked up in this house, she felt somehow powerless, and all this madness that was beginning to filter into her world was still outside the walls of this house, still seemingly just rumour. The birds still sang, the sun still shone, but here these two men told her all these terrifying things, and she did not know what to do with it. Arnsword was not evil, this she was sure of. Were they telling her this to convince her otherwise? She let her eyes wander out to the window where the sheep were scattered on the lawn, eating paths through the lush grass. How long before she sees for herself these evils they speak of? And what will she feel then, when she finally becomes witness to it?

"We are concerned of course, for your safety, and ours. No amount of shielding will keep an ogrein out of this house if it's determined to get in. I've been warned that I should not cast too much to attract anything nasty to our door, and that goes for you as well."

"I haven't done anything since, Since Wetherly," she said quickly, almost defensively.

"It's just a warning. I am going to cast one more spell before we fall into magical silence, so to speak, and that is to hide as best I can the fact that there are three casters in this house. We must live warily and modestly, for it's only a matter of time before the ogrein reach Lowhill and subsequently, my home," Edwith said. Ynith nodded, and sighed. Her desire to escape this place was now amplified, she wasn't sure of the reason. Oreth, and Ressa, they comforted her. But Edwith unnerved her, and his growing attachment and his desire to be protective was most discomforting. She nodded and pursed her lips and wordlessly left the two gentlemen to ruminate further on the mystery of the King and his magic.

Miranda Mayer

17. Ogrein

Ynith, growing increasingly claustrophobic, found ways to get out of the house in spite of the warnings from her host and his guests. The day after she was told of the ogrein, she slipped out into the gardens to get some air, perhaps to see if anything had changed. She hated being at the mercy of her host, and hated being forced to hear everything through their biased filter. The gardens seemed at first as the gardens always were, but what she did finally notice was a marked difference in the way the traffic of farmers and coaches on the main road had been reduced to nearly nothing, the way even the birdsong seemed tempered and hushed. The sheep were silent; the horses in the field were spooked, ears rotating as if listening for something. It was as if the world was hunkering down and preparing for an onslaught. She walked through the odd quiet like a wraith, clutching her shawl about her shoulders, the blustery wind twisting her skirts around her legs. She came to the rise at Lowhill, the place for which the village was named, a hummock of a hill dominating the eastern side of Bairesedge and climbed the gentle slope. There, one of Edwith's ancestors had built a round stone pavilion right at the peak of the gentle hill, so one could sit on the four curved benches and take in the prospect of the park, village and hills beyond Bairesedge.

She had seen this little domed construct, but this was the first time she'd managed to get out to see it up close. She sat down on the bench and stared out into the silent world. Far off to the edge of the horizon, in the direction of Teragaard, there was a long, looming column of darkness; a great mass of clouds the colour of slate hanging darkly over the landscape. All around her the world was impossibly still, save for the lashing wind. Here, the sky was flawless blue, and the sun dappled the earth through the branches of the trees; but the city itself was enrobed in a growing cloud of darkness.

She was startled quite violently by Edwith's arrival. He didn't make any noise on his approach and merely climbed up the steps to join her and sat down beside her. She was looking off towards Teragaard and she gasped loudly and made a shocked squealing sound that paled his face the moment she felt him beside her.

"I'm dreadfully sorry to startle you, Miss Ynith," he said quickly, his hand falling onto hers. She looked down at it, for he left it there to rest on her hand, rendered speechless by the thrumming in her ears and the speed of her heart from the shock of his abrupt arrival. Her cheeks and neck flushed in annoyance.

"I've come looking for you. I have something I wish to give you," he told her. She looked at his large brooding eyes, and then watched his hand move towards his watch pocket, reaching in the narrow slot with two fingers, he withdrew something shining.

He opened up his hand and a small trinket rolled onto his palm, falling face-up. It was a tiny cameo made from pink shell. It was set in an intricate frame of pale gold with a ring at the top to hang from a chain. The carving was unusual; the pale white shell on the pink background depicted a buttercup instead of the usual profile or figure.

"I've come to associate you with those little flowers now. All because of the other day, silly, I know. I conjured it last night as I thought of you. It is composed of an old piece that once belonged to my grandmother. I meant to make a profile of you, but my will; it produced the buttercup. It's but a trifle, but, I thought you would like it regardless," Edwith said, his eyes large and hopeful. Ynith's heart instantly pained her. She reached out her dainty fingers and plucked the cameo from his palm, studying it for a moment. She then put it back in his hand and reached up to unclasp the simple silver chain she wore now with the tiny square of garnet adorning her neck.

She slipped the cameo onto the chain and put it back on, clasping the delicate, paper-thin carving between her fingers, her eyes misted and her throat tight.

"I've never received a gift like this before," she said, glancing uncomfortably at Edwith. "Thank you," she finally said, overcome with confusion and emotion. Edwith looked quite pleased by her reaction.

"You are most welcome, lovely Ynith," he replied.

Before she could think or respond further, his lips were on hers, and his hands clutched her arms and twisted her so she would face him better. Her neck bent to the pressure of his lips and she stiffened. Immediately her eyes began to fill with searing tears. She tried to pull away but his kiss was desperate and needy, and he seemed oblivious to her resistance. He tilted his face, and parted her lips with his tongue, his hands sliding up her back to her neck. She felt her teeth part and he was kissing her as deeply as he could hope to, and she was so startled and shocked by it all, she could scarce react rationally. She managed to reach her hands up onto his shoulders and shove him back with all her might. Still he clung until he could cling no more, his eyes filled with passion when he finally withdrew. She wiped her mouth with the back of her hand and stood, backing away from him.

"That was n… not proper, Docent," she said, breaking into sobs.

"Yes, yes it was," he said defiantly, getting to his feet. "Why can you not see how much I treasure and adore you, Ynith? Why do you pine still for that… that inhuman creature who claims to be King? A man who would beset the full ogrein onto the world for no other reason but to secure his power? There is no good in him!" he snarled. Ynith's hand clutched over the pennant over her heart and she sobbed again. He stepped towards her, and she stepped back, her knees running into the bench on the other side of the palisade. He strode up to her and grasped her shoulders.

"I love you, Ynith," he said desperately. "Understand that all I do now is because I love and cherish you," he said. "You must come away with me; we will go further west, away from this as far as we can go. I cannot go on knowing you are in any danger, especially in danger of falling under the spell of this evil man as to lose you forever." His eyes were almost mad with emotion, and Ynith was frozen in both fear and doubt. He read this as something else and bent over her again, his lips devouring hers. Ynith remained stiff and emotionless, her eyes wide and shocked as he kissed her again; unable to decide what she was feeling. He clutched her to his body and wrapped his arms around her, and continued to embrace her. He took no heed of her hardness or reserve, he did not notice her eyes wide and confused because his were shut in bliss. All Ynith could do was stare past the face of this persistent, misguided man, and fix her eyes on the dark cloud slowly roiling over Teragaard.

Ynith's countenance over the next few days was one of even greater severity and hard-lipped silence. She seemed faraway and lost. Ressa appeared to be the only one who really noticed it. Edwith, somehow bolstered by the notion that he was secure in his situation with the woman he loved, was haplessly going about quite comfortable to touch her hand, to peck her lips in private, and occasionally run his fingers lovingly along her face. Ynith was as stone, eyes always wet and distant. In this crisis, the cloud broadening slowly across the land and rumours of ogrein getting closer to them with each day, the atmosphere seemed increasingly heavy in the house, at least for Ynith, and she reflected that darkness quite aptly. Ressa was very concerned, and spent most of her time with Ynith, reading to her, stitching while Ynith stared at the fire, lost inside her own thoughts.

Occasionally she would slip outside to get some air, to escape the suffocation of her situation. And when she saw Edwith withdraw to the smoking room with Oreth after supper one evening, and Ressa excused herself from fatigue, she slid outside onto the balcony of the back dining room and down the steps to the willow tree, and there she knelt down in the black of night, and cried. Her weeping was coarse and raw, there was nothing holding her back; she succumbed to her misery, her sobs falling into the darkness alone.

She hated what she was. She was the doe again, but she did not wish to be the chained beast either. She felt powerless and ashamed of herself. She could not contain her sorrow, and succumbed to it, her sobs and sniffles hardly muffled by the kerchief she had pressed to her open mouth.

"Simper simper, little flower," a voice hissed from seemingly all around her. "What dark troubles wrest your little heart so? To make you weep in the dark of night? Is it the prospect of inevitable death, perhaps? Or have you lost one of your pretty red slippers? O' such tragic things." Ynith's hackles rose and she twisted about to find the source of the mocking voice. She finally found it; barely a figment in the darkness, a pale, long face with a hawkish nose and two white long-fingered hands that looked like talons.

Her immediate instinct was to cast. She did so before she could check herself. Before she realized it, she had punched her consciousness through the chest of this creature. She found herself confronted with what seemed to be a source of infinite power; it nearly made her swoon. It was like staring directly in the light of the sun after being locked in darkness. With the power of her will, she pulled it towards her, across the span of lawn where the figure stood, and suffused herself with it. For a moment she was filled with a sensation of pure ecstasy from the weight of this power. She balled it up, and then threw it back at him with all of her might. She thought this would send him reeling away. The same explosive spell that had worked so well at Wetherly merely fell flat on him, in spite of the vibrant and heady power she could still feel vibrating through her bones. It took her a moment to realize she'd failed, and she had to gather her wits about her, still a bit dizzy from the elation of his power.

"Well, well, well, we are full of little happy surprises are we not, little flower with white petals?" the hand coiled up and twisted greedily before him. In his black cassock, this black-haired wraith approached, his eyes both simultaneously empty and curious at once. "I sensed some magic in this place, but expected nothing like this." Ynith stiffened. The towering, lean figure slid up to her almost soundlessly, just the train of his cassock rustling on the grass. He knelt, his spidery pale hand reaching up and clasping in its cool digits the side of her face, tracing the line of her jaw from her ear to her chin with the icy tips of his fingers. His thumb brushed the crest of her lips.

"Lovely creation, lovely, lovely," he hissed, his breath only gusts of air, no warmth, no scent. She saw his teeth now, a flash of sharp, pointed carnivore's weapons in a tidy white row, top and bottom. This was the first time she'd seen an ogrein up close. He was as terrifying as she imagined, but for different reasons than she'd assumed. It was a haunting, empty sort of horror she felt by his presence. He was hollow.

"You do not fear me?" he asked, his other hand tracing the other side of her face. He hunched before her like a carrion bird over a carcass, fascinated. "I suppose not, if you think yourself so full of power."

"I think no such thing," she snapped. He seemed delighted by her defiant reply and chuckled through his long nose.

"I felt you reach into me and steal some of my power, little one. But one cannot turn the power of an ogrein onto itself. You must know this if you know how to take it from others."

"I know nothing," she said, her voice betraying a shred of her fear. He hunched closer, his black eyes without reflection in the darkness of night. He was but a hovering head and hands, it seemed, his black cassock making the rest of him invisible.

"Hm... little flower," he said again, breathing deeply of her scent. "You speak lies to me, I feel your capacity for destruction, it's right here," he tapped her temple with his long, sharp nail."You've stolen power before, you naughty little thing," he said with glee. "I let you in, because I knew you could not hurt me. You could have turned my power against any other if you wanted. But you did not know that, did you, little blossom?"

"I did what my instincts told me to do, it was never calculated. I am of no threat to you." At that he laughed outright, and his hands dropped to hers, which he lifted from where they rested on her knees, and he turned the palms upwards so he could gaze at them.

"Such vibrancy, I can see it pulsing through you, like delicious light," he said. He leaned closer so his lips were but a shade from her ear, and whispered "I could sup upon you for days and if I were weak again, you would sustain me for many years," he then faced her again and slowly kissed the palm of each of her hands with his cold wet lips. She did not hide her disgust.

"But I cannot, because you are already marked, pretty flower," he sniffed her wrists each in turn, "not my flower to pluck. What a shame, but I cannot go cutting flowers in another man's garden," he said. He pulled her towards his face again, this time a bit harshly, his expression melting from amused to serious. She strained against him, pulling back with all her strength to no avail.

"You are the source of his very supremacy, I smell him on you. I smell another as well, you tawdry little blossom; whose heart are you most likely to break? Which heart will be most likely to destroy the world if you do?" She recoiled, and tried to yank her hands from his hard grasp again.

"Never mind the feigned squeamishness, I see it all, I've lived ages upon ages, you are all like books to read," he sighed intolerantly. "Lucky, the ones that love you, to love you," he said. "Fortunate for it, they are. They will be spared for your sake alone. But my white rose, know that I am watching you," he said. The ogrein let go of her hands abruptly and she fell back onto her bottom. She caught herself quickly with her hands bracing behind her, her eyes wide. He was on his feet and melting into the darkness before she realized it, leaving Ynith struck cold by his passing. What had just happened?

She scrambled to her feet and tore into the house as quickly as her feet could carry her, and found an unsettling normality awaiting her. Oreth and Edwith were in the drawing room both reading, both looking up from their texts, surprised to see her.

"We thought you retired for the evening," Oreth said with a smile. The room was filled with golden light cast by the fire and candles, the sight of it would normally be comforting and inviting. Ynith, dry-mouthed and flushed, shook her head, still unable to speak. Edwith noted her look of alarm.

"Are you unwell, Miss Ynith?" he asked, getting to his feet. Before she could formulate a reply he was ushering her to the door. "Come, I'll see you to your room," he said. And just as quickly, he led her out of the drawing room and up the stairs, into the darkness of the corridor. But instead of continuing on, he turned her to face him and reached up to grasp her neck, pulling her to him. She resisted, still struck dumb by everything that was happening, and unable to speak for the words were suffocated by his kiss yet again. By some strange instinct, Ynith's hand flew up and she violently slapped his face away. With a sob she pried herself free from his insistent grasp, ignoring his shocked face, and tore down the corridor to her room, her gasping sobs trailing behind her. Edwith stood with a look of shock and reproach on his face, unsure himself of what had just happened.

18. Laid Bare

Morning came and Edwith was astonished to find that Miss Ynith had risen before the sun and was leaving the house, a small trunk packed, the coach readied without his consent. Neither Ressa nor Oreth had risen yet, it was only by chance that he was able to catch her, sleepless and unnerved after what had occurred, he sought some tea to center his thoughts. He only saw her because he passed through the foyer with his teapot on his way to the library where he would contemplate.

"Where are you going Ynith?" he blurted, catching her just as she was about to exit the door, which was being held open by a very tired looking footman. She spun on her heel and faced him wide-eyed, taken aback by his appearance, her eyes taking in his loose shirt and white under-breeches and the banyan that hung limp on his body.

"I'm leaving," she said with finality. "I am sorry, but I can no longer stay here." She turned to walk out the door and Edwith plunked the teapot down on the center table.

"Under no circumstances shall you set foot outside this house, Miss Ynith, it is for your own protection."

"I no longer wish for protection, Docent," she said, stressing the formal appellation with a touch of acidity. "I am no safer here than anywhere else."

"You have our protection," he said of himself and Oreth, his face confused and lost.

"I can protect myself," she replied succinctly. She turned and went outside. Edwith followed on his slipperless feet, the pads slapping on the marble and then the granite of the stairs.

"Ynith I forbid you to go!" he shouted, losing control of his countenance for a second, his anger and alarm most evident. She halted, her shoulders squared and for a moment there was nothing but silence. But finally she turned around, her face a mask of rage like he'd never seen before in this normally docile, sweet creature.

"*You* forbid *me*?" she snarled. "How dare you! Back and forth, here and there, sit down Ynith, go rest Ynith, eat some food Ynith, practice your tricks, Ynith. You seem quite content to tell me what to do; where did you get the idea that it was acceptable for you to decide what's best for me, Docent? When was it decided that it was acceptable for you to force yourself upon me?" she flamed.

"Force myself..?" he stammered.

"I never wanted your advances, you have tried to turn my thoughts to you from the beginning, you have tried to suffocate me, tried to control me, tried to determine what choices I should make for myself, and…" her anger seemed to be building up with each word, her fury expressed in escalating screams, "and… and your uninvited kisses, your forceful hand, your complete neglect of my reaction. Your touch reviles me!" she shrieked. "I have been able to tolerate you for your kindness, but I will tolerate your advances no more!" tears streamed down her cheeks as she shouted. "I am no *flower*, no victim, no shivering, melting, simpering child for you to do with as you please. I can take care of myself. I always have! And if I am to be attached to anyone it will be someone of *my* choosing and mine alone!"

230

Edwith's rage finally surfaced. His quiescent nature evaporated the moment she said that she was revolted by him. Something snapped. "Get in the house," he snarled, his teeth gritted. "You are being stupid and irrational, and it must stop at once!"

"I will do no such thing!" she walked to the coach and flung open the door. The coachman and the footman stood in utter shock and discomfort at this exchange, and offered her no help as she lifted the hems of her skirts and stepped inside.

"Ynith, you will get back inside that house or I will be forced to make you do so at once!" She turned around in the coach and laughed riotously, giving him a victorious, challenging grin.

"Oh really, Edwith? You will force me to go into the house?" she asked in a mad, singsong voice. "Do show me how you plan to do that. Perhaps you'll use magic and attract some ogrein to your door?"

"I'll do whatever it takes, Ynith, to insure you are not caught up in the madness that the King has embroiled you in. I will not let you go to him!"

"Then TRY!" she screamed. She reached out and slammed the little door shut. "Get me out of here!" she shouted at the coachman, sitting down forcefully and facing forward. The driver looked to Edwith with trepidation.

"Go back to the carriage house, both of you," Edwith seethed. His staff members knew not to defy him, and Ynith felt the coach lurch as the driver stepped down, and she heard them both scurrying away.

"Get out of the coach at once," Edwith growled. She stared forward for a long, pointed moment and ground her teeth. With a deliberate slowness she turned to look at him; a blackness in her eyes he'd never seen before.

"Make me," she said levelly. The horses began to act disturbed and spooked, one of the team was dancing in alarm, and the other twitched and snorted, showing the whites of its eyes. They could sense the impending danger. Edwith's face turned beet red and with a violent sweep of the hands a white cloud formed from instant portals and swept across the coach like a storm, shredding the frame and body like kindling and tearing the cloth top to shreds; renting it all onto the driveway behind the coach and exposing Ynith. She on the other hand seemed oddly calm in spite of the coach being torn away from around her. The horses reared and began to lurch in different directions, one trying to run sideways, the other forward, both impeding one another, and causing further panic.

Ynith stood on the open coach and turned, her eyes locked onto Edwith with outright hatred. Her hands were clawed like the ogrein's had been, her white skin grew sallower, and her eyes remained fast on him as her face turned down so her chin nearly rested on her collar. She ripped power from him in a seamless, nearly invisible twitch of her head, and used it to cast a portal that blew outwards, sending Edwith back against the stairs. She dropped down off the lurching coach just before it was upset by the flailing horses. Finally resolved to escape the madness, they cooperated to run forward, taking the dragging assemblage of wheels and broken wood with them, tearing up the driveway and working themselves into a terrified froth until it finally broke away and they, still tethered together, galloped off around the back of the house.

Meanwhile, Edwith was righting himself, having been thrown violently against the steps of his home, a look of shock on his face.

"You think Arnsword set me free from Wetherly?" she asked, her voice chillingly soft. "You think he would have left me to languish after destroying the place? He was too busy trying to keep the Wetherly fools at bay, too busy fighting off the ignorant ones who choose to fear him rather than understand him. They kept him from me, they did. But I was never helpless," she said. Edwith listened, his mandibles rippling.

"*You* flattened Wetherly?" he muttered, incredulous.

"Yes. I flattened Wetherly," she replied, her cold haunting voice seemed hollow. She advanced upon Edwith, her gaze unrelenting.

"You lied to us."

"You expect me to tell you the truth? What could I have expected as a reaction to that, from you or even the Docent?" she asked, tilting her head inquisitively, her fingers still curled at her sides as she slowly walked towards Edwith. "What would you truly expect?" Edwith's expression suddenly melted from rage to something akin to betrayal or hurt.

"I expected you to know that I love you enough to understand, Ynith," he said. Ynith froze a few paces in front of him, for a second disarmed by his honesty, but then enraged by it.

"What I feel matters, Edwith. You cannot say you love me and expect me to accept that when I do not love you."

"How can you love him?" Edwith asked, gritting his teeth, fighting back his emotional response. Ynith paused, her eyes cast aside for just a breath, thinking of what transpired, from the moment she met him to last night, when the ogrein had found her. With deliberate effort to control herself, she smiled softly.

"The same way you can love me," she replied, and with that she lifted her hands, and bundled the air beneath him, lifting him off the ground with a sweep of her hands and a glare of her eyes. She threw him onto the grass.

"How are you doing this?" he shouted as he got to his feet. "How?"

"Never mind how," she snarled. "I'm leaving, Edwith."

"You will enable him to destroy everything that matters, everything that is civilized and good."

"No, Edwith, it's quite the opposite." Edwith shook his head and brought forth a rage that seemed to open the very portal of the world. He threw her as well, casting her onto the gravel, and sending her into a spray of pebbles. She grunted out in pain, but he did not give her a chance to recover. He picked up the shredded frame of the coach and threw it at her. Ynith shed it away with the sweep of a hand, and tried to get back to her feet. It was coming to her, the instincts, and the sense of how to manipulate her powers.

Edwith's hands rose again and the earth boiled beneath her, opening up to swallow her. She broke his connection by covering him in a shell of gravel, which he threw away within seconds, revealing a peppering of scrapes and cuts from the sharp stones. Ynith's gown was torn at the hem, one foot punched through, her elbows and chin bleeding. They were both breathing raggedly, but

Ynith was still filled with desperate anger and Edwith with something between horror and fury.

She roared and motioned as if she was pulling something down and a great chunk of the top of the roofline on the house gave way and the massive bricks pelted down at Edwith, who deflected them towards her. She was actually hit by one of the stones in the arm and she roared out in pain, and Edwith responded with an anxious cry.

Ynith was about to make the whole front wall fall upon him, motivated only by an instinctive rage caused by her misery and fury, when she felt something immaterial harshly crash down upon her and then whip her around. She then felt her powers drain and her senses flicker, and before she lost herself to unconsciousness, she saw the white, alarmed face of Oreth as he cast her into oblivion.

19. Recovery

"YOU NEARLY KILLED HER!" Oreth screamed, pounding his fist furiously on the sideboard. Ressa jumped at the noise and dabbed her eyes with her kerchief.

"Poor thing, why did you not simply let her leave as she wished? What right did you have to force her to stay?" she cried.

"It was for her own good!" Edwith snapped. "Where would she go? Except to be exposed to danger at the hands of the King or his minions, or the Wetherly Wizards."

"Or you," Oreth hissed, his anger was palpable. "She was most certainly in danger of you."

"*She* flattened Wetherly, I told you, *she* did it! She withheld the truth from us! I was in as great a danger as she!"

"Can you even begin to imagine how terrified she must have been? To discover the depth of her powers in such a manner, to be alone and without explanation or support; to know she could create that kind of harm with so little effort? It must have been horrifying. And then to come back here, and to tell you that she was responsible for that kind of violence, you expected her to feel compelled to tell us? If you think she could easily do so, then you know nothing of her character, Edwith. Nothing at all! Ynith is not fashioned that way," Oreth barked, his brows arched, his eyes wide, sparkling with his anger. "Your solution was to attack her?"

"I feared for her," he replied lamely, his voice breaking. "I allowed my anger to own me. When she retaliated, the powers consumed me."

"Then you failed the most fundamental lesson of the keeper of the ancient arts, Edwith. I am most disappointed in you. Most deeply disappointed."

"What of Ynith now?"

"She may have a broken bone in her arm, possibly more injuries I cannot know," Oreth replied with disgust in his tone. "How could you let it escalate to the point where she would sustain such injury? She is a young woman who has powers she barely comprehends. You should have called me the moment you saw her leaving. I could have tried to convince her to stay, or offered her an alternative that would not have led to what just happened."

"I suspect Docent Edwith was motivated by his own selfish desires, brother, I'm sorry I have to say it," Ressa snapped through her tears. Edwith glared at her, and Oreth sighed out loudly, shaking his head.

"I told you before you set foot into Gallevin that you should guard yourself and avoid attachments. Ynith has been hidden away at the Darvath, and does not know her loveliness, does not understand her appeal. I warned you," he grumbled.

Edwith sighed and rubbed his face and his throbbing temples with the flat of his hands. The magic had drained him, he was not apt to steal from others like Ynith and she had taken from him to supplement her destruction. He looked ragged from the battle with Ynith, and utterly defeated by the devastation of his heart. He had truly believed that she held him in the same regard as he did she, but how could he truly know? Her reserve and her timidity, although charming, were also deceiving. He had admired so much the little fire he'd seen flare up in her as he had given her instruction—but he could not know that seemingly harmless fire was fueled by a much greater source of emotion beneath her gentle façade.

Edwith's heart was truly broken. Had he known his kisses had repulsed her, had he any notion that she did not welcome them, he never would have pursued her so ardently and so clumsily. He blamed his inexperience and his ineptitude for what had happened, and thought that had he known the right way, he might have won her, he might have earned her regard and her affection, and he would not have lost his temper and his control and irrevocably damaged any chance to be near to her heart as he just had. Ynith was the only woman he had ever loved, and he was greatly distraught at the idea that he had just insured she would never love him. All he could do was try to shove aside the persistent memory of her soft lips on his, the sensation of touching her silken skin, and the scent of her hair. He threw himself up onto his feet from his hunched position on the edge of the seat and paced, running his hands with frustration through his disheveled hair. The Senior Docent and his sister watched Edwith in silence, both surely understanding his emotional state.

"With all due respect, not even you could keep from loving her, Docent. Nor you, my Lady. How would you expect a man of my age and my heart not to succumb to her as well? How could you blame me for surrendering to her charms, when you both adore her so much as you do? In your short time with her, you stand with her with the same fervent loyalty as you would stand by your own child, even when the man she continues to love murdered your blood sibling? You forgive her for that? You hold her above reproach, but you cannot see how I too might have fallen to her allure as both of you?" Edwith flared, his words filled with the passion he had in reserve for this young woman who had turned his life upside down.

The sister and brother's accusing glares immediately graded down into something more introspective and they both turned away from Edwith, seeing the truth for what it was. Ressa began to weep anew, and Oreth sat down, his bluster and rage dissipated like smoke. "She rests now; the physician will be here in the morning, if all goes well. Everyone is so reluctant to travel with the reports of ogrein roaming about the place."

"Your protections seem to be working, Oreth," Ressa said absently through her hiccups. "No ogrein have been knocking at our doors," Edwith's sigh was loud and heavy and he served himself some sherry and sat down at last, his drawn, sunken eyes and his wan skin a sign of his defeat. Oreth grunted in agreement with Ressa, and the three fell into a strange, empty silence while upstairs, Ynith lay feverish on her bed, wasted and injured.

* * * *

"A surprisingly strong, pragmatic little thing you are, my blossom," the whispered voice said to Ynith's ear. "Not at all what an old beast like me would expect and old beasts do covet the unexpected," he said amusedly. The voice paused. "Your choice was the right one, if not for you, for the good of the world. Yes, even from the perspective of one of the beasts that wishes to destroy all that it has become, I see this, my lovely flower." Ynith felt her wrist being encircled by cool, icy fingers. The strange, empty timbre of the voice that spoke was familiar to her. It was the ogrein, the one that had come to her so recently. She forced her eyes open and rolled her head to the side, where his frighteningly pale face hovered only inches from her own, his inhuman, skeletal hands quite bold as one held her wrist and the other smoothed the flyaways of her wild tresses from around her face with an astonishing gentleness.

She became aware she was in night clothes, her hair loose on her pillow and resting in curls on her shoulders, one of which hurt unimaginably. The movement of her head caused a sharp pain to shoot through her arm and neck, and she made a little grunt of discomfort and her eyelashes fluttered.

"What happened?" she uttered groggily.

"You were put down, so to speak, by the old one. He feared for you, and cast a rather powerful repose upon you," he explained. Then distractedly he added: "a surprising power that old man has, significantly more than that of his acolyte. Caught you completely unawares, which was good. Very good. He protected you."

"Oreth, yes, he did something," she muttered blearily.

"I know it is forward of me, little blossom, to break the repose, but I thought you might need fixing. We needn't have anyone discover that you've been damaged and react excessively, should we? No, no. We are no longer wasted, that is good, but I remember, we all remember the time before; it is not a place for mortals or immortals. We cannot have that happen, despite the advantages it might offer someone like me. We too, can be surprisingly strong and pragmatic, just like my pretty flower."

"Why should you care what happens to the likes of us? We are but food," Ynith uttered. His laugh was strange and wheezy; his bony fingers touching her cheek, lifting her elegant fingers, her hair. He hung over her like a specter, his face so close she could see the spidered veins the colour of soot just beneath his marble skin. His eyes had pupils like pinholes, the irises, in the light of the candle, were an otherworldly blue.

"Beautiful food," he simply said. He lifted her wrist again, higher this time, causing her upper arm to rotate and making her whimper in pain. He bent close and sniffed her shoulder, then the nape of her neck, his cool lips brushing her cheek. "Bones can be knit," he declared. "Food can be fixed. We mustn't give him reason to make it all darkness again." The white, bone-like hand slid over her throbbing shoulder and arm, and compressed the skin. She groaned in pain, and twisted her head away, her eyes clamped shut.

"Hush little blossom, hush. It will all be well." A sensation of heat enveloped her entire wounded side, encompassing her arm, collarbone, shoulder and part of her rib cage. The pain she felt there began to dissipate. She turned to look at his hand and at him again in the spare light of the candles. She realized he was performing an accretion spell much like her own, and was shocked to see that the matter he took was from his own body.

"We pragmatic beasts are blessed with such fast fixing, dear flower, worry not. What I take from my bones will be replaced in haste by the magic that keeps me," he assured her. She watched the stream of white flecks emerge from his skin and penetrate hers. With every passing moment, she felt better.

"Now you are perfect again," he said. The cool hands withdrew from her collarbone and shoulder, and laced instead around her hands. He lifted them to his mouth and kissed her fingers in turn. "Shame, shame, pretty flower," he hissed in a whisper, his eyes half-closed and his expression lamenting. He then dropped her hands and withdrew so that the light only touched the raised portions of his face; part of his forehead, his sharp cheeks and chin, his aquiline nose. His eyes had become but empty sockets.

"Do not wake until you are woken," he warned her. "And do not show that you have been fixed. Feign some discomfort for their sakes, or you will have to answer questions I am quite certain you won't want to answer. Questions that may lead to beasts." He withdrew completely into the darkness and soundlessly retreated into nothingness. Ynith laid there in the light of the candle stubs; the pain gone, she simply felt numb.

Morning came with the official removal of the repose by Oreth at the arrival of a harried looking physician. He seemed put out and agitated to be forced out of his hovel, and after some rough poking and prodding around Ynith's previously wounded areas, he declared there were no breaks, only possible fractures, and that the bruising should be treated with cool compresses, and possibly the application of leeches. He shoved a jar into Oreth's hands containing six or seven black, oily-looking fluke-like things undulating in the sloshing water inside the container. He then scurried away, hastily riding off back from whence he'd come.

Oreth put the jar on the table by Ynith's bed and looked at her with his kind, blue eyes. "I'm sorry I had to do that, Ynith. But I had to neutralize you to protect you."

"I understand, Docent," she replied hoarsely, reaching up with a wince, and gripping his lower arm. She gave him a look of understanding, immediately eradicating his look of worry. He smiled wanly at her.

"You are a powerful wielder, Ynith. I had no idea."

"Neither did I," she said with an ironic laugh. She tried to sit up a bit. The Docent took a pillow and helped her to sit up while he added it to the others behind her. She lay back again, and smiled weakly at him.

"I'm sorry I tried to leave. It was never a reflection on you, or Ressa."

"Rest assured, Ynith, we both understand."

"And Edwith?"

"He is inconsolable. Wretched. But he brought it onto himself."

"I allowed him to believe there was a chance," Ynith admitted. "I thought perhaps deep down there might have been, I don't know. I am partly responsible for encouraging his feelings by not stopping his advances the moment they occurred. I am at fault."

"Ynith this isn't a game of blame. It is just what happens when people interact. Hearts collide, some merge, others are broken. It is what it is. All I want is for you to get well. To find normality again."

"Docent, there will never be normality for me." The old man could not answer that without confirming this depressing notion. Ynith's eyes filled with tears and she bit her lip, her voice wavering. "What I would give to go back to the scriptorium; to take tea; to enjoy the peace that we had at the Darvath again. There's no sense in lamenting what's past, I know this now, but I long for it again so." She burst into sobs and turned onto her good side. The Docent's hand fell upon her shoulder and he patted it kindly, sitting on the edge of her bed.

"Well, perhaps those days are over, but I can do one or two things to make you feel better, my darling girl," he said, his eyes glistening. He too longed for the quiet companionship they shared. For her scratching quill and the sound of her when she leaned far back in her chair and stretched her arms and rolled her head to loosen her back and neck after hours at the writing desk. She twisted her head and caught him from the corner of her eye, her face inquisitive through her sadness.

"I will rustle up some tea—it won't be the summer pudding tea you like so, but it will be a good tea. And I will find someone who can make walnut biscuits for the two of us. I'll have someone come up here and dress you enough to be presentable and you will come down to the library and sit with me as we did. If you're up to it." She nodded and sniffed, wiping her nose with the top of her wrist, a strange grateful smile brushing her lips. She reached back and grasped her hand around the old man's fingers. He put his other hand atop hers and squeezed.

"It will get better, somehow," he tried to assure her.

But it did not get better. Remote and brooding, Edwith was cold and distant. Ressa was growing increasingly irritated by his coldness, and several mornings after, when Ynith emerged from the library with Oreth, she proposed they return to Gallevin. "We are his guests here, and now unwelcome guests. His bitterness is making me feel we must leave, and it cannot be pleasant for Ynith," she whispered to them both. "Who is to say he doesn't turn into something vengeful and summon the hunters here after her?" Oreth could not disagree, but he was concerned about removing to Gallevin where he was sure the hunters would find them.

"You can cast the same protections there as you did here," she assured him. They won't think we would bring her back there after all that. Otherwise, I can only suggest Hevranall; it's a smaller house, but it is reasonably comfortable, and it's away from here."

"Hevranall is a good idea, sister," Oreth exclaimed. "We shall go there. We can hire a coach to take us there, and send for other things should we need them. We should leave tonight if I can secure a coach by then," the old man said. He then rang the servant's bell and waited for the footman to arrive to take a message to the local livery.

Hevranall was another property of the Farnham family. It was a modest hall with only four bedrooms, however well-appointed, about thirty five miles inland in the thick of the Adjen forests, in the shadow of Mount Hale. It was located near the town of Rock Springs, which was a known spot for the visiting rich to take the strange-tasting effervescent waters, and to soak in the naturally heated baths. It was far enough from Teragaard that it discouraged the normal circles of society from traveling so far; forcing them to choose the similar baths and spring waters of Keradd twenty miles due east of the main city. This left Rock Springs rather pristine; a well-kept secret for those determined to avoid the seasonal crowds. There were a few fine houses belonging to great families peppered around Rock Springs, but nothing quite as grand or ostentatious as the city built around Keradd. In Rock Springs, there were no nightly balls, theatres or great tea-houses. There was the main elegant bathhouse, built by the Hervians three hundred years before, two or three rather nice inns for visitors, a few large houses set high on the rumpled, tree-covered hills around the village, a lovely park, also made by the Hervians before they were driven out by barbarians, the village market square, a few shops mostly for locals, and that was about it. Ressa was encouraged that perhaps this would be a good place for Ynith to rejuvenate and recover; to return the flush to her wan cheeks and at least some cheer to her sad eyes.

Ressa hadn't been to Hevranall since winter, and she was quick to send ahead by relay to announce their arrival to the caretakers. Oreth was successful in securing a livery to the post eight miles north of Bairesedge; however the livery was charging him twice what they normally would. They gambled that the post or some sort of transportation would be available to them from there, if not; they would stay at the inn and order the coach from Gallevin to take them.

Ressa helped Ynith pack, and thankfully, Edwith was brooding and distracted and did not even know they'd gone until his housekeeper brought him a note scribbled by the docent moments before they loaded up the coach and embarked. Edwith took the letter, but did not open it at once, staring blandly at the darkened window of his rooms; he finally opened the leaf of paper and read the note.

I apologize for our unannounced removal, it seems untoward of me to perform such a thing in this manner, however we feel that perhaps we are guests that have become a burden to you, and we do not wish to further impose upon you.

We take our leave with gratitude for your hospitality, and hope you can forgive me for this unkindly manner of departure. I will write soon.

Oreth.

Edwith's hand dropped to his knee, still holding the letter. He threw his head back and sighed, shaking his head. His jaw rippled and he chewed his mandibles, the letter was crumpled between his fingers and was thrown with deliberate vitriol into the fire.

The post-coach had been suspended. A note was immediately sent to Gallevin to send the coach, with specific instructions to be discreet. The three of them waited in the grubby inn, Ynith distant and quiet and Oreth watchful and concerned. Ressa had nothing better to do than to fuss over Ynith. It made the young woman realize how fortunate she was to have them. They had become her family.

The next morning the coach was waiting for them, and they loaded it up and headed towards the foothills of Adjen.

20. Rock Springs

Hevranall was a home that appealed to Ynith. She decided if she were to ever have a home of her own, she would want one just like this. It was not Gallevin, grand and imposing; it was a fine house but with a sense of humility and restraint. Made of brick and embellished with carved stone, the broad, flat face was arranged with grey-stone framed windows – five on the second floor and four on the first, the front door centered between them. A grey-stone portico shaded the door, which was painted snow white. The wooden mullions in the windows were also painted white and arranged in attractive diamond frames where the bubbled glass panes rested. The roof sloped back from the face, with three dormers spaced evenly along the front. Cheerful windows peered out onto the cobbled street which was only several long strides from the front door, separated only by the low river-stone wall that was flocked in a calico coat of mosses and lichens. Two chimneys rose on each gable of this simple rectangular box. One smoked cheerfully. Reddish brown ivy climbed up the left face of the house.

"It's so lovely!" Ynith exclaimed, surprising Ressa, for she'd been largely silent the whole time. The late afternoon sun cast down onto the willow tree that hung heavily and sorrowfully over the street, its trunk situated on the right front of the house squarely between the two windows, and screening the upstairs windows from the street with its cascade of leafy branches.

"I do like it here. It's *cozier* than Gallevin; the rooms more compact and the space better economized, but I do like how humble it is," Ressa agreed. "Let us go inside, you will like it more."

An elderly woman greeted them at the door; she seemed particularly happy to see Oreth, who she exclaimed in a hard eastern accent that she hadn't seen in ages. The door opened to a small foyer with an unpretentious stairway leading to the upper floor. A formal parlour occupied the left front of the house, visible through a broad archway. The room was appointed quite beautifully, and above the intricately carved mantel featured a painting of young Ressa beside her late husband holding a young child in her lap. To the right was a less formal room, where Ynith knew they would spend most of their time. A dining room occupied the back area behind the formal parlour and the kitchens were behind the stairs. A small library and office was annexed onto the sitting room facing the back of the house.

Ynith was led upstairs and given one of the front rooms, which was small in comparison to her apartments at Gallevin. This was a single room with attached wash chamber, but compared to her room in the Darvath dormitory, it was spacious and private and beautiful. She examined the refined woodwork of the elegant pilaster bed, the slipper chair, the vanity, the marble basin in the wash chamber where she could bathe, and she was most content to call this home for now. She set to unpacking her own trunks, understanding that there was only the housekeeper here, and nobody else to do this for her. She was accustomed to doing these things for herself, and found an odd comfort in being returned to that state of self-sufficiency she didn't realize she actually missed living in the great houses of Ressa and Edwith.

The three were served a simple supper, and they settled in for the first night; all three quite satisfied with the decision to come to Rock Springs.

Ressa was aware of a peacefulness that immediately shrouded Ynith the moment she entered this humble house. In spite of all Ynith's challenges and worries, she seemed calm and at peace. She liked the house; she enjoyed the sense of normality perhaps, the feeling that somehow by being in this unpretentious place, she had less pressing upon her. It was evident, and something both the elders noticed in one way or other.

Oreth had muttered something to Ressa about how serene Ynith seemed. At Gallevin and at Bairesedge, she was quiet and watchful, but always unnerved and on edge. Here, Ynith moved with an easy grace. It gratified Ressa to see her feeling less burdened. She wondered idly how the child would react to being out of the Darvath and among her family again, if that were ever to pass. Given the optimistic view, and the crisis that bound the land would somehow abate, what would become of Ynith? Would she be on edge, and watchful among strangers?

The second evening, while the three huddled in around a fire, staving off the first of the cool early autumn nights, Ressa looked up at Ynith, who had been reading, but had dropped her book to her knee. Her large eyes were trained on the dance of the flame, her chin propped on her hand, her elbow on the arm of the chair. She was lost somewhere inside her head. Ressa's voice startled her, and she dropped her hand and turned to face her when she spoke.

"Ynith, I may be overstepping, but I am curious. Oreth mentioned you had a legacy, something to sustain you after you leave the Darvath." Ynith's eyes slid to Oreth, who at that moment snorted out a little bit and twitched. He'd fallen asleep in his deep wingback, his pipe dangling precariously from his fingers over the arm of the chair. She marked her book and closed it, placing it on the side table beside her.

Ynith stood and plucked the pipe from his hand, placing it on the beautiful glass tray designed to hold it. She then reached for the warm woolen throw that was folded and draped over the back of his chair, shaking it out and letting it drift over his legs and lap, taking the time to tuck it around him. He barely stirred. Ressa watched this with a soft smile brushing her lips.

She had come to love Ynith. She imagined it was difficult not to, ultimately. She however, like Oreth, had a developed a deeper understanding of Ynith than anyone else and she empathized and respected the girl. Here she was, a sheltered, guileless soul, never exposed to situations like all this that had so recently occurred, never being required until now to face the facets of herself she was least familiar with. Ressa suspected Ynith was surprised by what was inside her; not just her powers, but her inner fire, her temper, her strength, her sense of defiance; even now, as she idled in a state of calm and patience when the world seemed to be falling apart outside the door. Ynith finally looked to Ressa and faced her, casting herself into a silhouette against the fireplace.

"I do have a legacy. A sum of gold and assets, kept by an uncle I've only met twice, and who writes me almost as infrequently. He protects this legacy. I am not sure how large it is, but I am not too concerned. If it is enough for me to find a place for myself, something humble, like this," she looked around her with overt appreciation for the cozy room. "I do not require the opulence and luxuries of the great houses, like that of Gallevin and Bairesedge; like those that once belonged to my parents and are now occupied by my relatives," she said. She turned and made her way to the sideboard and poured herself some water, offering Ressa a glass before sitting down.

Ressa clutched the cut glass goblet, observing the girl with the beautiful face, cast in golden firelight, and then turning the glass that shone like a golden gem against the firelight. "Assuming when all this is past, you will seek your own home then, Ynith? Shall you not renew connections with any of your family?" Ressa asked. Ynith snorted derisively and shook her head.

"Those people are of no connection to me. Perhaps there is a weak one by birth, but in the end, what does that really mean? Were they connected to me when they descended upon my parents' estate like a flock of carrion birds the moment news of their death found them? Did they show any connection to me when they stripped everything my parents possessed bare? No. Only one relative cared enough to think of me; to secure some part of what was left to ensure I would not be left utterly bereft of anything and anyone, only one relative cared. He did not adopt me into his household, however. He hid me away. They do not want me. My uncle says they would fear me, because of my title, and the fact that I could take everything back if I wanted to. He said that I could truly be in peril from my own relatives. I do not want them. I do not care for my title, or my birthright to the Shalmeen line.

"No. I have grown up in a way that has prepared me for self-sufficiency. I have grown up in a small room, repairing my own garments, stoking my own fire, and dressing without a maid. All that I need when I leave the Darvath is a home to call my own. And I will be well, by myself. Perhaps I can find some occupation to challenge my mind; tutoring perhaps, or transcribing for someone. As long as my legacy can help me keep a humble roof over my head, a cottage of sorts, I can be content and rely upon myself alone, as it was meant to be."

Ressa found her words most saddening. She realized that Ynith had never imagined a future for herself that included anyone's company. She had imagined a future alone, depending on herself—with no true, meaningful connections to bind her, no husband, and no children. Ressa supposed it was only natural to think such things when most of her life was spent in very much the same state; mostly friendless, no family, and no romantic attachments. *Poor, poor dear*, thought Ressa.

"When the time comes, and all this passes, Ynith, you will come here, to this house. You may let it from me, if you like; we can negotiate all those silly terms when that happens. I see how much you like this house. You will also love this village just as much."

"You would let me live here?" Ynith's eyes glassed over.

"Goodness my girl, of course I would let you live here. It would be silly not to. Here, you have most apparently found some qualities to soothe you, even in this strange state the world is in. This house is beloved to me, but it is one of four houses I own. I do not come here enough to justify leaving it empty. Especially knowing there is someone I can trust to care for this place. Hevranall isn't grand enough to attract my children or theirs. Indeed. As long as you could tolerate the occasional visit from myself and my brother for a few weeks in winter; but even that is not obligatory."

"Ressa…"

"And know, my dearest girl, that I understand that family is not something you seek, you've been given every reason to want nothing to do with that, but we, Oreth and I, we will always be here for you, now and when you are away from the Darvath. I do hope you know that we consider you family." Ynith turned her face away to hide the emotion that washed over it. Ressa stood and walked to her, bending down and pecking her on the forehead, patting her hand.

"You are a good girl, Ynith. Would that my children were even remotely as worthy as you." She then sat down again and took up her stitching. Ynith just turned to the fire, not even bothering to pretend to read now. Oreth snorted again and harrumphed before slipping back into his quiet slumber.

A few days passed in peace. Ynith feigned a recovery from her bodily injuries while her bruises slowly changed colour and began to mend. She allowed herself for just a few moments here and there, to forget that the rest of the world was in turmoil. For some reason at Hevranall, it was easier to do that.

Rock Springs itself was gloriously unaffected so far. The people of the village were aware of the goings on, slightly set on edge by the idea, but they were preparing for the storm in the way they could, the magic bearers even consulting with Oreth once they discovered he was in town and had knowledge of the most recent happenings. He busied himself with local wizards during the day, leaving Ressa and Ynith to sometimes explore the town, other days to sit idly by the windows while reading or stitching, and watch the slow signs of autumn coming upon the land. The first to show was the large beech tree on the side of the property, one of very few deciduous types growing in and around the house and town. Here it was mostly conifers. But the ones planted by people were slowly turning colours, picking up hints of gold and yellow.

"Already a season is passed," Ynith said in wonder. Ressa smiled.

"We'll have some more time of good weather still," she assured her. Ynith glanced at Ressa, unsurprised her lament was lost on her.

Then one morning, the world crashed down upon them. A casting war broke out between some local wizards and a group of ogrein and dark wizards that had arrived sometime during the night. And then, to Ynith's horror, a clatter of hooves drew her to the window only to witness a horde of men riding by wearing the telltale navy blue and red-embellished capes of the Wetherly hunters. They thundered past at great speed, heading for the town.

Ynith tore down the stairs, worried for Oreth who had been since early that morning out in the village community hall. She vaulted past the last step and found Ressa, still in her dressing gown looking alarmed.

"Did you see them?"

"Yes. You should hide!" Outside, a great deafening boom sent all the birds reeling into the sky, and the ground trembled for a moment. Ynith's frightened eyes were wide and searching. She peered out the window, but the village was not in sight of the house.

"Oreth, what of Oreth?" She could not hide the panic in her voice.

"He can take care of himself," Ressa assured her, unsuccessfully concealing the worry in her voice. Ynith's hands balled into fists.

"Not against a horde," she replied. "If he casts something powerful in the presence of the hunters…" she left it hanging as the realization washed over her as well. Without taking any shawl or covering and without taking leave, Ynith simply bolted out the door towards town in nothing but the slight pale pink morning gown she'd just put on, her drab slippers and her hair simply tied up into a tail on the back of her head. She ran down the street towards the noise and chaos, cresting the edge of the hill and looking down to see a building ablaze and people running about in panic. She headed for the main street, finding herself immediately pulled into a tangle of horses and people, ducking at flying debris as Wizards flung whatever they could find, cast columns of fire, swarms of blighted insects, whatever it took to keep the powerful ogrein at bay. She skidded to a halt just in time for a chimney stack to collapse mere steps from her, and explode across the cobbles in a shatter of angled stone and mortar. She picked her way through, focusing on getting to the hall.

There were more ogrein than Ynith imagined; their black robes and pale faces seemed to be everywhere. They cast mostly with their hands, and their long, spindly fingers were continually pointed anywhere there was a flash of navy blue. She did not see the ogrein she knew amongst them. These were formidable fighters and one could match many mortal fighters quite easily.

She learned from her ogrein acquaintance that she could not tap them to cast magic against them, it was fruitless. She focused instead on the mortals, accounting for as many as she could in brief glances as she struggled to get past the bedlam to Oreth.

The people who were not magic bearing were huddling terrified in their shops, or trying to escape the madness. One man saw Ynith and took her arm, trying to drag her into a building for safety.

"Miss, you must come away from this. You will be killed!" He shouted. Ynith's brow knit in defiance and she pulled herself from his grasp.

"Thank you for your concern sir, but I have to get to the great hall." He watched her gingerly jog away, and then retreated into the smith shop where some of the villagers retreated.

Ynith lifted her arms to block a spray of glass from a shop window that was violently shattered by some sort of thrown magic. She cringed aside as a hunter's horse reared beside her, his flailing hooves coming within inches of her head. She bit her lower lip, and forged on, deflecting some flying bricks with a flick of her hand and her own power.

Ynith dodged through the anarchy towards the great hall, where in the doorway she spotted Oreth and another elderly wizard pushing back a wall of flames by casting some sort of invisible shield over themselves. They were both struggling under the weight of the spell.

Ynith witnessed a wayward blast from a hunter render a market stall into wood shards that exploded outward in all directions. One of the large splinters impaled Oreth in the leg. The shield did not protect him from projectiles. He crumpled to the ground, gripping his thigh and grimacing in pain. The dome that protected them shrank by half, and Ynith's self control at that moment was lost.

She threw her hands up and then pushed them out, thrusting out of her chest a peppering of portals that broadened so quickly and so widely the air crackled. The wiggling strands that fingered out from the portals reached out in undulating tentacles, latching onto the chests of the hunters and dark wizards within her immediate vicinity. It was a violent tapping, not like what she'd done at Wetherly, where it was a more passive drain and then an explosion. This time, the bolts rented the power from the men, jarring them violently, yanking their power into Ynith with a brutal jerk. Their forms wavered and their magic fizzled immediately.

Once filled and practically glowing with strength, Ynith reached up and gestured with her hands as if capturing something. While she did, the great wall of fire that threatened Oreth and his companion began to form into a great ball. She then, both mimicking with her hands, while the flaming sphere followed her movement, directed it in a fiery projectile towards the dark wizard that was casting it. He fell back and covered his face before the fire fell over him. Ynith did not pause to watch the effects of her casting.

She thrust out again and projected her stolen power, bursting from her body in a sizzling series of spoked arcs that followed the paths carved by the first tentacles, back to the mortals that fueled her, sending every one of them flying from their horses and off the ground, throwing them yards from where they had stood; the tendrils did not discriminate which side to attack, they threw both hunter, dark wizard and even the odd ogrein was caught in the crossfire. Ynith's palpable anger, like Edwith's, had taken over. She was not herself. As wizards and ogrein scrambled to their feet she began to sweep things at them. Bales of hay, barrels of beer, objects littering the market area, whatever she found; all done with astonishing ease and a graceful dance of her arms and hands as she somehow directed the magic to do her will.

A number of the ogrein and dark wizards that were out of range of Ynith's spells, looked upon her aghast. The ogrein were odd figures that did not belong in the light of day; they stood like a stand of dark willowy trees, their eyes fixed on the inordinately beautiful girl in soft pale pink who had just momentarily stunned the entire phalanx of Wetherly enforcers and a good portion of the other faction.

As the hunters and other mortals began to gather their wits about them, they began to focus on the source of this destructive magic, and were beginning to retaliate against her. She was mindful and quick. With almost thoughtless gestures as she picked her way across the ruin that was the square, she invested several souls in the debris they had made, she threw two men aside like rag dolls and cast some bolts of light that connected with the eyes of her attackers, blinding them. When she felt weakened, she merely took from the power all around her, reveling in the heady, almost delicious sensation of the ogrein energies, which were vastly stronger and purer than anything the mortals offered.

When the fighters all had been sufficiently quieted for her to safely cross the square, she ran up the steps of the great hall to Oreth's side. The sight of him in pain brought her senses reeling back, and her emotions came to her at once. Burning tears filled her eyes and she fell onto her knees beside Oreth. She ducked under his arm, wrapping it around her shoulder, and with all her strength, she hoisted him to his feet. She was sniffing and trying to bat away the tears that were filling her eyes.

"Ynith, you've just announced your presence to all."

"I could not leave you to their mercy, Oreth. The fighters are so careless and reckless they do not care who they hurt. I cannot believe how thoughtless the hunters are. Look how much they've destroyed, and how many people they've endangered. They are a greater threat to us right now than the ogrein and the dark wizards." She helped him down the steps to the square.

"Hurry, we don't have much time," she gasped, faltering a bit under his weight. With urgency, she half-dragged him, surprised at her own strength, never thinking to use her powers to help her. They staggered to the edge of the square, coming between two ogrein who did nothing to impede them, but instead watched them pass with open puzzlement. Once she had turned the corner out of the main square, and had managed to support Oreth several streets away from the thick of the fighting, the battle of magic resumed in all its noise and destruction. She dragged Oreth back to the house without hindrance, and once inside, she helped Ressa sit him down and then ran from room to room, yanking all the heavy curtains closed while Oreth was seen to by his sister. When she was done, she returned to them, her hands trembling, and her face pale and filled with sorrow.

"I don't want to leave," she said in a half sob to Ressa. The older woman looked up at her sympathetically and put the piece of wood she'd yanked from her brother's leg on the table. "Not again, not from here."

"Ynith, fetch me some water and have Venna cut strips from a bed sheet for me." Ynith did as she was told, returning with a bowl and a cloth, which Ressa used to clean out the wound. Venna arrived sometime later carrying some cloth bandages which Ressa carefully wrapped around Oreth's leg. She'd cut part of the trouser leg just below the groin with her little embroidery scissors and then tore the rest free. Oreth's stockinged leg stuck out from the chair while his sister bound his thigh. She stared at the wound, which was not too severe, but enough to make her queasy. Oreth seemed rather clear of mind however, and he reached out and took Ynith's hand.

"This will follow us wherever we go, Ynith, it is spreading. This is nothing, it is the fringe; in the core, closer to Teragaard it must be much worse. Our friend Edwith must be overrun by now." Ynith's tears flowed freely. She was tired of this. Tired of running. She wanted only the normality that everyone wanted. It was too late. What Arnsword had begun would not be changed now. The sides had been taken, even if he tried to end it tomorrow, the war would wage on. She pulled up a chair and sat next to Oreth, still clutching his hand. When Ressa was done she too sat, and they listened to the noise outside, which seemed to be slowly moving away from them.

"The village is a shambles," Ynith said to Ressa. "The whole square has been decimated. The villagers are terrified."

"The people who are without powers, they will begin to organize and rebel, it has happened again and again in our history. It is inevitable. This is the way it goes. I am not sure what Arnsword means to do with the book of Hadris; but the knowledge that it is in his possession has sparked a terrible war that will likely not end for a very long time. The possibility of unchecked power is too great for one side to ignore and the idea of losing control is too dreadful for the other side to bear. How this will end, I do not know."

"Unless Arnsword ends it," Ynith concluded.

"How would you suggest he do that, except to do something worse than has already been done?" Oreth asked.

"I don't know. I don't know!" Ynith snapped. In the gloom of the darkened room her eyes darted about the nothingness in search of answers that were not there.

21. Inevitably

The inevitable arrived at their threshold within hours of the morning incident. Oreth had been helped to his room, and given a draught for the discomfort. He was sleeping. Ressa was at the small table on her writing slope, anxiously scribbling out a letter to someone, relying on the light of the candle since the heavy curtains remained drawn. Ynith stared at the covered window and waited.

Ynith was prepared for their arrival. Oreth had warned her. And they had chosen not to run, not with the chaos going on outside. Ynith had pondered both fight and flight, and was unable to decide. However, she did not seem to grasp that she was not quite the mistress of her own will. And all it would take was the sight of Edwith to set her nerves on edge and start the cascade of events to follow. He arrived with a group of hunters and several of the southerly wizards they'd told her about before.

The skirmish in town had migrated slightly north towards Ellsborough; however there was still violence occurring in the town of Rock Springs. Wizards were pouring from the woodwork it seemed, dark ones, ogrein and brotherhood bearers alike, in an endless fount of explosive energies, drawing those who were gifted but hadn't chosen sides into the fight. But since the battle had gone mostly out of town, the brotherhood now had the luxury of addressing the reports of the rogue lady caster who was using forbidden magic with great power. And leading them, bearing a hard, cold expression on his face, was Edwith. She was astonished to see him there—more so shocked by the hard, cold glare he cast upon her the moment he saw her face. There was no softness, no kindness, no recognition; nothing but a hard resolve and vengeful anger.

Ynith stood at the door, looking at him, not sure how to react for a moment. Her first thought was the safety of her friends, and her second thought was that the large contingent of hunters, at least twenty of them, was trying to tap her. Edwith had warned them about her. They were also quite well armoured against her immediate, retaliatory attempt to tap them back. She could see their cheeks colouring, and their chests swelling as they stole her strength and it infuriated her. She clung to the door, glaring darkly at Edwith.

"I've done nothing wrong. You will leave," she said through a tight jaw, feeling with every moment the increasing weakness they were causing her.

"You will come with us. This war must end, and you are what will end it," Edwith said frostily. She swooned for a second, glancing back at Ressa who now stood two paces away, reaching out to Ynith tentatively, her eyes on Edwith.

"Leave her alone, Edwith. Leave her be, you don't know what manner of trouble you could cause by taking her. Don't you see? You could make it all much, much worse."

"She is coming with us, and she will remain drained until Arnsword relents," the younger docent hissed.

"You could kill her, Edwith," Ressa gasped. Edwith's eyes were hard and icy when he turned back to look at Ressa.

"Take her," he snapped. Three of the hunters advanced. Ynith, her legs failing her, felt one of them lift her up into his arms, and carry her out the door.

"No, please," Ynith began to sob. Ressa was also weeping, clutching the doorframe. Ynith looked back over the shoulder of her abductor at the older woman, the genuine love and concern in her face, and then Ynith's eyes widened. Behind Ressa, a looming, pale, black figure appeared in the gloom of the darkened interior, unnoticed by Ressa or anyone else. He was in the house, unbeknownst to them all.

The effect of his proximity was immediate, and the ogrein openly offered his power up to her. She felt the essence of her sinister friend infuse her. She felt his power also shielding her, cutting off the tap lines that were draining her. Immediately her strength returned in a steady, electric stream.

With an angry, unladylike roar, Ynith threw herself from the hunter's grasp, and swept the lot of them onto the street. The force of the magic spooked some horses, and sent them clattering down the cobbled path away from the town. Edwith landed, and immediately regained his footing, reaching towards her with a clawed hand he struck back. Ynith felt like a talon had clutched around her heart and she screamed. The force of her scream was magnified by the ogrein's power and transformed it into a sonic weapon, sending Edwith to the ground in an agonizing squirm, his ears ringing, momentarily deafened. All of the bearers were stunned. But Edwith was determined, and bitter and furious, and he was no longer compelled to any sense of protection over Ynith. His anger made him powerful. He was slighted and hurt, and all he wanted to do was hurt Ynith as much as she had wounded him.

His control was lost, and his conscience was impaired. With angry, tear filled eyes he threw out his hand again, and clutched at her again, almost feeling her furiously beating heart clenched in his fingers, struggling to beat as he increased the pressure upon it.

Ynith gasped and lurched forward, short of breath and wild-eyed, unable to scream, she did what she could. She created an arc of flame that sprang up from the earth and radiated outwards, catching the still stunned hunters and enveloping them in flames. Edwith was quicker to protect himself, distracted only enough for Ynith to suck in a wheezing breath. But immediately, he clutched out again and she lurched forward, the pallour washing over her face as she fought to breathe and fight.

"You will do as I say, Ynith or I will kill you!" he said hoarsely. Ynith whimpered and dropped forward onto her hands and knees on the street. Ressa cried out and stepped towards her, only to feel herself being pulled back.

The ogrein's pale hand reached up and grasped her waist, and he gently guided the horrified and shocked Ressa back into the doorway. He then emerged into the daylight, walking so smoothly on his robes it was as if he were floating. With a fearsome snarl, he threw himself forward onto Edwith. Ynith's lungs painfully filled with air and she fell onto the ground flat, her chest rising and falling as her heart attempted to recover from the pressure that had been crushing it.

The ogrein and Edwith did not bother with magic. This was a fight of physical blows, and the ogrein flashed his row of razor teeth before burying them into Edwith's shoulder. Edwith's scream was fierce and feral. The two were a tangle of limbs, pale and living, fists and claws. The ogrein's protections had faltered, and Ynith was again being drained. Her eyes took in a few of the hunters, still rolling on the ground as well, but a few trained on her with malicious glares. She felt as if her very life was being sapped from her, and she was starting to lose her senses. Her vision seemed to flicker, and she gasped agonizingly, her heart still faltering, perhaps too damaged to continue.

And then the sky seemed to fall.

A blast of wind hit the ground with the force of a granite wall. The earth trembled, and Ressa, in the doorway, fell onto the ground. The trees swayed and the gusts blew the capes of the hunters awry. A great sonorous, deafening boom exploded just left of Ynith, and a black, hunched-shouldered figure appeared in a swirl of grey smoke.

The figure was fuming, and every soul on that street could feel it. It was like a searing fury that burned. The tall, lanky, dark shape hugged himself, and when he opened his eyes, he dropped his arms, and looked down on the ground, where the form of

Ynith lay barely moving; the soft pale pink muslin of her gown whipping around her legs.

She was barely breathing, her skin so wan she looked dead. Her eyes were glazed and her fingers, white and fragile were twitching. The stork-like figure stooped and dug his arms beneath her, rolling her onto her back and then pulling her onto his lap. Her head hung listless, her eyes partly open, she mouthed weakly.

"Ogrein," he whispered. The ogrein struggling with Edwith responded immediately, withdrawing from the fight, his face covered in blood, he obeyed, looking to his new King and then down at the girl in his arms. "Fix this." The ogrein nodded and stooped beside them both, gathering Ynith up he lifted her and carried her, limp and frail into the house. Arnsword then turned and faced Edwith and the hunters. The ones that were cogent enough to even attempt to battle were not given the slightest chance. With a clenched jaw, the King lifted his gaze to each one, and with a jut of the chin, they were wasted into nothing but ash, each in turn. He turned to Edwith and glared at him. The wizard attempted to cast, but Arnsword possessed the power of the Hadris for himself. Edwith had no chance. He might as well be a powerless mortal, his portals never even originated. Arnsword looked upon him, and sneered.

"Your thoughts contradict themselves, you pitiful man. You feel love for her yet you tried to murder her," he hissed. Arnsword looked more like an ogrein now than he did a human, his hair, black and lank, fell against his pale skin, his harsh, angular face made more severe by the drawn eyes and enraged set of his lips. The influence of the powerful magics had made him even harder-looking. "Hunters are of no use against me, and you, pretender, think yourself worthy of the forbidden powers," he snarled. "If she dies, I will exact a punishment upon you and all humanity that you will regret for eternity."

The ogrein stood aside, a strange, irritated look on his face. Ynith was resting on a settee, her feet on a bolster, Oreth's throw resting on her body. Ressa had moved a small chair to her side, and was patting down Ynith's disheveled hair, sniffing away the tears. Oreth had come downstairs, limping in on a cane, disoriented and groggy from the draught he'd been given. He looked confused at first, at the sight of the ogrein hovering over Ynith's pale form, but then his concern for Ynith took hold, and he pushed by to look at her.

"Docent," Ynith's soft voice intoned. "You should go lie down."

"Don't be silly girl, what in the name of Kadros happened to her?"

"Edwith tried to kill her," Ressa said flatly, her anger barely contained. "The ogrein, he did something."

"He healed her," Oreth concluded.

"As best I could. Her heart was damaged, some of her organs starved of what the heart provides. I have interlaced her flesh with some of my own," the Ogrein added. "She will need to have access to the same sources as we ogrein do, in order to continue living. My presence is the only thing that sustains her right now." Ynith, although weak and slightly disoriented could not help but notice that the whimsical madness had left the ogrein's vernacular, and he answered in straight comprehensible phrases. She laughed hollowly at it, but nobody noticed.

"Someone must summon the ogrein source for her?" the old man asked, filled with wonder. "She is part ogrein."

"I wouldn't say quite say that. She is mortal. She will need to eat and to drink to live. But to make what is of me function within her, she must have a source of magic to maintain it."

"You are speaking of me as if I wasn't here," Ynith muttered. Ressa laughed in relief and kissed her cheek. Oreth sat on the edge of the settee and grasped her hands, smiling at her.

"It's chillingly still out there," Ressa noted. Ynith's brow arched and she remembered the battle.

"What happened?" The ogrein sneered,

"The King finally decided to make an appearance."

"The K.... Arnsword!' Ynith pushed herself up with some difficulty, still pale and shaky, she got to her feet. She pushed away the helping hands offered by the elders, and grabbed onto the Ogrein to steady herself before releasing him and making her way to the entrance of the house.

The door was still ajar, and there she witnessed Arnsword and Edwith. Her beloved had the young docent suspended in the air, watching him writhe in agony with a satisfied sneer on his face.

"Arnsword!" Ynith declared groggily. There was the sound of a body falling to the ground and the King turned to see Ynith standing in the doorway, clutching the frame. She stepped forward, as did he, and they met.

"Oh Arnsword," Ynith's sobbing exclamation was one of relief and release, and she stumbled into his arms and nuzzled her face against his chest. "Where have you been my Arnsword?" she cried. His knobby fingers slid into her hair, his hand cupping the back of her head, and he bent down to embrace her. A wash of glorious bliss rippled from them like a pebble thrown into a pond. Ressa and Oreth felt it inside the house.

He pulled away to gaze at her beauty, at the look of devoted adoration on her face, to feel for himself the grip upon which she held him, to see that she was terrified of being parted from him again.

"I am so very sorry to have left you to the wolves as I did, my beloved Ynith. I knew you were strong enough to fight them, but I never anticipated someone like this fool would love you and hate you alike." He turned and glared at Edwith's groaning form on the ground. "I will end it quickly for him now."

"No, Arnsword. I do not wish to bear any more death my account. He is pitiful and angry but of no threat to you. Please," Ynith whispered. She looked up at him, her eyes wide and pleading. The King reached up again and ran his fingers through her hair, pushing back some tendrils that had fallen into her eyes. With a loving look on his face, he nodded his assent. He did not doubt for a second the sincerity of the gaze she bestowed upon him. He complied because he loved her more than anything in the world.

"Come. I will take you home to Teragaard."

"She will need a summoning. She possesses a part of my flesh now that must be kept alive," the ogrein said. Arnsword nodded stiffly and coolly, and with a wisp of smoke, they were both gone.

22. Small Allowances

Oreth locked the archive doors and picked up the snuffer on its long iron pole. In silence he methodically wound through the shelves of the archive, reaching up to extinguish the candles on the great candelabras hanging aloft. With each movement, the scent of wax and wick intensified around him, and dot of light by dot of light, the archive fell into darkness. He had arranged his route carefully so the last lights to extinguish were on the wall sconces along the wall by his offices. He proceeded through his space to the transcribing room, where his eyes fell momentarily on the desk Ynith had occupied for so short a time, but seemed to still belong entirely to her. Her ink-stained apron was folded on the seat. He snuffed the candles, banked the fire, and returned to his cozy offices, picking up the kettle and stoking up his fire in the office, looking about the room with a critical eye while he waited for water to heat up.

He then picked up his service table and set it between the two chairs, putting a plate of small white cakes with raspberries on the table along with a delicate flowered cup and saucer, and his own blue striped cup and saucer. He prepared the tea leaves, and the steeping pot, while the kettle began to steam.

"I do hope you're making a white tea at this time of evening, otherwise I'll be awake all night," a familiar voice intoned. He glanced up from his task and a smile cracked on his lips. Ynith stood by the doorway as if she'd just stepped through it. She was resplendent, beautiful, and fashionable but also, a little bit sad in the eyes. He straightened and reached out his hand.

"Of course it is," he replied. She tilted her head and smiled, her eyes twinkling at him with the unmistakable expression of affection and love. She stepped forward and took his hand, allowing him to guide her to her chair. She sat down gracefully, her pale, lace embellished hands resting on her silken lap. She was wearing a fine silk gown of a red so deep it was almost black. Her neck was encased in a shallow, sheer ruff, and the broad, square neckline of her gown was filled with the same sheer white worked fabric. Her ears were adorned in two modest diamond pear-cut pennants, and her hair was intricately curled around her face and piled artistically on the back of her head. Her long sleeves covered the top of her hands; the white lace cuffs brushed her knuckles. She looked like the nobility she was born to, but her face was still Ynith, still the sweet, lost child he knew. Her eyes were wizened, and touched with a sadness, which pained him to see. She seemed so happy to see him in spite of the touch of sorrow.

He took the hot water kettle from the fire and filled the pot, his eyes smiling at her. She watched him perform his ritual and proffer her the plate of cakes. She picked one up with her pale fingers and bit into it, closing her eyes in delight.

"Ynith, Ynith, what I wouldn't give to have you, even occasionally, in the scriptorium again. My new assignment is a bit of a disaster at the table, although I will admit somewhat competent at the archiving process; creates more work for me in the end when it comes to transcribing. I wish I could keep him focused on what he is good at."

"Docent, you would have me transcribe again?" she asked incredulously. The Docent snorted in laughter as if he thought the idea was silly himself, and was raising his hand to dismiss it. "No, no, I'm just surprised," she laughed, her air easing about her. "Do you think it advisable for me to be here during the day?" That she was even entertaining the thought, let alone speaking of it with a positive lilt to her tone pleased him immensely.

"Well, if it were to happen, I can assure you that nobody will bother us in the writing room. They never do." Ynith blushed, thinking of Arnsword, who had very much barged into the quiet space without leave. But it was a unique situation. This room was reserved for the Docent's appointees only; he determined its occupants. She leaned forward and accepted the edge of the saucer upon which her tea-cup rattled. The Docent had just filled the cup with the steaming liquid. She leaned back in that forsaken sinking chair she had learned to sit in gracefully, and pondered for a moment, sipping gingerly from the hot liquid.

"I can't see why I can't come and do some work with you, ultimately," she replied at length. The Docent's eyes sparkled again and he smiled broadly. "As long as it doesn't create problems for you," she said in a warning tone. He nodded enthusiastically and sighed.

"It is so good to see you, Ynith," he admitted.

"Likewise, Docent," she replied warmly.

"I'm glad you agreed to renew this little ritual of ours," Oreth declared. She arched a brow and smiled.

"I do not feel complete without it," she said matter-of-factly. "I was so happy to receive your message." Her voice wavered when she said the words, as if it was almost impossible for her to believe he had sent her a message to begin with. That he could forgive her, and still offer his friendship after everything. It meant such a great deal to her; she could barely contain her emotion. She managed to wrest her feelings back and took a tick or two of his old clock to gather her wits about her. She lowered her tea cup to her lap and smiled stiffly. "How is Lady Farnham?" It was a tentative question, as if she partly feared what the answer would be.

"She is well. She does miss you terribly. She would be envious to know what we are doing today," he confessed. He first saw a flash of relief cross her face, and then a shadow of darkness, but it passed quickly. She nodded.

"Do you think I could see her someday?" she asked; her voice weak. He nodded with a wave of the hand, as if it was silly of her to even ask. Ynith's reserve melted a bit more.

"…and Edwith? Is he well?" she added, eyes averted. The Docent was sipping his tea when she asked, so it took him a moment to swallow it down and speak. He only did so when he'd clinked his cup back into its saucer.

"Edwith is no longer serving here. He has gone to Adrulath, to the brotherhood," he said, unable to hide the dismay in his voice.

"As long as he is well," Ynith added. Her voice broke. The Docent quietly understood Ynith's feelings, and decided it was a matter that should no longer be discussed. With a cheerful tone, he went on.

"Your former classmate Treen applied for your position here. She's a nice girl on the most part, but a little too smug and opinionated for my tastes," he quickly changed the subject. Ynith, grateful for the segue, had no doubt Treen would have jumped on the opportunity the moment it arose. She imagined Treen must have been quite disappointed when Oreth chose another. She suspired. Poor Treen.

"She will find other ways to distinguish herself. She is quite brilliant."

"Indeed. She may find a place among the faculty someday." Ynith lifted her cup to her lips and sipped, her eyes falling on the old Docent who she'd come to love so much.

"So when am I to begin at the transcribing, Docent?"

"As soon as you like, Ynith. Your apron is on your chair waiting for you. You can begin as soon as tomorrow if you like. Come when it is convenient. Just be kind enough to send me some notice so I can ensure that I am supplied with the biscuits and cakes you favour. I recently ordered some of that summer pudding tea you enjoy so."

"I will come tomorrow, I think," she decided. "I will choose how often afterwards. I have missed the peace of the transcription room. I have missed you." The Docent's eyes beamed with contentment and he leaned back into his chair. He was happy now, with his Ynith sitting where she belonged. Her expression was one of growing comfort and ease. With a happy sigh, the Docent picked up the pot and refreshed her tea.

"Have another cake, my dear. I will have fresh walnut biscuits for you tomorrow in celebration of your return," he said, proud to have remembered her penchant for that particular sweet. "Ressa will be enchanted when I tell her to send them." She responded by reaching forward and snatching the little cake from the plate with a delighted smile.

A simple linen gown, covered by an ink-mottled apron, such comfort in the sound of silence and scratching quills, the clink of ink-bottles, the astringent scent of the paints mixed with the aroma of leather. Her beloved crow quill, small and black with a violet sheen was still there in the spray of feathered tips protruding from the cup on her desk.

He never prodded her about her world beyond her hours with him in the scriptorium. He never questioned her when she sat in his office, taking tea. There was a simple, easy comfort to her time with the old man.

Nobody would ever suspect that the new Queen of Teragaard spent some of her days teetering on a step-stool, wiping down the dust from the cluttered shelves of the Docent's office. Nobody knew that on rare occasions, when she sat at the transcription desk, a smear of ink on her cheek, a lock of her hair fallen from the loose bun behind her head, her hand moving across a page cast in the golden afternoon light, that she was watched quietly by a dark, brooding figure, seated in a chair by the fire, a harsh figure with unforgiving angles but tender eyes only when they were resting upon her. The Wizard King and his coveted queen, eating walnut biscuits and drinking tea in the company of the only mortal who could, ultimately, truly understand and let them be.

Nobody except Ynith knew that another figure hovered nearby as well. She sensed him; she was connected to him now. He watched them all with an envious eye, licking the tips of his razor-sharp teeth, biding his time. This figure was the only one who had truly seen the aptitude for devastation this otherwise gentle, sweet creature could wield—and he was drawn to her dual nature like a moth to a flame. He watched over her, and clung unseen beside her with the same avaricious possessive desire as the man who now had claim on her. He was the only one of all those that surrounded her, who was truly tacit of Ynith's motivations and her choices. There was an unspoken understanding between the two, in spite of their hardly ever crossing paths. She knew when he was there, and he delighted in knowing this. Only he seemed to understand how pivotal Ynith was to the tenuous, imperfect balance that held the world right now.

Outside the walls of the Darvath, and beyond the city of Teragaard, all around them, the war continued between the King's supporters and the brotherhood of Wetherly—the magic, albeit restricted in its power by the Wizard King, was still damaging to so much of the world they used to know. But there was never quite enough for one faction to ultimately destroy the other. It was a violent, destructive stalemate. But somehow, it struck some kind of balance now where people could eke out a living and find some semblance of normality in spite of the fighting.

The mortals, although now resentful and rebellious against any magic bearers, as Oreth predicted, lived in fear of their tyrant King, and dared not defy him. They attempted to function on under the duress—life finding a strange, disjointed rhythm.

Little did anyone really know, that the only object that prevented the war from being abruptly ended fully in favour of the King—what prevented the world from being transformed into something worse than it had already had become, was sitting at a transcription table, carefully copying artful texts to carry forward into an uncertain future.

She was the only thing that provided some normality for the people of the land. Because it was what she most desired, above all else; even if it meant it would cost her everything she had quietly hoped for. She gave everything up for it. But she held onto this one thing. This mundane task, this time with the old man and his sister. It was all Ynith had left that was hers. Every other cherished thought, the future at Hevranall, the simple, solitary future she'd seen for herself was no more.

With a meaningful glance shared with Oreth, she dipped her crow quill in the raven ink and followed her careful pencil tracing. Outside, the bell rang, and the sound of tramping feet rose up from below as students left classes.

"Summer pudding my dear?" Oreth asked. She paused in her rendering and smiled softly.

"As if you have to ask." The Docent offered her a happy smile and shuffled off to retrieve and fill the kettle. She took the moment of his absence to put down her quill and to slide out the thin drawer at the base of her drafting desk. There, in the shallow trays of the drawers, she reached down and touched her finger to the delicate shell cameo adorned with the shape of a single buttercup blossom. She gazed at it momentarily, and then slid the drawer shut.

With moist eyes, she reached out and grasped her quill again just in time for Oreth to return with the full kettle.

Miranda Mayer

About the Author

Miranda Mayer lives in the Mount Hood territory of Oregon. A polyglot, artist, avid historic costumer and lifelong equestrian; her interests are broad, and edge on geekery most of time. She is married, and is a new mother.

Miranda's stories range from Science Fiction to Urban Fantasy to Fantasy. She writes from her heart, imbues her writing with her quirky humour, and tries very hard to make her characters as real and three-dimensional as possible. Her unpredictable and rather Attention-Deficit-Disordered nature guarantees that her stories will take readers to unexpected places.

Miranda Mayer

Other titles by Miranda Mayer

The Trilogy of Tinna:
Tinna's Promise
Tinna's Might
Tinna's Reign (TBP)

The House of Black (TBP)

The Belletrist

Blackroot